Am I
Allergic
to Men?

BOOKS BY KRISTEN BAILEY

Has Anyone Seen My Sex Life?
Can I Give My Husband Back?
Did My Love Life Shrink in the Wash?
How Much Wine Will Fix My Broken Heart?

KRISTEN BAILEY

Am I Allergic to Men?

bookouture

Published by Bookouture in 2022

An imprint of Storyfire Ltd.
Carmelite House
50 Victoria Embankment
London EC4Y 0DZ

www.bookouture.com

ISBN: 978-1-80314-120-6
eBook ISBN: 978-1-80314-119-0

For Nick, who doesn't think I'm very funny at all.
Well, you married it.

PROLOGUE
AUGUST 2010

'Y'all right?'

    'Yeah.'

    'What's your name?'

    'Lucy.'

    'You don't want to ask me my name?'

    'No.'

    'Rude.'

    'Not really. I don't care what your name is.'

    'It's Craig.'

    'I said I don't care.'

    'What are you drinking?'

    'A drink I'll buy myself.'

    'Nah, seriously. I'll get you a drink.'

    'Craig, thanks but no.'

    'Bitch.'

    'Excuse me?'

    'I was just trying to be nice.'

    'Hold up.' I pass my bag to my sister, Emma, who's standing next to me and looking slightly ashen with nerves.

    'So you come up to me, Craig... a man coming up to a girl, in a club. I've not met you before and you expect me to be friendly and accept drinks off you? I want to be cautious and because I refuse, that makes me a bitch? What if I'd accepted the drink? Then you would have expected something from me. You'd have wanted payment for your niceness. Right? What would you have wanted in return? Or was this a purely altruistic act because I look thirsty?'

Craig's mates behind him start to chuckle. *Of all the girls to offer to buy a drink, Craig.* Craig continues to stand there, wearing a dazed look but also my pet hate of midwash denim and a mint polo shirt.

'So when a girl decides to buy her own drink and not engage with you, Craig, maybe she's just looking out for herself and not wanting to get involved with someone who looks like his mum still cuts his hair,' I finish.

Emma lets out a huge sigh of despair. Beth, our other sister at the bar, shakes her head and gets in between Craig and me.

'Lads, she's tanked up. You don't want to go there,' she says, putting a protective arm across me. Beth can talk. We've just been in the loos and she snogged a sink.

'Not worth the drama,' Craig retorts.

'In your dreams, home haircut...' I continue. He puts an anxious hand over his mop of hair. Emma is very close to clasping her hands over my mouth. My sisters put their bodies between me and the group of lads and we continue to lean over this bar, waiting to get noticed and served. I could have got a potato and made the vodka myself with how long I've had to wait. Am I tanked up? Hell, yes. We are in a nightclub. It's the law. I let out a huge burp that tastes like mixed berries.

'I need another drink!' I cry out, exasperated.

'But do you?' Emma asks.

'Beth, be a dear,' I say, one leg in the air, my arm around her neck. She levers me onto the bar and I scramble to my feet. That group of fellas look on and I'm conscious they have a view right up my skirt. Emma tries to block that view with a coaster. Lordy, it's high, I can see the world from up here. Emma's hands are firmly around my ankles and I can't tell if she's pulling me down or keeping me upright but this will get us served. Or kicked out.

'SERVICE, GARÇON! IF YOU PLEASE!' I shriek in a posh voice, my arms rising to the air like a soprano's.

A bartender looks over, laughing. 'LUCY! Mate! Get down before you fall down!'

He saunters over and half the bar give me evils. *Not my fault you lack my drunken creativity at the bar.* I jump down a bit ungracefully and fall into Beth, who creases over in laughter.

'Philip!' I exclaim.

The bartender leans over and gives me a kiss on the cheek while home haircut next to me flares his nostrils at having to wait longer. Well, I have good reason to go first: a) it's my eighteenth birthday b) I aced my end of year exams and c) ladies first, lads. Have some manners. Lady Lucy, I like that. I can change my name to that now I'm of age. From this day forth, I'm a noble wench.

Philip, I know because I've seen him in this club, Oceana, since I was fifteen and I used to sneak in here with a fake ID under the name of Lavinia Limone and a picture of a forty-year-old woman. This is where all us sisters used to come so it makes sense that before I fly off to university, we all come together in this place of dancefloor worship to say an official goodbye to our youth and welcome me into the world of being a vibrant young adult person. Philip scans down and notices I'm wearing a giant badge that says 'Birthday Bitch'.

'Babes, that was today?'

'Yes? You forgot? Get out! Seriously!' My hand is pointed to the actual exit and Emma watches it, wondering how and why I'm insulting the staff.

Instead he knocks his head back in laughter. 'What can I get you, Luce?'

'Sambuca shots, eight of them, and two jugs of Sex on the Beach, many straws...'

'Could I just have a Coke?' Emma asks, her hand in the air. 'I told Simon I was only going out for the one drink...'

'No, ignore her,' I tell Philip. 'And don't serve her if she asks for soft drinks or I'll tell the manager that you're stealing from the till.'

Again, he laughs but I am deadly serious. It took me several hundred phone calls, threats and messages of emotional black-mail to get her out and she's not allowed to spoil my evening by being sober. Emma pulls down the short skirt we made her wear after she showed up at our house in bootcut jeans and a baggy hoodie.

'I don't think Meg is drinking either, Luce,' Emma informs me but I turn and point to the dancefloor. Whatever. Meg and Grace, our other sister, are throwing shapes in the best possible way. Meg is a new mum and an ex-party-girl so today is about release, fun and shots. We should have just wired her up to an alcohol drip. Grace is here to dance but also supervise and ensure Meg doesn't hurt people with flying limbs.

'Come on, Ems,' Beth says, sliding a shot in her direction. 'Drink, drink, drink, drink...' she starts chanting. I join in, as do the men standing next to us. The peer pressure works and she downs it in one.

'If I fail my cardiac anatomy exam then it will be your fault,' Emma says, her face wincing as the alcohol hits the back of her throat.

'You won't. You're amazing.'

Emma gazes at me. I can't quite tell if it's in admiration or judgement but she grabs my face and kisses me on the forehead. 'We're not all like you, some of us have to actually study. How the hell did you get those results?' she asks, referring to my four As.

'Luck, genius and good looks,' I say, dancing on the spot. And so this night is deserved. I will have a good time tonight, a truly excellent time. I look up at the ceiling, howling in delight. Philip notices and laughs as he takes Emma's debit card to process the drinks order. I hand over shots to the other sisters.

'To universi-titty,' I say, slurring. I take a shot, down it and stare into space.

'God help them,' Emma says.

'You OK, Luce? You going to vom?' Beth asks, opening her clutch.

I shake my head. 'No, I will not give him the satisfaction.'

Both sisters look at each other, in a slightly more sober state than me to handle this situation.

'Him? Craig?' Emma asks.

'No, Josh,' I inform them. My boyfriend. The sisters suddenly realise why I may have gone both barrels at poor Craig. 'But we're not calling him that any more. We're calling him Dickface. We had a huge fight about me about going away to university. He said I'm not allowed because I'll be leaving him and he was a proper king-sized dickhead. Like, I'm surprised he could fit in the room because of the size of the monumental bellend attached to his face...'

Both of them study me as I start to dance with even more animation but also sway like I'm at sea. It's a lot of movement.

'He did that on your birthday?' Beth asks, horrified.

'But he's not going to crap all over my evening so shush...' I say, putting my finger to my lips. 'The plan is to drink it all away and dance with all my sisters and my mates and celebrate madly...'

Emma and Beth watch as anger and alcohol sweep my words out of me. They know to play along, and I refuse to let Dickface Josh get in the way of this night. I did my nails. I spent money on my nails. Contrary to what Emma said, I did work my arse off at school and I deserve to be able to celebrate without his insecurities getting in the way. The song suddenly changes and Beth screams, scaring a young man and making him pour a drink down himself.

'TUUUUUUNNNNE!' she yells.

TLC, 'No Scrubs'. What an absolute banger. We all attempt to nestle as many drinks as we can into claw-like hands before going to meet Grace and Meg, who are in the middle of the dancefloor – now a huge, sticky, noisy mess of people and lights and alcohol-laced sweat seeping out of everyone's pores.

Meg sees us and squeals. 'He's also known as a...?'

'DUSTER!' I squeal back and we all laugh, remembering how Emma misheard that lyric, and join in, singing along and grinding, shades of an old dance routine we learnt as kids being brought before the masses without shame or care. Grace throws her arms around me, Beth's smile is as big as the moon, while Emma is tasked with holding Meg upright.

Oh my life, I love these girls. I love being the youngest and having this ready-made army of brilliant siblings. Look at Meg, she's got a baby now, she has a proper little person. I'm an aunt. We're all aunts. Emma's a doctor, she's so smart it hurts my heart, and soon, like Beth and Grace, I'm going to be at university too. We're taking on the world, all of us. Like proper adults. And who knows where my little troop goes from here but the chapters are all unwritten. For now, I just want to forget about Dickface and dance to TLC, so wildly and loudly that the walls of this place shake. Grace gets a camera out and she turns it on us so we can take a picture. Click. The song changes and Meg breaks out another turbo-charged dance move.

'I BLOODY ADORE THIS SONG!'

Because it's Beyoncé. She's our queen. Grace and Beth double over in laughter. *You dance all those sleepless nights away, girl.* I look at Emma and point disco fingers in her direction. *You're feeling it, too. Come on, Ems.*

'LUCYLUCYLUCY!'

The moment is, however, interrupted by a pair of hands on my waist. I turn sharply to see it's one of my best mates, Farah. The bling and the eyeliner are both on point. Tonight, she wears a skirt that I think once had a past life as a belt.

'Faraaahhhh! Where have you been?' I throw my hands around her but she pushes me away.

'Hun, you've got to come, yeah. You will not believe what I've just seen. Like properly, I can't believe it. Oh my god...'

The way she shouts the words above the music sobers me up for a few seconds and the sisters turn to see what the commotion is about. Farah takes my hand and we all weave through the dancefloor towards the gents' toilets.

'We can't go in there,' Emma instructs us but Farah doesn't care. Her hand wrapped around mine, she charges in, sisters in tow, as the men standing at the urinals all panic, trying to put their tackles away and inevitably peeing on their shoes.

'Farah, what was it? What did you see?' Grace asks, panicked.

Farah pushes at the stall doors to reveal one man with his trousers around his ankles, eyes wide open in shock. We go back outside and she scans the room until she finds what she's looking for. They're standing near a column by the cloakroom, half plunged in darkness, half illuminated by the lights of the club. *Are you seriously joking me?*

'I am so sorry, babes,' says Farah. 'I'm not even joking. I was in the gents' before, don't ask, and he was there literally in one of the stalls with his hand in her pants, didn't even close the door. It's Chloe Hilton, she's in the year below. I'm fuming for you,' she says, not even stopping for air.

By the column is Josh, face attached to Chloe, plus the rest of his body too, from hips to legs to hands. We literally only had that fight half an hour ago. We've been dating for a year. We're official on Facebook. You told me this was for keeps. Forever. Is this what this is then? You little piece of...

I don't know this feeling. Is it heartbreak? I thought I would feel that more in my chest. This overtakes every cell, it simmers in my blood like some potent chemical reaction. And the tears form in my eyes and roll down my cheeks without ebb. It's a horrific feeling. But oh my word, IT IS... ON. Like Donkey-effing-Kong. I storm over and grab at his shoulder.

'JOSH! WHAT THE HELL!'

I don't know where Farah is running to but I hope it's to get me a big stick. The look Josh gives me in return is pure contempt. We fought, I hurt his little fragile male ego and now this is how he's going to hurt me. Try harder, Dickface.

'Excuse me?' says Chloe, her hands in the air. I glare her down. Yeah, like don't even try.

Josh's face drains of colour. 'Luce, chill. It's nothing...'

'So this is what you want?'

'Yeah...'

'You're breaking up with me on my birthday?'

'You're selfish,' he says. 'You don't love me, you don't love anyone. All you love is yourself.' He remains stony-faced, completely devoid of emotion.

Chloe laughs and, for one moment, I pause. Mainly because I'm summoning up enough vomit to projectile all over the both of them.

'What the hell, you jumped-up little prick!' The voice comes from behind me and the fire that radiates through it is big mama energy. Meg. She squares up to Josh and points a finger in his face. 'Apologise to her now...' she warns him.

'Or what? You're going to take me on with your nursing bra?'

He said that, didn't he? Meg grabs a drink from someone next to us and throws it at both of them, cider dripping off their faces, hair and Chloe's super-cheap plastic-looking handbag.

'OH MY GOD! YOU BITCH!'

'What did you call my sister?'

'Are you replacing that drink?'

'You tart.'

'Calm down, bird!'

'You pea-bollocked wanker.'

'I've seen better fake tan on a garden fence.'

It's a huge collection of voices and noise but all the while Josh stands there staring at me, sticking his tongue out the corner of his mouth. He's smiling, isn't he?

'It's none of your business anyway,' Josh tells Meg.

Did he just shove my sister? MY. SISTER. Grace tries to get in between the two of them, another fella's drink falls to the ground. Emma tries to pick it up and act as referee. I think she says sorry about five thousand times. Never apologise, Ems.

I storm over and slap Josh, hard. The crowd cheer.

'Piss off, you are so dumped.'

'I'm dumped?'

I find another drink to throw at him. The men next to us really need better reflexes. Meg is just ranting at this point, splinters of spit glowing in the lights of the club. *You're just a cocky, jumped-up little boy. Who are you, telling her what to do with her life? In ten years' time, she'll be flying and you'll still be here with your dick in your hand.* Chloe has a handful of Beth's hair. Someone gets punched. Someone screams. A bouncer in black combat trousers and an earpiece comes storming over and he grabs at Meg. He's got the wrong person.

And like some crazed jungle lynx, I launch myself at him, obtaining tremendous height to attach myself to his back. He spins to try and release me, getting gradually faster like I'm going to launch into the air like a discus. Nice try. I cling on, trying to pull him off Meg. The spinning isn't great. The people and lights around me rotate like I'm at a fairground. Is this what it means to be an adult? Where will I land? I just need to hold on as hard as I can. But I taste sambuca in my throat, frothing up, in the roof of my nostrils. It's going to happen, isn't it? And with that, a loud, high-pitched scream comes from the bouncer, and the faces of dozens of people gurn in slow-motion disgust as I spray cocktail-coloured vomit all over everyone in the corner of the nightclub like a garden sprinkler. I release my grip as the bouncer realises it's all down the back of his neck and I crumple to the floor where Emma catches me.

'Lucy, Lucy...' she says, wiping my chin down with the edge of her T-shirt.

Are you laughing? I clutch down at my chest and she panics, thinking I'm going to throw up again.

'Are you OK? Are you hurt?' asks Emma.

'Some shithead stole my Birthday Bitch badge...' I say, pouting. I see relief in her face, which quickly switches to fear as the bouncer finds me. He has a stance like he's about to rid this place of some strays.

'One thing...' Emma says.

I nod.

'Happy eighteenth birthday, Lucy...'

I laugh. I then throw up again.

1

OVER TEN YEARS LATER

'Stickers are for babies! I don't want your stickers.'

When is it acceptable to drop kick a child? This one is about eight. I don't think I'd be able to kick him very far but he stands in front of me, pigeon puff to his chest, hands on his hips and a look on his face that you know he's had since birth. *I don't understand why I'm on this planet? It's cold. It was warmer in my mum, put me back.* I bet he stares at broccoli like this or when he opens a Christmas present with the wrong price tag. *This isn't real Lego, Mother!* You can tell he's a reluctant party guest too. *This woman before me is also not a real princess. She is an imposter. She told me her dress was sewn by woodland creatures and fairyland magic. It's quite blatantly from Amazon.* His mum is the slim one in the sports gear and the Louis Vuitton tote bag who showed up with a green smoothie. Look at her, waving her arms about, animatedly talking about their next trip to Mustique, and how they had to fire the nanny because they caught her drinking the San Pellegrino when she should have been drinking water from the tap. I hope that smoothie gives her the squits.

'Well, I'm afraid that's all I have. Stickers or fairy dust...' I say, throwing a handful of glitter into the air. I use the glitter because it will make the clear-up harder and that's not in my job description.

'That's rubbish. Where are the sweets?' the kid asks. 'You lot always have sweets.'

'There are no sweets, little boy. Now jog on to the face painting,' I say, breaking with character, my tone loaded with a bit too much sarcasm.

'You can't talk like that to me.'

'I can. It's not *your* birthday and I ate all the sweets. All the Haribo and they were bloody delish, I tell you.'

He glares at me. This could go two ways now. He could be one of those clever kids who'll fake tears and run to his mum, and I'll get the sack. Or maybe, just maybe, I'll have taught this little toad a lesson.

'I'm going to have your job,' he whispers into me. Oh, he's a mini sociopath. This gets better. I put a hand to his shoulder.

'What are you going to do? Write to my boss in crayon?' I say in sing-song tones, best party smile on.

His eyes narrow. I really hope he's not an important child, a politician's son or European royalty. A figure approaches us from behind his back.

'No one even cares about you anyway. Cinderella? None of the girls like you. They're all going to Belle and Snow White. You don't even look like a princess, you're really ugly.'

'Are you sure you don't want a sticker?' I say, my head cocked to one side.

'I told you to keep your stickers. Bitch.'

'CHRISTIAN!'

The look on Christian's little face drops. *Ha. Got you.* The voice comes from Estelle. Estelle's daughter is Ophelia and it's Ophelia's birthday today. Estelle is rocking a midi dress and Alice band vibe today and looks immediately perturbed. Too right, Estelle. Drop kick him, go for it.

'That is no way to talk to Cinderella.'

Estelle hasn't used my real name all day. I'm Cinderella and Hayley (who works in a sex club on Thursday evenings, has a nice side hustle on Twitch and whose black hair is completely out of a box) is Snow White.

'But she was being mean?'

I fake shock and put on my best Disney tones. 'Oh, I think Christian was disappointed by the stickers. They weren't quite what he was expecting.'

Estelle shakes her head at him.

Face it, Christian. You have nothing on me. I'm a fair princess and take Les Mills fitness classes twice a week. I will have you.

'You can come with me, young man, and we will talk to your mother,' she says, taking him by the hand. 'Cinders...'

Oh, that's me. The level of familiarity has reached abbreviations now.

'Could you help me look for Ophelia? The photographer wants to get some pictures of her with the bubble machine and I can't find her anywhere...'

'Of course. Bye, Christian!' I say, waving, my best party princess rictus grin on view. He looks over his shoulder. He then sticks his middle finger up at me.

Oh, London kids' parties. They really are quite the thing now. I was the youngest of five sisters and Mum sometimes didn't even do parties. *You have all these sisters, there is no room for any more people in the house.* So she'd make a cake and we'd play pass-the-parcel except the parcel was my gift and she'd always time the music so the gift landed on me. They were efficient parties. There were always sausage rolls and jam in the sandwiches and my mum would pop on her kids' party CD that kicked off with the *Ghostbusters* theme tune.

Today, we're in Somerset House in Central London so this is a next-level kids' party, not a pink wafer or plastic banner in sight.

Oh no, they've got hand-sewn bunting, pink macaroons that have initials hand-pressed into them, proper teacups and an actual horse called Frou-Frou who plaited his mane for the event. My job is to mill around, pose for photos and occasionally burst into song and teach all these little girls how to be the perfect princess. The poofy dress action and ringlets are strong in this courtyard.

There are also boys. The boys are being taught how to be knights by my mate, Darren, whose sword skills were learnt from his time as an extra on *The Witcher*. Except the swords are made of balloons. I've had to open jars of pickle for Darren before because he has such weedy forearms. So, kids, you should be looking at me if you want to know how to fight.

The excess today kills me, as does the gender stereotyping. I do hope one of these girls nabs a sword and goes on the run. I hope a boy comes over and asks me to put some lipstick on him. But then this is the job and the job is paying me ridiculous amounts of money to occasionally go over to Darren, break into a waltz, swoon at how handsome he is (he's not; his wig gives him long hair like spaniels' ears) and curtsey like I might mean it.

'Mate, have you seen Ophelia?' Belle asks me.

Belle is Cass. I live with her, and see her regularly eat baked beans cold out of the tin and fart with wild abandon so she's maybe not the best person to teach these kids about regal flair and etiquette.

'No. If she's clever, she's run away,' I reply. Cass tries to stifle her giggles. 'Are those crumbs on your bosom, Belle?' The joy of these princess dresses is that they also hoik up our boobs so the dads in attendance can grab an eyeful.

'Oh, shit!' she says, dusting them off with her satin-gloved hand. 'Mate, have you seen the bloody smoked salmon in the catering? I tell you, when the kiddywinks have cleared this place, I am going in for the doggy bags.'

Cass has always been very driven by where her next meal is coming from but she says all of this in a delightful Disney voice. She'd sing it if she could. They really haven't written enough Disney ballads about bloody smoked salmon. Belle swishes her dress at me. It's all part of the role play. This is what princesses do.

'The dad at four o'clock with the jeans and the dress shoes offered me sex before,' Cass tells me.

I put a hand to my chest and chortle. 'The one with the cap and the boat shoes?'

'Why yes, Cinderella. He's even asked me to keep the dress on...'

'Oh my. Is that his wife in the jumpsuit?'

'But of course...' she says. 'I bid ye farewell, my fellow maiden. I am going to steal some scones.'

We both curtsey, Cass burping under her breath as she does. From the corner of my eye, I can still see Christian being told off by his mother. I curtsey in his direction too. If looks could kill... But hey, he's eight and I am twenty-nine. I will but brush them away with a twirl of my princess hand.

'Can I have a picture?' says a tiny Rapunzel, tugging at my skirt.

'Why, of course you can. What's your name?'

'Hero Beaufort-Charles.'

Of course it is, little lovely. *Have you seen Ophelia? You two could start a Shakespearean pop duo.* That's the problem when you get further into Central London: the names become posher and the children look like they regularly book in for spa days. It's a world apart from what I knew as a kid and the children in my family. All my nieces and nephews feel like normal kids – ones who don't mind a chicken nugget and who don't spend the weekend learning Latin and the cello.

'Oh, there's a photographer – how marvellous,' exclaims

Hero's mum. 'Now remember, Hero, lean and smile, no teeth. Chin, find your angles.'

Oh, she's a stage mum. That's why this girl's teeth look like they're coated with gloss paint. I lean my head into Hero's as Mum huddles into the photographer to see if she approves of the images.

'Oh, that's lovely. I must get that one off Estelle for her portfolio. Thank you both so much.'

It's the sort of thanks I always get, through gritted teeth because they have to communicate with the hired help. We both nod in reply and the photographer comes over.

'Did she just say portfolio...?' he asks.

'She did.'

Photographer man is dressed like a bargain Simon Cowell. He's not ugly, though the beard is a little sculpted for my liking, but seriously, do up the shirt buttons.

'I'll take it this is your first children's party gig?' I ask him.

'I normally do weddings. This is genuine weirdness.'

'Oh, I've done worse. I've done this on ice before. A child went face first into the ice and broke their nose and there was a lawsuit. Fake snow though. And Slush Puppies.'

He chuckles under his breath but I see his eyes scan down to my décolletage.

'I'm Reuben,' he says, not offering out a hand.

'Cinderella. Close friends call me Cinders,' I say, curtseying.

He pauses for a moment. 'I noticed a room out the back if you wanted to take a break,' he whispers in gentle tones, leaning into me, his breath on the side of my neck.

Oh, Reuben. Is this his trademark move at weddings too? A nice-looking bridesmaid, guest or band singer? I know that prolonged gaze and raised eyebrow. And it's not like I've not hooked up with single dads at parties before. I have. It's one of the perks of the job. But I've always been professional. We did the do after the party end time on the invite and never within the vicinity of children. I mean, that's just wildly inappropriate. Reuben thinks he has charm. He has a bare chest, that's about it. He also has a wedding ring, which means any charm vaporises into the breeze and is replaced by sleazy smarm factor.

'I don't take breaks, Mr Photographer Man.'

'Well, what about when the clock strikes twelve? We could go somewhere. I could show you my pumpkin,' he says.

There are many ways I could respond to this: fear, disgust, worry. But no, he's just compared his manhood to a pumpkin. If his penis is round, swollen and orange then I am definitely not going near it. So I laugh.

'Mine's the Tesla out the front. See you after?' he replies, mistaking my laughter for flirting.

'Or how about after this, you jump in your Tesla and go back to your wife.'

'I'm not married.'

'And I'm not a virgin princess. Go and take some photos or I'll shove your long lens up your piss pipe.'

He scowls at me and wanders off through the party.

'Trouble, young maiden?' says Darren, strolling up next to me.

'Yeah, some crap knight you are. You're not fending away the monsters.'

He makes a tactical turn to shield himself from the group and pulls a wedgie out of his arse. I told him to go with the leather trousers but he was worried about getting too warm. Now he has the problem that my tights are getting stuck up his crack. He can keep those.

Darren and I have been on the books for this talent agency for the longest of times. We once did a very cool Aladdin party where I had to paint him blue as a genie. I may have used the wrong sort of paint though and he had to spend a weekend indoors because people were calling him Papa Smurf in the street.

'Have you had any mums come on to you yet?' I ask him.

'I've had a number slipped into my sheath.'

'Oo-er.'

'My sword sheath.'

'I knew what you meant.'

'Is the photographer a sleazebag then?' he asks, his eyes following him around the courtyard.

'The worst sort. Also, the birthday girl seems to have done a runner. We've all been told to keep an eye out.'

'Like, out of the venue?' he asks, a little worried. 'Do I need to find my noble steed and gallop through the streets of London to find her?'

'Last time I saw, you have a Fiat, mate.'

We both smile at each other, still in character of course, him bowing and me curtseying while I wander through the courtyard trying to find Ophelia. I wave to all the children, nodding to Belle as she sits at one of the tables pretending to teach little girls how to hold a teacup but, in fact, getting herself in position to scoff the petits fours. I also see a child with the latest iPhone. As my phone has a cracked screen and is held together by tit tape, I do not like this child. Who the hell are you calling at eight years old? And don't say your Pilates instructor.

I scan the area. Ophelia definitely is not here. Damn. Maybe we should be making more of a fuss? Like, she could be on a train at Waterloo by now. I try to think where I would go if I was eight. I used to hide under tables. I was the youngest of five so it was the best way to bite ankles and annoy sisters older and stronger than me. Or maybe, just maybe...

I slip past catering staff, through the corridors of one of the buildings. It's silver service so it looks like they've been shipped in from Downton Abbey and, through the cracks of the kitchen door, I see a group, yes, a *group* of people trying to work out how to get the cake through the doors. That's not just cake. That is mammoth, obscene amounts of confectionery. Good luck trying to wrap a slice of that in a napkin and send it home. You'll need a chainsaw to buzz through it.

Past the kitchen, I notice the toilets themselves have been themed as Princesses and Knights. The Knights one has a portcullis and a dragon at the door. Not a real dragon, obviously, but I kick it just to be sure and a puff of smoke comes out of his nostrils. Or is that air freshener? I enter the Princesses and get on all fours to scan under the stalls. At the end, glittery ballet shoes dangle off a toilet.

'Hi... Ophelia?' I say in my friendliest tones. The shoes withdraw themselves. 'I just saw your feet, honey. It's all good. It's just me here.'

'Who's me?' a voice whispers.

I get up to my feet. A door swings open behind me and a mother and daughter appear. Christ in heaven, they match and not in a good way. I don't know in what kingdom princesses would wear matching Burberry like that.

'I'm afraid you can't use these toilets,' I say swiftly, blocking the entrance.

'Why ever not?' the lady says, the tone putting me, Cinders, in my place.

'I...I...' She tries to push past me but I stand my ground. 'I didn't get to the toilet in time. There's a huge puddle of wee in the middle of the floor.'

Both mother and daughter look completely horrified, the mum glancing down to my skirt. That was one of my worst excuses ever but, hey, I'm not sure I care. I can be that anecdote she tells others at the school gate: the pissing princess.

'The Knights toilets are open. Fare ye princesses across the way.'

The mother turns, unimpressed, grabbing her daughter's hand. Good riddance. I barricade the door with a chair and head to the cubicle where Ophelia is hiding. As I approach, I knock tentatively.

'It's me, Cinderella.'

'Did you really pee in the middle of the floor?' a voice whispers, half laughing, half trying to catch her breath.

'No. Was that an awful lie?'

'You could have said the toilets were broken.'

'Right? I'm just not as smart as you. You OK?'

The door unlocks but doesn't open. I push it slightly ajar. She looks a little how Cinderella looked when she was told she couldn't go to the ball. What's worse is that I know she's been crying, thanks to the puffiness, the ruddiness in her cheeks. *Oh, you poor fair Ophelia.* She pops herself back on the closed toilet and I lower myself onto the floor, making a note to dry-clean this outfit later.

'It's your birthday, you're supposed to be having the most fun that any girl could ever have in the whole entire world.'

She gives me a puzzled expression in reply.

'Did I overdo the princess there?'

'Yeah. Do you have a real name?'

I smile. She's seen through all of this: the extra blusher, the decent bra, the synthetic dress that warns me I shouldn't stand too close to naked flames.

'Lucy,' I say, holding out my hand.

'Pleased to meet you, Lucy.'

I pull some loo roll out of the holder, bunch it up and wipe down my pits. This triggers more of a laugh from her to see a glimpse of me out of character.

'It's tiring lugging this dress about.'

'Is it heavy?'

'Kinda but I once did a medieval fair and had to be Anne Boleyn. The dress was made out of curtains and had hoops and everything, that was heavy.'

'Did they cut off your head at the end?'

I chuckle, impressed that this girl knows her history. I went out with Henry VIII from that gig for a month. His name was Jay, he was authentically ginger and had a thing for golden showers. She doesn't need to know that though.

'They did. It stung but they reattached it with superglue. Doctors can do marvellous things these days.'

She laughs and the sound breaks the sadness hanging in the air. I hear someone try and push the door open.

'DON'T COME IN! CLEANING IN PROGRESS!' I shout over the cubicle. This makes her smile again.

'That was Penelope Stanton before,' she says. 'That woman you stopped from coming in here.'

'Queen Burberry?' This induces a bigger laugh. 'What's Princess Burberry's name?'

'Saskia.'

'Sassy Stanton. I think I know what sort of girl she is... Not a fan?'

She takes a little pause before answering that. 'She's not very nice to me. She calls me Boffy Offy and a sad case. Mum doesn't see it. She thinks this is one big party so she can show off to the other mums. I didn't even want this. I've not watched a princess film in years.'

'What did you want?'

'Trampoline park.'

'Oooh, they're mega fun.'

'Right?'

'I took two of my nieces once. We went on the night that they turn off the lights and your teeth glow.' Trampoline parks are handed to me as most of my sisters' pelvic floors can't take it.

'How many nieces do you have?'

'Seven and two nephews.'

'That's a lot. Are you the fun aunt?'

Like I said, super smart, this girl. 'I like to think so.'

'That's cool.' Ophelia goes quiet for a moment and my heart

bleeds for her. You can almost feel the sadness radiating off her. *Tell me everything*, I want to say. *But there's only so long I can stay in this cubicle, lovely. I can't make this better for you, not here.* That thought alone makes me a bit upset.

'I could trip Saskia up? Throw a cupcake at her like a base-ball? I've got good pitch.'

She cups her hands to her mouth at the thought.

'I'm sorry she's such a cow. Is her mum a cow? Usually they come in pairs.'

'Her mum was the first female vice president at JP Morgan. She recently split up from her husband because she was sleeping with her barre teacher and they had to sell their holiday home in Marbella.'

'Oh, so a primo cow then?'

She giggles again. I shift into a crouching position and take her hands in mine.

'Ophelia, you will come across women like that sometimes. Ones who are not very nice at all. I will never get them, ever. But you can't let them bring you down, you just can't.'

'I heard her mum make fun of my teeth before. I know they're a bit wonky but she told me that a princess would never have teeth like mine.'

I see her tongue scooping at the inside of her mouth, young, self-conscious shoulders slumping down.

'A grown woman said that about you? So she's not a cow, she's a different sort of animal.'

Her eyes widen. 'Like a female dog?'

'I never said that. Don't repeat that.'

She shakes her head in what I think is awe and wonder.

'Next time she says that, you reply with "Well, I can fix my teeth, it's a shame they can't fix your personality."'

I say that cocking my head to one side. There's a little spark in her eye. That's not even my best retort, I have lockers of the things. Thank the sisters for that. My wit is as razor sharp as they come, literally like a new razor, out of the box. If she wants, I can go out there and take this girl and her mum down for her. I wouldn't even charge extra on top of my normal fee.

'Can you talk to your mum about this?' I ask.

'My mum and Penelope play tennis together.'

Of course they do. I bet they play a light match where they don't break out in a sweat and then sit in a sauna together and end the date with a Caesar salad. Without the dressing or the bacon.

'I think you are more important to your mum than Penelope Stanton.' The look she returns makes my heart break a little. Oh, Ophelia. 'It can't hurt to at least say what's been happening?'

'Maybe. I just need to get through this circus first,' she says calmly.

Who is this child? I like her. I wish I could take her to a trampoline park. We could go dressed like this, imagine how high our skirts could fly up.

'What about sisters? Brothers?' I ask.

'My brother, Lysander, is in boarding school. He got in on a chess scholarship. We don't see him much.'

I don't know how to respond to that. Does Lysander play his chess in a velveteen feathered cap, write with a quill and own a very small beard? Instead, I extend my hands and pull her up.

'Well, let's get through the next hour or so. You are very welcome to stand by me and tag along. I'll look after you.'

She looks up at me, almost as if no one has ever said those words to her before. I squeeze her hand that much tighter and reach into my purse, getting out a Mac lip gloss. I reapply and then reach over to give her a smidge. It's glittery but that's because I am a princess, I do this shit right. The moment is interrupted by hard knocking at the door of the room.

'OPHELIA! ARE YOU IN THERE? WHO IS IN

THERE WITH YOU? WHY IS THIS DOOR CLOSED?
HELLO?'

Ophelia rolls her eyes at me, pushes past and moves the
chair that was blocking the door. Behind it stands Estelle. Do
not give me that look, Estelle. If you want to throw this down
then I can take off these gloves and do it here. Game on.

'What is going on here?' she asks, condescension in her
tone.

'My hair came loose, Mummy, and Cinderella helped me
fix it again. I was really embarrassed. I didn't want anyone to
see.'

Her mother examines it for loose bits of fringe. 'Well, crisis
averted. Thank you, Cinderella. Penny gave me a different
version of events,' she says, looking to my crotch. 'You should be
out there, darling. It is *your* party.'

'It's not though, is it?' the girl replies. From the look of her
mother's face, you can tell that Ophelia doesn't do this much:
answer back, stand her ground. It makes me beam though, any
time a girl finds her strength and it starts to beam out of her like
sunshine.

'Excuse me? We have spent a lot of money on today, we
raised you to show gratitude, young lady.'

Ophelia side-eyes me. *Keep going, honey. You got this.* But I
sense what we got was a little spark, a flicker of hope, that one
day she'll be able to tell her mother everything. Just not today.

'Thank you, Mummy,' she whispers and pushes past both of
us to exit the room.

Estelle turns to the mirror to check her make-up is still in
place. 'Thank you, by the way, for finding her and sorting her
hair. I told the hairdresser to use more hairspray.'

She slips a twenty-pound note onto the sink space in front
of us. What would she like me to do now? Hand her a towel and
a pump of hand lotion? I stare at the money. Then I look back
to her.

'She's such a sensitive girl. Her eyes will be all blotchy now, maybe we can Photoshop that out.'

Never mind Christian outside, I've found a new person I want to drop kick. I remember a party my mother threw for Beth in a village hall once. I was tiny but there was a boy there who said Beth had ugly shoes (this was not incorrect, we did have a lot of hand-me-downs). This made Beth cry so my mother didn't give him cake because 'nasty little boys don't deserve cake'. *That* is how you mother at parties.

'I think she was crying because of something else, perhaps?' I feed her the information hoping there is some sort of maternal instinct in there. But it's not there, is it? Not even an iota of the stuff. I could leave this here. This is not my fight and certainly not a fight I want to start because my rent is due and I need somewhere to live. But I'm also Cinderella, I know how to get over evil villainous creatures. Someone hold my glass slipper.

'Ophelia saw something before which was quite upsetting for her,' I say, making it up as I go along. 'The photographer and one of the mums were possibly doing something a little inappropriate in the bathrooms.'

This seems to pique her interest.

'One of the mums?'

'Yes.' I am such a good actress when I need to be. 'She was in Burberry?'

'PENELOPE? She was having sex at my daughter's party?'

'I didn't catch her name.'

'The photographer is my brother and he is married.'

Oh. That took a turn. Still, he was a complete creep and that is not a lie. I nod in the mirror, feigning horror.

'I know she's single now but there are some people that are just off limits. How very dare she!'

'I'm sorry. I didn't mean to cause drama. Maybe the best thing is we carry on as normal and you can tackle this later? For Ophelia, at least.'

She studies my face in the mirror. I can't quite tell if she thinks I'm lying but, Estelle, I'm a princess. We don't shit stir. It's all starlight, true love and musical numbers.

She nods. 'You are so right. Thank you.' Her eyes point to the money and she puffs her hair out one more time before exiting, stage left. I look down at the money. I leave it where it is.

2

I remember a time when the after-party used to be a kebab, a spliff and a drunken snog in someone's front room. That may come later but, for now, we've waved our hands and curtseyed to every damn person in this place so we're rewarding ourselves by sprawling across the marble floors of an empty event room, enjoying a picnic of goodies that Cass stole from the kitchen. Naturally, this event was also not without alcohol so we have stolen a few pitchers of Pimm's. Cass isn't even using a glass but linked up some paper straws to one. I cast an eye over the finger sandwiches and tartlets but I don't fancy any of it. I fancy crisps. But princesses don't eat Pringles, do they? Hayley enters the room, looking like she may want to stab someone or something.

'I hate rich people,' she mutters, taking a cupcake and running a finger through the icing. She takes off her Snow White bow and drops it to the floor.

'Trouble?' I ask.

'Just people who don't know the value of things. One woman wanted to hire me for her daughter's party. I could have said £3K for the hour and she'd have blindly written me a cheque. Also turns out the daughter is one. I'm being paid to sing to a room full of babies.'

Cass and I giggle, having had our fair share of the Pimm's already. Cass's worst party experience was a room full of two-year-olds, one of who pooed down her dress because someone forgot to put pants on their child. Darren and I were once expected to dress up like lions. We wore gold catsuits. We had a *Lion King* routine all mapped out and then we got to the party and we were not what was expected. They wanted real lions. For a children's party. They demanded we leave the venue immediately and we couldn't get changed. We had to go back on the Tube dressed like that.

'Waste of money, these big parties,' I mumble.

Darren laughs. 'Says she who is having the biggest party for her thirtieth.'

I gesture a hand at Darren for pouring shade on my party plans. In a few months' time it's my thirtieth and I am going for broke. I've hired a field in Hampshire and I am turning it into LucyFest. It'll be like a Glastonbury celebrating me, we're having a small stage erected, an ice-cream van, and everyone is bringing their own tent, firewood and alcohol. Emma, my second eldest sister, is far from impressed because I'm forcing her to buy a sleeping bag but I have perfect visions of dancing around a camp fire, drink in hand, and bellowing into the sky to celebrate thirty whirls around the sun.

'Babe, you know that's different,' I reply. 'It will be hardcore raving in a field, not a fluffy cake in sight. Just dancing until the sun comes up and getting smashed off our faces.'

'With your face on all the T-shirts?' Darren jokes, though I'm glad he sees the funny side of that as he'll most likely be the one helping me iron all the transfers onto them.

'And? Not even Ophelia had merch today.'

'No, she gave everyone Pandora,' Cass adds, getting out an

impeccably wrapped party favour she seems to have possibly stolen. 'I was tasked with handing these out.'

Our jaws all drop to the floor. 'Charms for the girls, leather bands for the boys and a note in calligraphy. Not a Tangfastic in sight.'

We all let out a collective sigh of shared despair and resignation. None of us have a desire to be in the party business forever. We're here for the money. The money pays our bills, keeps our noses clean (maybe not Hayley's; there's also a certain irony that she is Snow White) and off the streets. We supplement parties with waitressing, film-extra work, bar work and aforementioned side hustles on the internet. Darren works at Costco every Tuesday too but that's mainly to get the free hotdogs. They're not perfect jobs but they also supplement our hopes and dreams of seeing our names in lights. Better to aim for doing something in life that will make our souls sing. That's the quiet underlying reasoning about why we're sitting here looking like the world's saddest Disney reunion film.

'I don't ever want to be that rich,' Hayley says dolefully. 'If I become the next Adele and win Grammys then you all have permission to slap me back down to where I belong if I become some highfalutin bitch bag.'

I nod earnestly. Cass salutes, half scanning something on her phone.

'Urgh, how is this even possible?' she says, gagging. 'That pervy dad at the party has found my Insta page and has just messaged me.'

We all grab at our phones. 'Name?' Darren asks.

'Frederick Bell.'

You've never seen fingers move quicker. Hayley cackles with laughter.

'The bell stands for bellend. Those berry red chinos are a LOOK... Check out the hunting pics, what a knob. Fiver says he's into kink involved with that,' I say.

'I always get the old man freaks. You two get the fit dads...' Cass cries, stuffing a quarter of a sandwich into her mouth.

'I get the married ones,' Hayley reminds her. 'I'm the bit on the side, it never ends well.'

I nod in agreement. 'These are not hunting grounds for boyfriends. It's either single dads who've been dumped on their asses or blokes in stale marriages who want to re-live out stuff they've seen in porn.'

Hayley nods. Cass is not like me and Hayley. She's still looking for that happy ending where someone will pick her up, pledge undying love and whisk her away to a new-build semi in Surrey. The sort of world Hayley and I inhabit, the semis and happy endings normally end on our faces.

I grab Cass by the cheeks and give her a massive kiss on the lips. 'One day your prince will come.'

She pouts. I mean, he'll probably come via Tinder as opposed to on a white horse but hey. Our phones all pinging with messages suddenly get our attention.

'Dickweasel warning,' Hayley tells us.

We flare our nostrils. It's Richard, sometimes known as Dick but his proper full name is The Dickweasel and he's the owner of the agency where we all get our ridiculous party jobs. The nickname is pretty self-explanatory. He's a sneaky diva, never pays us on time and likes to bore us with his fake stories, like the time he sat next to Tom Hanks on a flight and they shared some nuts. Never happened. He calls us his kids like we're some sort of family but we're not here for him and his terrible acting tips, we is here for the moolah.

'They need an Elsa in half an hour over the river. The girl booked has shown up drunk and thrown up,' Darren says. 'Well, that's me out.'

'I dunno, D. You have the legs for tights,' Cass says, looking down at his calves, the hairs sticking out of the Lycra at unsavoury angles like a very bald rug.

I'm studying the message, while Cass and Hayley look to me. I know why. Elsa is my speciality. I can let it go like no one you've ever seen. I'd like to say I've won awards but no. Kids tell me I'm great and sometimes I get tips and extra cake for my time. Today, they're paying double to get someone down straight away and I think about my very overdrawn bank account.

'I can help. I got ready here – I can do your hair?' Hayley says, rooting through her bags. That's the thing about princesses – the costumes are interchangeable. Cass is already taking her Belle gloves off for me in case I touch stuff and it turns to ice. Hayley whips off her white cape. All I need is a French plait and I'm pretty much good to go.

'Two parties in a day, that's pretty much your forte,' Darren says, winking at me.

'You want to come along and be Hans?' I ask. 'We can ask the kitchen here if they could give us some ice.'

'I'd say yes but these tights are making my balls sweat buckets,' he says, pulling at the gusset. 'You'd better hustle. How are you going to get over there? There are those roadworks right outside,' he reminds me.

'I'll run?' I tell him, slipping off my glass slippers and changing into my Converse. It'll add to the drama, me running across the Thames, my skirt and cape billowing in the river breeze. It'll be nice for the tourists.

He smiles, knowing last minute is my life. 'I'll text Dick and let him know you're coming.'

'Bring it on,' I reply, gloving up and going through Hayley's make-up. We will need glitter, all the goddamn glitter.

* * *

When I get outside, I realise Darren wasn't joking. London is famous for this – traffic that not only weaves its way through three different lanes but also is governed by traffic lights that make little sense and usually end in couriers being where they shouldn't and black cabs swearing at them with added hand gestures. It's early June and a midsummer heatwave means the warmth simmers up from the pavements, thick and unrelenting. Whoever's booked a *Frozen* party in this weather is feeling the full force of irony today.

'Y'all right, Elsa?' says a man in a black cab, winding down his window.

'How long have you been sat there then?' I ask him.

'Days, mate. I've had kidney stones that have left my system quicker than this shitshow. Where do you need to go?'

'South Bank,' I tell him.

He sucks air sharply through his mouth. 'Bridges are rammed too. Can you get on the Tube like that?'

I could but running feels like the better option. I salute him and escape down a staircase to try and tackle Waterloo Bridge. I'll be hot and sweaty Elsa but at least I won't be drunk and vomity Elsa. As I look down the bridge, black cab man wasn't far wrong. It's also the weekend and the tourist vibe is strong. I stand here wondering what to do.

'Hello, thank you, please?'

I turn and a group of European tourists are grinning and pushing their kids towards me. Oh. I'm not one of those street artist people. But the kids look up at me, wide-eyed with excitement. I guess... I bend down and smile next to a boy in a Union Jack T-shirt. This better make the DVD photo reel they show Grandma. The dad, in a figure-hugging lemon yellow polo shirt, then gives me a pound. I won't be able to get a can of Coke for that around here? They all wave at me. *Danke, merci, gracias.*

Are you on your way?

It's a text from the Dickweasel.

Yep.

Make sure the mother comes through on the paying you extra in cash. She also wants some singing. Be a love and belt out a couple of favourites?

If we were singing my favourites then it would be numbers from the Cardi B back catalogue. *Come on, kids, let's be bad bitches and beat up them piñatas!* I don't reply. I'll do a stand-up job because I care.

I lean against a railing as I bring up the address again on my phone. Shit. I'll need Usain Bolt speed to get there in time. I could jump on the Tube. Sometimes the Tube is quick, sometimes it's a bloody lottery.

'Excuse me? May I?' a young man suddenly asks me.

I look down and realise I'm propped next to a line of rental bicycles and he is trying to return one. There's a young twenty-something casual vibe about him, like he's just been on a tour of London to buy sourdough bread and marvel at the architecture, and I immediately resent how relaxed he looks. He's even had time to turn up his jeans. The young man looks at me curiously. *It's Elsa with a rucksack.* And his point is? Where else is she going to put her stuff if her dress doesn't have pockets?

'You look lost?' he says quizzically.

'Not lost, just trying to work out the best way to get over the river.'

His face says it all. *I don't think you're dressed for a bike, love.* But seriously, I've ridden these before (usually at night, drunk). Tourists ride them with selfie sticks and go live on their YouTube travel vlogs. Sourdough boy's look aggrieves me, like he doesn't think it even possible that I could get on a bicycle. Only one thing happens when someone does that to me, it's a challenge. I get out my phone and book a bike.

'I'd jump in a taxi,' he suggests.

'Party is in half an hour, too much traffic.'

I can see what he's trying to do. Rescue me. Yeah, mate, if you watched the film, you'll see that Elsa does not need saving. She needs a sister.

'Well, good luck,' he replies, puzzled.

I tuck the sides of my skirt into my knickers and take off my cape and stuff it in my rucksack. We all know that capes can be disastrous. The trainers will help. Hell, I may even take a selfie because this is the stuff that makes Instagram stories interesting. #elsawithherlegsout. Done. Right, time to ride this bad boy out of here.

My sister Grace taught me how to ride a bike. It was along our street on a hand-me-down bike where the plastic basket had been eaten away by the fact that we sisters had often tried to sit in it to catch rides on the handlebars. I remember her pushing me down our road and her shouting at me to pedal. *Your legs have to go round super quickly!* I pedalled for my shitting life. I still remember that grimace on my face, having to make my legs work that quickly. I remember crashing right into the neighbour's Astra and leaving a scratch down the side that we blamed on the bin men.

That memory is brought to the fore as I pedal like a maniac now. Five minutes ago, I was completely romanticising this image. I thought I'd be floating over the bridge like romantic heroines do when they're cycling through fields of French sunflowers in well-fitting sundresses with no bras. I'd wave at tourists, have my breath taken away by the iconic London skyline and make someone on a bus laugh. However, the reality is that this is a bloody slog in this heat and I'm grimacing. And sweating. A black cab toots his horn and I can't tell if it's because I'm revealing a lot of thigh or because my cycling's a bit wobbly. He can bite me. Oh, I know why. It's because I'm not in the cycle lane. I'm cycling along with the actual traffic. That's brave, if stupid, as the cycle lane is empty. I won't get over that barrier.

Double pay, Luce. Focus on the money. This will be a great anecdote to tell the nieces. They will love this story. I stop next to a bus where a young child kneels up on a seat to gaze at me. The eye contact is completely unnerving. They tug on their mum's sleeve, who turns to stare at me too. She looks worried for me but she's not completely perturbed as this is London so there are crazier things one can see in this mad city. I once saw a man walking a pig. But you can tell she's also trying to come up with a feasible explanation for what I'm doing. *You see, in the summer, she needs to get around on a bike. A sled is useless. As are crystal slippers when you have to get around town and be practical.* I wave. The child waves back. Please be one of those little girls who imprints this vision into your mind. That time you saw a real-life princess towing her own arse around town and doing the work, under her own bloody steam.

I put my feet back on the pedals and push off to a start again. The traffic starts to crawl, which makes my job a bit easier, and I see a gap, manoeuvring my bike along a stretch of clear road, the sun on my face. This is the part where I'm supposed to close my eyes, put my arms out and freewheel my way into freedom and a better life, isn't it?

'Oi! Oi!'

Oh god, it's some sports-loving tribe of men crossing the bridge, possibly on a stag do. I'd like to think I'm cycling fast enough for them not to notice me but I'm now weaving around cars at a standstill and using my feet as brakes.

'Mate, is she your stripper? Thought she was showing up later.'

I slow down. I shouldn't as I need to get to a party and have quick tidy and wipe-down before I appear in front of the children but certain things get my back up, casual misogyny in the street, for example.

'You wish, you doucheface.'

I turn to face him and give him the bird, which shows incredible feats of balance from me. He and his rubbish hipster beard don't look impressed as, naturally, he's lost his alpha status because I dared to answer back so now some of the group laugh.

'Oooh, she's a feisty one... What you doing later, love? Say ten-ish?'

Oh, you can eff off too. 'I'll be at home laughing about you and your needle dicks. Toodle-oo.'

And with that, a gap in the traffic appears and I ride off at a moderate speed without having to worry about men in loafers chasing me, just leaving words in the breeze as my legacy. I really hope they're not chasing me.

I pedal a little harder. I cross lanes thinking I'm some sort of cycling ninja. Look at me like I'm in the Tour de France. A male tourist, possibly European because there's double denim involved, screams something in a foreign language at me.

'Elsa, ACHTUNG! *VORSICHTIG SEIN!*'

'And to you too, my friend!' I reply, laughing jovially.

But before I can work out what he means, it just appears out of nowhere. That's an actual bus. And I panic. The side of my dress to my right thigh falls out, I can't grab it and brake at the same time. It gets tangled in the wheel. Oh, you fricking idiot. No, no, no. Boof. And then air. All this air beneath me. Like I'm flying. Does Elsa fly? I don't think she's that sort of princess.

3

'LUCY! IF YOU CAN HEAR ME, SQUEEZE MY HAND! IT'S EMMA! LUCY!'

Why is Ems shouting? Like, you're right there, stop shouting at me. Did I not set an alarm again? What day is it? If she's woken me up to make her a cup of tea then she can naff right off. Why do I have to squeeze her hand? I'll squeeze it all right. Maybe I should dig a nail in. I feel my thumb clasp around her fingers gently. Why don't my hands work? Squeeze, Lucy. I must be *really* hungover if I can't even attempt a minor physical assault on my sister.

I open my eyes and look at a strange perforated ceiling divided up into a grid like a giant noughts and crosses board. I'm not at home, am I? And why does it feel like my eyes are being stabbed by the light?

'Ems? It's bright. I can't. Turn off the lights.'

'Oh my god... oh my...'

I feel her throw her body over mine and envelop me. I don't think she's hugged me like this in her whole entire life. Has she? Maybe when Lexie and Mark died in *Grey's Anatomy*. God, is she crying? What the hell has happened? The lights dim and I open one eye again to try and make sense of things, to take in the sounds.

'Ems, why are you crying?'

'Ring everyone. Tess is downstairs in the cafeteria, tell her to send her parents back. They were just about to jump on a train. Mum and Dad went home. Oh my... page Dr Elliott because she'll need to do tests and arrange for an MRI.'

They'll have to do a what? Who? Emma's tears run onto my skin and dampen my shirt. Wait, not a shirt. I seem to be wearing paper. I'm in a hospital? Emma gallops through giving instructions to a man next to the bed who could be a doctor but he's also got a hand on Emma's back like he's comforting her. Is he crying too? Why is he crying? Who is he?

'Lucy. How are you feeling? Have you got any pain? How's your breathing? Do you need oxygen? Jag, get a nurse in and let's get you on some oxygen,' says Emma.

'Ems... just give her a moment.' The man's hand goes to her back again.

'Why am I here? Ems?'

I force my eyes open again and take in the room, the faces, the air around me. I'm in a room with a television on the wall. I don't remember watching that television. I wriggle my toes. It feels important to make my toes move. I saw that in a film once. I hold my hand up, seeing that a needle is running into my hand and the crook of my arm. And who's been drawing on me? There are pictures on my arm. I sit up, short of breath. Why? Ems sits down next to me and encourages me to calm down. I claw at the tubes going into my nose.

'Lucy, you were in an accident. On Waterloo Bridge. You were on a bike. In a dress. You are so lucky. You got hit by a bus, dressed as Elsa,' Emma says in loud, accentuated tones like she's talking to a foreign grandma.

'Who?' I gasp.

'You. You were hit by a bus,' she replies.

'But who's Elsa? Are you a doctor?' I say, turning to the gentleman in the room.

'I'm Jag?'

'It's nice to meet you.'

He looks over at Emma tentatively.

'She's just confused. Lucy, you suffered quite a traumatic head injury. They operated, they had to put you in a medically induced coma to control the swelling to your brain. You've been asleep for weeks.' She explains everything slowly, holding back tears. I was on a bike? Like, Dad's bike? Who the fuck is Elsa? She sounds German. German... I remember a German man. Do I?

'We've been taking it in turns to come here and sit with you. I mean, you're awake. That's everything.'

I reach up to my head, it's bandaged. My hair. Someone cut my hair? I hope it wasn't Meg. She did that once and gave me some pretty rubbish levels on my fringe. I was in a coma? I rub my tongue along the underside of my teeth, everything is dry and fuzzy. I study Emma's face. She looks different. Sad, yes, but there's something else.

'When did you get old?' I ask her.

'You're such a cow,' she replies. She throws herself over me again, laughing but crying and not really caring too much about the fact she's snotting all over me. So grim. 'Oh god, I don't know what we would have done had we lost you.'

I pause to take that all in. They nearly lost me. I nearly died? The man called Jag keeps looking over at me. Whilst Emma's face reads relief, you can tell he's thinking things through a bit more. All I'm thinking is that I think I'm wearing a nappy.

'And if I look old as hell, it's because you've probably aged me ten years, that's why.'

I look down to a badge on her shirt. Emma Callaghan-Kohli. Who?

'You're a paediatric cardiologist?'

'Yeah?' she replies.

'Fancy.'

'Well, her sarcasm mode is still in good nick,' Emma says to Jag.

I am silent as my mind whirrs through everything. How long have I been asleep? I cough. Everything feels stiff and unused. There's a window that overlooks the river and I see sky. It's so blue. No clouds. And a hint of buildings, a line like on an Etch-a-Sketch. I look down at my arm again. Someone didn't draw on me. That's a tattoo. What the actual mother of shite? That's a bloody leopard. Why have I got a leopard on my arm? Why does he look slightly drugged? My eyes shift about the room.

'Luce, it's Mum and Dad,' says Emma, who's on the phone. 'They want to speak to you. Mum won't believe it until she's seen it.'

'LUCY!' My eyes focus on a phone screen to see my parents in our living room. They're on the phone. Like a picture? No... they're moving. It's a video. It's so clear. And when did my sister get this posh phone? This must have cost a crapload of money. When did this happen? Dad is sobbing, his hands cupped over his face. Mum has one hand to his back but her eyes stay fixed on me, studying me intently. I can't say a word. They look older too but Mum's hair is still the same, the same bob she's had since forever.

'Lucy, we're going to make our way down now. We will be there really soon. Stay awake for us, love, OK?'

It's very Mum. When her girls do good there's a nod of the head, a clench of the jaw, a fire in her eyes. She doesn't crumble, at least not in front of us. I don't know what to do so just wave. Can they hear me?

'Emma, is she comfortable? She doesn't look comfortable? What does this mean? Why is she so stunned? Is she on some sort of new drugs? She looks pale. Someone make her a cup of tea.'

That is also classic Mum but the sound of her voice is soothing.

'I read that sometimes people have a surge before they die. Is this it? Is this her surge?'

I hear Emma loudly whisper back at her that she's ridiculous and that I can still hear her and then they argue. But strangely, this is also familiar and I think I might laugh.

'Just get here, Mum. Her vitals are good. She's a bit confused but the more people she sees, the better it will be. Get in an Uber. Use my account. Don't you dare drive, you're emotional and you'll both get confused about the congestion charge. Mum, I said don't drive...'

An Uber? Their call ends and Emma exhales deeply as Jag rests a hand to her shoulder. She sees me, smiles and comes to sit on the side of my bed.

'Classic Mum,' I mumble.

Emma laughs. She reaches for a small plastic cup of water and a straw.

'Small sips. You had a tube in for at least two weeks.'

'I think I have one in my flaps?'

'That's a catheter helping you wee. They'll take that out in a bit. Just let it do its job.'

'I can't pee when he's in the room,' I whisper, gesturing over to Jag.

'Hun, I've been out with you and you've crouched down between two parked cars and taken a wee before. You set off one of the alarms you peed with that much force.'

'I did?'

'At Beth's birthday thing? Though you were smashed so I doubt you remember.'

That'll be it. But when I cast my mind back, it feels like

there's a blank page there. It'll come to me, I'm sure, but all the words are fuzzy.

'There's a lot going on. You have a large scar on your skull, some cannulas for drugs and fluids. You were intubated so that's why your throat will feel dry. Though Meg did joke you were used to having things rammed in your mouth...' she jokes brazenly.

I don't reply but return a look of horror. 'I do?'

'We removed the tube last week, the doctor was confident. Take lots of sips. We need to check your reflexes and up your fluids.'

She smiles at me, throws me a look of reassurance and puts a hand to my cheek. Her phone rings and she goes to answer it.

'Oh my god, Gracie – yes!' She bursts into tears. 'Don't cry. She's fine. Get yourself over here with the girls. Do you want to talk to her? Breathe, Gracie. She is fine. She is awake.'

My eyes light up to hear that name. Grace. I know her. I want to see her.

'Hold up, Gracie...' Emma cups her hand over her phone. 'I need to calm her down. Understandably, she's not dealt with this very well. Give me a mo, Luce.'

Surely no one's dealt with this too well but I get it. Emma and Jag move to the end of my bed, chatting like they're on some conference trading call, my eyes and ears bouncing between the two of them. *Gracie, this is nothing like Tom's coma. Come and see her. I can meet you at the door with the girls. Will, she's up!*

Grace, I know. Who is Tom in the coma? And there's a Will? *Will and Grace*. That's a show. We watch that show together. I want to see all the sisters now. I want to absorb all that big sister energy like a huge collective hug.

A nurse, in the meanwhile, enters the room, observing my machines and taking a few notes.

'Morning, Lucy. I'm Zahra,' she tells me in a soft lilting West African accent. 'Can I take your blood pressure?' I nod and let her take my arm and wrap the band around the top of it. All I can hear is the scratch of the Velcro. It tightens. A beep.

'How are you feeling, Lucy? Any nausea? Pain?'

'I feel drunk.'

She laughs and it's a welcome, joyful sound in a room of machines and panicked phone calls.

'Well, Beth did joke that we should push neat vodka into your cannula. That would wake our Lucy up for sure.'

I glance over at Emma. 'I bet they freaked out, the family...'

'They tried everything,' Zahra tells me. 'Your favourite music, they would read to you and dance and paint your toenails. They've been coming down here in shifts with your parents to sit with you. A different one every night. We don't mind too much, they bring us all biscuits and cake. I've never seen a family like it. You are very loved, young lady.'

I pause for a moment to take that in.

'Your brain and your body have been through a lot, Lucy. Give yourself time to catch up. Simple things first, deep breaths, let your eyes adjust to the room. If you can feel your toes and fingers then move them, move your neck from side to side too. We will get there.'

My breaths feel slow, shallow. Breathe, Lucy.

'Did Emma tell you, you'd made the news, too? It went viral. All these pics and videos. Kids were crying because they thought Elsa was dead. The headlines in the papers were that you had "frozen" the traffic.'

She laughs under her breath.

'Why was I on the bridge? On a bike?'

'Emma said you were on your way to a party? It's what you do – you dress up as princesses and perform at parties.'

'I do? I dress up?'

'You do. But they had to cut your dress off at the scene to rescue you. That is why you also made the news. You were in a thong and Converse and someone got a picture on their phone, a less than conventional princess.'

'I wear thongs?'

She laughs again, with her whole body. 'Emma told us it was lucky as normally you prefer to go commando.'

I do? I am pretty sure I don't as Beth told me that spiders can crawl up my minnie while I'm asleep. Their leftover legs then stick to you and become pubes.

'Emma told us you were the funny one.' I grab Zahra's hand suddenly and she grabs it back. 'She also told us you were a fighter. The feisty one. Classic Lucy to take on a double-decker in fancy dress and stop the traffic. But she had no doubt that you would wake up. I'll go and chat to your doctors to see what we do next. The call button is here if you need me but I think this lot have it covered.'

I glance over to Emma. I'm very much drawn to her feet. Emma, those are old lady moccasin shoes. Mum has slippers like those in burgundy velvet. She does look different. She goes in to hug Jag and they look over at me, HOLDING HANDS. Emma! She has that jerk doctor boyfriend called Simon. I've seen him ogling my boobs before. Have they broken up? Has being in a coma and nearly losing me meant she thought long and hard about the love she deserved and hooked up with this Asian dude? I like him. I don't remember him though. Jag? The door suddenly whips open and Meg surges in, dropping her bags to the floor and launching herself at me.

'Oh my LUCY!'

I put my arms around her but, in truth, words scream inside my consciousness even louder. MEGGSY, YOU ARE FRICKING ANCIENT. Is that grey? Behind her is a man I recognise. That's her husband, Danny. I never quite got the physical appeal of him as I thought he looked like a sad lumber-jack but now there's a paunch there. Did he stress-eat while I was in a coma? Meg pulls away from me and studies my face.

'Don't you dare do that to us again, OK? We have been out of our goddamn minds.' Her eyes fill with tears and she cups my face.

'Meg? I don't get it.'

My breathing becomes more shallow as I look into her face. You're Meg. You're definitely Meg. But you're old. I have a tattoo and wear thongs. I am really confused. My lip goes and I start to cry, using the palms of my hands to wipe at my tears. Meg grabs me harder and I rest my head on her shoulder. This feels the same. This definitely feels the same.

'I didn't mean to shout at you. I just... Lucy.'

'She's been through a lot. She's really out of it...' Emma says. 'I'm sorry, Lucy. I got so excited. This must be so much for you to take in.'

'Danny and I were just about to jump on a train when Tess called...'

'Yeah, Meg ran back, actually sprinted. Only time she ever does that is in a Next sale,' Danny jokes.

Meg narrows her eyes at him. I can tell she's been running from the sweat patches under her boobs.

'How are you feeling? What don't you get?' she asks, wiping a tear from my face.

'I just don't remember being on that bike at all...' I continue. 'Why the hell do you look so middle-aged?'

'Well, that part of her isn't broken at least,' Meg says, laughing. Another person stands in the doorway. She's young, a teen, and carries a takeaway coffee. She stands there in denim shorts and a cropped top, a checked shirt tied around her waist. She certainly likes her eyeliner.

'Aunty Lucy?' she says, her face beaming.

I look up at her, my mouth open. She looks just like Meg. Just how Meg looked but slightly different. My stare seems to scare her though. Jag looks over at Emma as she starts to work it out.

'Lucy, you know who this is, right?' she asks me.

I shake my head.

'It's Tess... my daughter. Tess?' Meg says, almost like I may be joking.

I still stare blankly. Tess comes over to squeeze my hand and I burst into tears. 'But... you're a baby. The last time I saw you. You were a baby.'

Emma and Meg don't utter a word. Tess runs back and hides in her father's arms, distraught. Don't cry. I didn't mean to scare her.

Jag comes to the end of the bed. 'Lucy, do you know what time of year it is?'

It must be the summer. The sky is blue. Meg's in shorts. She's not shaved her legs but I won't bring that up. It's the summer. I remember it being the summer. I still can't say anything. Why can't I remember?

Jag approaches the side of my bed as Meg stands to hug Emma, both of them lost for words. For once. This is normally not the case.

'Spit it out, you guys. Is this some sort of really bad joke? This is not funny. Who is that girl? Tess is, like, tiny. She has really fluffy hair. She looked like a duck.' Jag puts an arm to mine, trying to calm me down. 'I don't even know who you are. Where's Simon? Emma was going out with some other doctor called Simon?'

Emma looks absolutely mortified that I'm saying his name out loud. Jag smiles and shakes his head.

'Emma divorced Simon,' he explains to me. 'Emma and I got married a few months ago. In Bristol? You were there?'

I don't even remember her marrying Simon. She's been married twice? I bury my face in my hands. I love a wedding. I'd remember a wedding.

Jag takes my hands gently. 'Lucy, I want you to take some really deep breaths. Do you know your full name?'

'Lucy Victoria Callaghan.'
'And when were you born?'
'August twenty-first, 1992.'
'And how old are you?'
'I'm seventeen. I'm pretty sure I'm seventeen.'

4

My name is Lucy and this much I know. I'm seventeen years old, a few weeks off my eighteenth birthday. I'm off to study Theatre Studies and English at Birkbeck University come the autumn. The last thing I remember is Mum telling me to get my accommodation forms in order otherwise they'll put me in a leaky bedsit in East London above a minicab office that doubles as a meth lab. We were having conversations about saucepans. She said she'd treat me to a trip to Ikea to buy clothes pegs and frying pans and I told her I wouldn't need such things. She laughed. What would I fry eggs in? I told her I would buy my fried eggs from the many London cafés and she told me this is why I would end up with no money. But Mother, I told her, I will have my looks, my smarts and my spunky outlook on life. That doesn't fry eggs, Lucy, she replied. And she laughed and exhaled in both despair and adoration because I'm her favourite daughter. We all know it.

What else do I remember? Lady Gaga? Obama is President. David Cameron is the Prime Minister. My life's ambition is to, one day, snog Robert Pattinson or join the cast of *Glee*. I left sixth form a few months ago so I'm in some in-between stage of working and partying, spending days as a waitress and behind the bar at The Shy Fox, which is a crappy gastro pub that's managed by Fergus, who sits in the storeroom in his breaks and watches porn on a laptop. I have my mates at school. Farah's my girl. My go-to party mate. And I have four sisters. One brother-in-law. One niece. A boyfriend.

These are all answers to questions that people keep asking me. The psychologist, the neurologist, the phlebotomist, they all end in -ist and someone needs to help them find better shoes. They ask me to talk at them, draw circles, show them that I know my left from my right, my blues from my reds. I sing and spell and I'm a fricking queen at their flashcards. They poke and prod me. *Right*, they say. *I'm just going to call in another specialist who may be able to advise*, and I get passed along to the next person like the bowl of peas at a roast dinner. *She was always quite tricky to work out*, Dad jokes with a pained expression. Mum thinks I'm faking and keeps telling me to stop messing about. *This isn't funny at all, Lucy.* Grace cries with worry. Emma seems fascinated, like I'm a science experiment to her. Because I'm not seventeen. Apparently, I'm nearly thirty and, fuck me, I can't remember any of it.

When you're the youngest of five girls, you get used to being talked about a lot. I am the baby of this clan and, as such, I've been forced to grow up far quicker than most. I found out about periods before I was ten (I walked in on Meg changing her pad; I thought she was bleeding to death), I found out about sex from reading Beth's diary (she lost her virginity to some boy called Christian who she thought looked like Orlando Bloom, but he didn't know where to put his willy) and I first got drunk with Grace after being insanely jealous that our sisters were going out clubbing without us. We got hammered on Bacardi and Ribena. Ribena is not a suitable mixer by the way. My mother will tell you that because we both threw up. Grace didn't make it to the toilet in time either and chucked up purple in the hallway over a basket of freshly washed laundry. Dad had to repaint.

As the youngest, you become the butt of the jokes. You're the accident. *Mum and Dad never really wanted you.* The one on the end. To combat that you acquire the best of skills, the loudest of voices, the snark is off the scale. You're the one who has to shout the loudest to be heard otherwise you'll be forgotten. You think that's an exaggeration but it isn't. When I was ten, I went to the supermarket with everyone and was tasked with wheeling the trolley back. THEY DROVE OFF WITHOUT ME. I'm not even joking. They only noticed when the car hit the dual carriageway and they had cracked open some crisps and realised there was an empty seat.

Am I a rebel? Maybe I've done more at a younger age than most. I mean, I had four sisters at university. I've heard all the sisters' stories. I've been invited to visit and partake. It's been a running theme my whole life. *Let Lucy tag along.* And I did. I absorbed all that experience into my soul. Because of this, people talk about me.

She's overly confident, Mrs Callaghan. She defies authority and is abrasive in her manner.

She threw a full can of Coke at my daughter's forehead.

I am afraid we will have to ban you from the village hall after the party you held here last week. We have not seen carnage like it.

I think Lucy slept with Danny's brother-in-law at my wedding.

MUM! LUCY STOLE MY SHIT AGAIN!

They're doing it now. I can hear hushed whispers from the corridor chatting about me, thinking I'm still in my coma, believing I'm still the baby on the end who needs protecting, who's still vulnerable.

'How can she think it's 2010? That was over ten years ago?'

I don't know who is in that huddle but amongst them is my brain surgeon, Mr Gomes, who came in earlier and asked me a bunch of questions and shone a lot of light in my eyes. He does this a lot and inspects my scar, looking by and large extremely proud of his work. When he came in, I fully expected one of the sisters to be married to him. Maybe I was married to him. Maybe I fell in love with a Portuguese doctor who has a rounded paunch like a teapot. Maybe we have kids called João and Inez and a house full of cats.

I don't know who anyone is any more because it's 2022. I've literally lost years and no one knows why. Am I scared out of my mind? Yes. This is like the future. Are the cars flying yet? Because the phone technology is crazy. Is Justin Bieber still a thing? I had a whole season of 30 Rock saved on the planner. Did anyone get rid of it? But I daren't say this out loud because I should feel lucky to be here, to be alive. It feels like a hangover. A really terrible one. I watched that film. I remember that film. We all wanted to shag Bradley Cooper after that except Emma, who was strangely drawn to the singing, toothless dentist.

Or maybe I'm a traveller in time. Like a female Michael J. Fox. Like maybe a bus hit me into another dimension or forward in time. Yet all my theorising, all my worry, is also mingled with suspicion because I know what my sisters are like and this could possibly still be a very elaborate joke. Those cows told me for years that my real father was Giles from *Buffy the Vampire Slayer* and that he had to leave the actual country to be a Watcher because he was so ashamed of me. They loved the pranking.

I've been introduced to so many children. One nephew is literally months old. His name is Jude. Nieces and nephews for days. They all seem to like me very much and I'm surrounded by their artwork so I'm glad that whatever has transpired in the last ten or so years means I've been a quality aunt. But the life stories, the sheer amount of extra people we seem to have acquired, makes me think this could be a very elaborate set-up. These are all actors, perhaps. Maybe the sisters have gone to extra lengths to prank me. A prank that has seen Beth go up a few dress sizes, Meg dusting her hair with talc, Emma pretending to be a qualified doctor. If it is a prank then there is a lot of attention to detail, almost too much. This means there is only one outcome here and that is my brain has shut down the last ten or so years of my life. It's literally forgotten them.

'The brain is a very curious mechanism and amnesia like this is not something we can ever hope to understand. It could be brought about by injury or the trauma. I would need to do more investigations. The earlier MRI showed no clots or other injuries that could be causing this,' explains Mr Gomes.

'So is this permanent?' Meg.

'What if the MRI missed something?' Grace.

'How can this be happening? She remembers everything.' Beth.

'Emma, is this the best neurosurgeon we know? Is it time for a second opinion?' Mum.

'I can't answer that for sure. Sometimes these things can be temporary. I've had people in comas who've woken up with accents, new personalities, the deficits and changes can be so different. I can't say anything until I've done more exploratory tests,' continues my poor brain surgeon.

I wonder what those tests will be. Will they involve needles? Then again, I must be OK with needles because I have these tattoos. Not just the leopard. I have some flowers down one shoulder that trail along my bicep. I have an actual Tweety Pie on my ankle. Did I do that as a bet? I close my eyes for a second. Come on, Lucy. You were on a bike. Remember the bike. It must be in there. Maybe it's like a maze. I have to open up all these doors and channels to remember anything. Try harder.

'All I know is that her initial reflexes and observations are good. Please give her time to rest. Don't inundate her. It may just be some sort of fog. We need to let the fog clear. I'll let you know when I know more. For the meanwhile, I'm going to ensure someone from psychiatry comes down too.'

'You think this may be caused by some psychiatric disorder?' Emma.

'What she has been through is traumatic, and when we have no organic answers for why Lucy's amnesia has happened then we have to look to other psychological mechanisms to explain things.'

Lucy. She always had a touch of crazy about her. I try and piece together what I've just heard. So the brain is intact. That's good. But maybe there are some screws loose. Christ, this could be a hallucination of sorts, some form of psychosis. I've not left this room. What's outside this room? Maybe there's nothing. I'll know if I start seeing twins dressed the same and twisting staircases, right? This could be a truly excellent episode of *The X-Files*. What was the last thing I remember? What did I last eat? What was I wearing? I don't have a bike. There is certainly no bike. I clench my eyes closed. Come on, Luce.

'Are you in pain? Are you wincing, my dear?'

The door of my room is open and Zahra stands there in an apron and with a trolley.

'No. Come in... I was just closing my eyes to see if I could retrieve my memory.'

'Well, that is one way of doing things. Has it worked?'

'No.'

She leaves the door ajar as my family continue to fire questions at poor Mr Gomes. Zahra watches me listening, taking in all these words about my poorly working brain, about a part of my life I'm desperately trying to find.

'Is Mr Gomes safe? Are they coming at him from all directions?' I ask.

'Haha, I am sure Mr Gomes can handle himself.'

'You've not met my family...'

'I can tell them to move into one of the rooms down the corridor if you don't want to hear anything? It can be a lot to take on.'

'It's fine. This way I get to earwig. I'm good at that. One of my best skills from being the youngest. Have they at least stopped crying?' I ask.

'Your dad is still quite bereft. Him and Grace are standing there holding each other.'

'Grace apparently lost a husband recently. His name was Tom. My sister must have been through so much. All that grief and I can't remember any of it.'

I look thoughtful at saying that out loud and Zahra comes over and puts a hand to my arm.

'All these beautiful children they've brought into my room too. I didn't want to scare them because they're so tiny so I hugged them all, but I don't know them either.'

'I need to tell your sisters to take it easy on you. They're all so happy and relieved that you are well, I don't think they realise that you've been inundated with so much.'

She wipes a tear from the side of my face. 'I think I feel guilty, Zahra. I feel bad I've put Grace through some repeated trauma of losing someone, of having no recollection of any of these people.'

'Hush now. That's the last thing you should be feeling. Now the focus should be on you.'

'And Emma... is divorced? Did you know Simon?'

Zahra pops her head around the door to see who may be listening.

'Yes, he was famous in this hospital for all the wrong reasons. I'd seen his penis and I hadn't even slept with him. If you ask me, we thought your sister had some sort of brain injury herself for sticking with him for so long...'

I laugh and cough a little and she sits me up in bed to steady myself.

'Jag is a good guy. I went to a party after they got married. They hired a restaurant, it was lovely.'

'Was I there?'

'I don't recall. I think I would have remembered you.'

For the minute, I seem to be clinging to Zahra. Everyone else is firing information at me and waiting expectantly for me to react. *These are my daughters. I got married. I'm dating a bloke I met on a plane who looks like Aquaman.* And I stare back at them wondering when and how everyone got so grown up. And who on earth is Aquaman? Shit, does your new boyfriend have webbed feet?

Zahra doesn't lay that on me. She pauses for a moment to take my pulse and observe my monitors as Beth walks into the room, her small baby, Jude, in her arms.

'Is it OK if I just take a chair and feed the little one?' she asks.

I smile. 'Of course, you numpty.'

Beth beams to hear my reply and I watch as she removes the little man out of his sling and retreats to a corner of the room. Beth came in and, like Meg before her, launched herself at me before realising she had a baby strapped to her bosom. Beth has a baby. Scrap that, she has two babies. How is that possible? To me, she's my sister at uni who came back at Christmas and told us she'd shagged a lad in the laundry room on top of a tumble dryer. His name was Paul. She showed us a picture and Meg said he looked hairy like a hobbit and then Beth threw a Rubik's cube at her face and cut Meg's lip open. This is the stuff I remember.

'How old?' Zahra asks.

'Two months.'

'Is it Jude like the song?' I ask her.

'Naturally.'

Beth was the muso sister. She made mix CDs for everyone and gifted them us at Christmas and most of the time we told her she was a cheap bitch for doing so. But she lived her life for gigs and festivals and she'd be the person who you'd want on your team for any music-based quiz.

'How is it I remember all the lyrics to that song but I can't remember you having your baby?' I ask her.

'Everyone knows the lyrics to that song. It's something all of us just learn subliminally through time.'

I hum it to myself. 'Tell me the story of how he was born,' I ask her.

'It was May. We didn't even make it to the hospital. Jude was eager to get out into the world so I birthed him on the floor of our flat. Will delivered him. He had Emma on FaceTime...'

'Way to go, Mummy...' Zahra adds.

'FaceTime is the phone call on the screen thing, right?' I ask.

Beth nods, trying to piece together what I do and do not know.

'And Will...?'

'Is my boyfriend. We got together when I was twenty-four or so.'

'And he makes you happy?'

Beth pauses for a moment to adjust Jude on her boob. 'Very.'

Did I ever envisage my sisters with all these kids, boyfriends and husbands? In my mind, I always thought at least one of us would bag Zac Efron.

'Can I ask a question, B?' I mutter.

I take a deep breath, almost too scared to hear the answer.

'Sure, hun.'

'What have I been doing in the last ten or so years? Am I still with Josh? Is he coming to see me?'

Beth's face tells me the answer. 'Josh Reid? That footballer you used to date? The one with the acne and the Vauxhall Corsa?' I can't tell if she wants to turn this into a joke or play it seriously. 'Luce, no.'

As soon as she says it, I feel a crushing sensation in my chest and exhale deeply, my bottom lip quivering.

'Oh, Luce... I'm so sorry. I don't know how else to put it. You and Josh broke up before you left for university. He wasn't kind to you at the end.'

That part feels like an arrow to my very soul. What did he do? Zahra looks over at Beth to tell her to maybe stop. I loved him. I'm pretty sure he gave me a ring. Like, not an engagement ring. It may have been from Argos but I'm sure we were destined for something more. He looked like Beckham. Even if he was prickish to me, why do I feel so sad? Because I don't know what he did. It's like my heart being broken for a second time by the same person.

'So, did I have a boyfriend? Kids?'

'Not exactly. You have friends. Lots of them. Out of all of us, you are busy. You work and party hard. You have... fun.'

I look at her quizzically. 'Are you saying I'm some sort of slag...?' I ask her, almost aghast.

Zahra tries to intervene. 'Lucy, I'm going to start washing you. We have the physio coming in a bit. I can come back later if you want to finish your conversation?'

'Nah, you're good,' I say, studying Beth's face. 'Go on, you were telling me I was a bit of a ho.'

'Not that at all,' Beth says, trying to backtrack. 'You just... out of all of us, you've almost shied away from that traditional relationship stuff. You worked hard at your career, you've spent most of your twenties at university, doing courses.'

Zahra undoes my gown and slips a flannel down my back. 'But my career? I thought I was some sort of second-rate party princess. That doesn't sound like I'm doing much with my life?'

'You do all sorts. You do a lot of auditions, you've been in a lot of musicals and shows. I saw you in *Rent*. You were brilliant.'

'Oh... so basically I bed-hop and work-hop and have nothing stable or of any concrete value in my life. Do I own a flat? A house?'

'You live in a house share in Herne Hill.'

'Do I have a car?'

'No. You failed your test five times and your instructor said after that you may be a lost cause.'

'I remember him, his name was Robert. He said I was good at driving.'

'You gave him a concussion after a touch of road rage where you drove into a Domino's delivery moped.'

'I don't remember that.'

Beth goes silent as Zahra holds my gown up, trying to protect my modesty. I peel it off completely.

'Please, she's got her boobs out, what are two more?' I say. 'You join in whenever you want, Zahra.'

If you have four sisters then you're not really allowed to be shy. You have to embrace the nudity in enclosed spaces and all the body hair, tampons, farts and screeches over shared lip balm that come with it.

'You have wonderful tattoos on your back?' Zahra says.

Beth nods slowly.

'Christ, I'm a fricking easel. Of what?' I ask.

'I think it's a tree?' Little Jude rolls off Beth's boob and she pops him on her shoulder and clips her bra into place. 'Here, let me get a picture for you.'

She comes over with her magic phone, takes a pic and shows me. That's not a tree, that's a bloody forest on my back and a sexy woman in a beret with a devil tail. Who's she? Before I hand the phone back, the camera comes on again and I take a look at my face on the screen. I've not done this yet. When I woke up, they were so keen to do their scans that they wheeled me straight into MRI and I caught a glimpse of someone in a lift. Someone with a bandaged head and bruised eyes like she'd been in a fight. She had no hair. Oh my god, that's me. I recognise her. Has she aged? She looks like she's seen stuff, her eyebrows need work, but her eyes are still the same bluey-grey colour.

'So I've also spent the last ten years doing stuff to my body. Anything else I should know about? Is this a *Girl with the Dragon Tattoo* thing? Am I a spy? Am I really bloody good with guns now?'

'I wouldn't know if you were a spy. I don't think you're a spy. You're terrible at keeping secrets in any case.'

My shoulders slump. I'm not scrapping that theory though because that's what happened with Jason Bourne when he fell off that boat.

'When did you get your piercings done?' Zahra asks.

'My what now?' I say, reaching up to my ears.

Beth winces a little, not quite knowing what to say. 'Oh, well... you nearly broke the MRI here because when you came in you were unconscious and naturally they didn't think to look for your piercings,' she explains.

'Where the hell are my piercings?' I ask.

Zahra reaches in a cabinet under the bed and pulls out a cardboard basin full of metal bits that look like they're the fittings for a flatpack wardrobe.

'A nipple, I think, and then you had a clitoral hood thing too... I had the pleasure of removing them. Someone suggested a metal detector to make sure we hadn't missed anything.'

I reach at my private areas, Zahra laughing.

'But why? How? Have I got holes in my minge?' There's a grin I can't quite explain on Beth's face. 'Why are you laughing?' I ask her.

'You got it done one summer because you heard it increases sexual pleasure,' Beth explains.

'It does?' asks Zahra.

'I wouldn't remember...' I reply. I remove my gown to take a look at my naked form. Now this has changed. I have a softer stomach, my legs look fuller, my pubes are bristly. 'So I told you all about my fanny piercing?'

'You have a habit of broadcasting information. Some family dinner and no one believed it so you got your bits out in one of the bedrooms and showed us. Grace asked if it jingled when you ran,' Beth informs us, bursting into laughter, tears in her eyes. 'You literally just pulled your knickers down in that room, no shame. Emma fell over from the shock. She told you to douse your bits in salt water so it wouldn't get infected. You said it stung and Meg and her just looked at you because they'd had babies so we got a rundown of their vaginal traumas.'

Like, why isn't that burnt into my memory? Surely something like that would stick to the grey matter? 'Do I pee funny now?'

'I wouldn't know, Luce. We share a lot but there are limits.'

I laugh. Oh, Bethy.

'Luce, it's who you are. There's a real freedom about you – courage, adventure, nothing was off limits. You were always the one at the top of the tree and one of us would have to come get you, you gave bullies what for, you defied everything. It was part of your magic and, in your twenties, it was a running theme. You lived your best life.'

'Lived my best life? Did you just come up with that?' I ask her.

'No, it's a thing now. People say it a lot. I need to catch you up with the lingo,' she says, patting her baby's back as he falls soundly asleep on her shoulder. *Look at him, Beth. That's your baby.* 'And when you're telling your nurse to get her boobs out, when you swear and ask me if you've got holes in your minge, then that's my Lucy. It's unapologetic, slightly... no, *very*...

coarse but you were open and honest. So honest and funny. You were the tonic we all needed.'

'Well, obviously. You bitches were kinda boring, even back then...' She smiles and comes over to sandwich me in a hug again. 'Beth, we're squishing your baby again...'

'He won't mind... Is this a good time to tell you you've got a peach tattooed on your right arse cheek too?'

5

Things they don't tell you when you wake up from a coma: you don't just spring up out of bed like a grandparent who's found a Golden Ticket. After all the relief settles that you are alive and semi-kicking, you're still a physical shell of your once former self. You've been lying down for weeks, crapping in a nappy and have multiple tubes coming out your orifices so it takes some time for your body to return to normal. I also ache everywhere because my return to normality is being controlled by Igor the physio man. When I'm done in this place, I am going to make a voodoo doll out of him and ensure that every night I stick pins in his crotch. Blunt pins. Lots of blunt pins.

'Just a few more steps, Lucy,' he says in his strong Eastern European accent, which makes him sound like a Soviet gymnastics coach.

'Piss off.'

'Igor, I am so sorry,' Emma intervenes, horrified.

'I'm not. If I could actually control how I pee and I can't because I've had a tube up my bits for a month then I would pee everywhere and mostly in his general direction.'

Emma shakes her head for the shame. Meg laughs from behind a hand covering her mouth.

'It's all right, Emma. I get a lot of abuse. An old lady hit me with a walking stick yesterday.'

'I like this lady,' I say. 'Me and her can be friends. Give her my number.'

I push my walker (yes, my old lady walker) a few more steps and glare at all of them. Are you not entertained? I did the walking. Now let me rest and watch some bad television.

'Have you been doing the stretches like we discussed?' Igor asks me.

'Yeah?'

Meg raises her eyebrows at me and I stick a middle finger up at her.

'I'm putting down that your middle finger still seems to work,' Igor says, scribbling in his notes. He's not just into torture, he's also into sarcasm. If only my lower leg had the power to kick him in the balls. 'These exercises are important. You're leaving here soon. I want you to have some basic mobility back for the everyday. To be able to take a shower, turn on a kettle, write a letter?'

'To your mother, telling her that she bore a son who is a harbinger of pain?'

'She loves a letter. Nice quality paper, please. Her name is Magda.'

This would be a worthy exchange if he was in the slightest bit good-looking but he has hair like he belongs on the cover of a romance novel – proper eighties Bon Jovi locks with a bit of a curl.

'Lucy, I got in Igor because he is the best at what he does. He's right. We need to get you back into real life and ensure all your muscles don't seize up. Please listen to him,' Emma pleads with me.

'But I quite like the sponge baths in bed and people

bringing me hot drinks and sushi. I don't need to do anything. In any case, I can't work. I don't think I can really leave the house because my head is all shaved and stitched like a Frankenmonster so essentially I'd be lounging around anyway, waiting for my memory to come back.'

'So you basically just want to be a lazy bitch?' Igor says.

Meg sniggers again, quietly.

Seriously, Emma? She's paying this man to hurt and insult me?

'I'm allowed. I got hit by a bus. I'm owed some time off and to be waited on hand and foot.'

'For a while but you still need to do some things independently that require mobility,' Igor continues. 'To get to the toilet? You want someone changing your tampons forever?'

'Some people might find that kinky,' I reply.

Emma is on a high blush now. Did she not warn the physio man that I come with a tongue? The knock I got to my head clearly did little to level out my disposition.

'Well, that's one lucky man who'll get to do that for life.'

It won't be you. Don't worry, Igor.

'Well, we are done, Miss Lucy. I will see you again tomorrow. I will leave those hand-grip trainers on the table for you. Please use them.'

I smile. 'Thank you. I'll see you tomorrow, Igor.'

'You will and you will love it,' he replies.

I hate you. He gathers his belongings and Emma walks with him out of the room as I pull faces at his back.

Meg is still laughing to see me so riled. 'You do know that in the last ten years, you were a total gym bunny. You did classes and stuff. You ran races. You were the fittest person I know.'

'Well, naturally. I'm super fit. It's the giant staples in my head, I reckon.'

Meg rolls her eyes at me. 'Do the exercises.'

'But they hurt.'

'Says the girl with the pierced nipple.'

The family take it in turns to be with me at the moment. Dad brings me photo albums hoping it might jog something, Mum brings crisps and lectures about wearing bike helmets. Beth brings music and Grace brings me medical journal articles on case studies of amnesia, including the story of a man who got amnesia from herpes, which made me check my lady parts with a mirror. Assorted friends drop in; some I know and some I don't. Farah did a video call and it turns out she's not my go-to party girl any more. She's married with a son and living in Amsterdam. She still loves me dearly but liquid eyeliner and drinking until we fall down is not the priority any more. She's changed. They've all changed.

'Why don't you do one of those colouring books like he suggested for your fine motor skills?' Meg suggests.

'All right, Mummy. Only if you do it with me,' I say in a whiny kid's voice.

'Are you going to draw cocks and balls on everything again?'

'Yes.'

'Well, we will tell Igor you tried.'

I like Meg for the dryness and the camaraderie. I think the two of us are kindred spirits in how we regularly test Mum and the limits of her patience. Meg snuggles into me and starts colouring in a panda. I give the panda a willy on his head.

'How is Tess?' I ask. 'I have a feeling I scared her on that first day. Is she OK now?'

'She has a lot of questions but she's just worried. You and her were quite close to be fair. She came down last month to spend some time with you. She wants to get into theatre so you showed her round your manor.'

'I did?'

'I have a feeling you did much more than just show her around various backstages but she adored you after that trip.'

'She wants to act?'

'Costume design,' Meg continues. 'Turns out the girl can draw. All from her father, those skills.'

'Or maybe from me, look how well I can speed-draw a penis.'

'Beautiful colouring, Lucifer.'

I laugh and she allows me to rest my head on her shoulder. She started calling me Lucifer the day I first learnt how to bite. To me, she is Big Meg because she was always taller and bigger and more mature. The day she first kissed a boy, she came back and told us all the detail: how he slipped her some tongue and she nearly bit it off in shock. We all sat there in our matching nighties (that was a thing, it saved our mum time) like the Von Trapps, in giggles and admiration of the biggest one of our lot stepping out into the world and coming back with morsels of gossip. If we could we probably would have sung about it. *Boys in Adidas who know how to sing, these are a few of our favourite things.*

'I have a question, Meggsy?' I ask her.

'I suspect this will be a running theme for a while.'

'What's with the high-waisted baggy jeans? You look like Mum from when we were little.'

She looks at me and shakes her head. 'I'm not too old and you're not too unwell that I can't slap you.'

'It may bring my memory back.'

'These are nineties chic. You know fashion, it goes full circle. All the cool girls are in mom jeans. Anyways, they're high-waisted and tuck in my gut.'

'Yeah, I noticed the gut.'

This time she does hit me. My memory does not come flooding back. What I do want to say though is that she kinda reminds me of Mum. But if I say that, she'll kill me. She'll push me off the bed and say it was an accident.

A knock on the door gets our attention and Meg welcomes

the people in. *We know them?* It's a man and a woman, a couple?

'Hi! We're mates of Lucy's. I live with her. I'm Cass. Your sister down the way told us to come on in.'

Cass is busty and brunette and her companion has boy-band curtains and holds a bouquet of flowers in his hands. Curtains made a comeback too?

'I'm Darren. Lucy? Hi, how are you feeling?'

Christ, I have no idea who they are. I study them both. I can't quite tell if his chinos and Converse with the white socks are a complete fashion fail or if that has also come around again. He has tears in his eyes. *Did I break your heart? Or are you in shock at my appearance?* It's a trackies and vest thing with no bra. It's a look.

'I bought you mochi. I had no idea what to bring and I thought, Lucy likes mochi,' Cass spurts out, with a bag in her hands. 'Like, nice ones from a Japanese bakery. Maybe I should have brought doughnuts but I just didn't know what to bring.'

'Thanks,' I say, turning to Meg.

'You have no idea who we are, do you?' Darren says, studying my eyes.

'I'm really sorry. Did we go to university together or something?'

Cass looks a bit taken aback but Darren smiles. 'We all worked together, gravitated towards each other as mates. We went on holiday several years ago to Ibiza.'

'I've been to Ibiza?' I enquire.

'If anything you are well remembered in Ibiza. We went on a yoga retreat and got kicked out because you laughed through all the sound baths and then got your revenge by stealing one of their goats.'

'What did I do with the goat?' I ask.

'You called him Greg. We sold him to a family in town who I suspect ate him but hey...'

'That's awful,' I reply.

'It wasn't one of your best ideas...'

I smile at him, trying to work out if there's a thing here. Cass clings onto him, almost scared.

'We're sorry too. We were there that day. We should have made sure you got to that job safely or done things differently. We were still at the venue, someone told us there was an accident on the bridge. Someone dressed up as Elsa on a bike. And then Darren realised it was you. He ran. He actually ran across that bridge when he realised...'

'You were the one who called Beth...' Meg suddenly realises who they are.

Darren nods his head, obviously taken back by the memory of it all, and grabs my hand.

'I can't believe you got on a bike, you silly tosser...' he says.

It'd be nice to say it feels familiar or there is some cosmic connection here but it just feels like a hand, a hand that cares at least.

'Oh, we've also got you a gift from the Dickweasel... He's our boss, of sorts,' Cass explains, reaching into her handbag and pulling out a gift and an envelope. 'And the day of the accident, you did a party for a girl called Ophelia. She wrote you a card and sent it to the agency. I may have had a read and a cry. I'll leave that here...'

I study both of them again, hoping some recollection of who they are may return to me. Nothing. 'I'm sorry I can't...'

'It's fine,' Darren explains. 'You're alive. That's what matters.'

'Do I live with both of you?' I ask.

'Just me,' Cass says. 'And six other people. It's a bit of a commune vibe, truth be told, which is why your sisters weren't sure if it was the right thing for you to come back straight away.'

I nod. It was agreed yesterday that I would soon be discharged but I couldn't go back to a house that was unfamiliar.

In that sense, I need to return to the only place I know, 25 Elm Road, the house I grew up in.

'I packed your stuff for you and dropped it off this morning. And Pussy, too. I don't think your mum was expecting Pussy.'

'Pussy?' I ask awkwardly, blushing to hear her talk so frankly.

'She's your cat. She's a cat you adopted...' Cass shows me a picture on her magic phone. It's of me in bed, kissing the top of a ginger cat's head except the cat doesn't look best pleased by this. She looks quite pissed off by the physical contact. 'I mean... come back when the time is right. That house isn't the same without you. And any time you need either of us then you know where we are, yeah?' She bends down to hug me and I hug back. She really has quite the rack, there's some cushioning in that hug.

'What are they? Like, double G?' I ask.

Darren laughs. Cass gives me a look like her boobs may have triggered a memory. They haven't.

'They are. You groped them all the time. You told me to go into porn...'

'You're in porn?'

'No,' she cackles, looking deeply into my eyes. 'You're still in there though, aren't you?'

I never really left. I just don't know who half of these people are and that's starting to upset me because they look like fun and it feels like I've missed out.

'Can we come see you at your mum's house?' Darren asks.

'I'm sure Mum will be fine with it, especially if you bring mochi,' Meg adds.

There are final hugs, thanks and exchanges of telephone numbers before they take their leave and I'm left staring at a bunch of tulips on my side table.

'They're your favourite flower,' Meg tells me.

'I have a favourite flower?' I ask.

'That's something that seems to happen when you become older. I'm a fan of hydrangeas. You like the comedy element of tulips.'

I look at her blankly.

'Two lips. Like a vagina,' she says in embarrassed tones.

'I'm glad I still remained mildly hilarious in the last ten years then?' I mutter.

Meg smiles.

'Sometimes the joke wears thin. But half the time, it's actually needed. The funny. Especially in the last two or three years. Sometimes it's been hard to find anything to smile about.'

This is something that's also been drip-fed to me. Another thing I've erased from memory is that in the last couple of years, there were moments when the world shut down for a while, a time when we wore masks and kept a distance from each other.

'You kept everything buoyant in that time, Lucy. You'd do family Zooms in fancy dress to entertain the kids. When Mum was crying at how much she missed us, you'd crack an inappropriate joke about flatulence. When I was exhausted and anxious, you told me I was dramatic and that I looked like shit and would distract me with stories about a man you'd met on Tinder who'd catfished you and told you he was Tom Hiddleston.'

'I didn't understand half of that last sentence. Tinder? Catfish? Tom who?'

Meg just laughs in reply and cradles my broken head in her hands. 'We have so much to fill you in on.'

'Did I sleep with that Darren guy?'

'Most likely.'

'Was that my bar? That feels like a semi-low bar.'

'No comment. Open your gift and your letter.'

My fingers claw at the paper of the gift from the suspiciously named Dickweasel, which reveals itself to be old lady soaps. The envelope, however, is a lot classier. Inside is a thank you note unlike anything I've ever seen before. It seems to be personalised and on weighted card like a wedding invitation.

Dear Lucy,

I hope you don't mind me writing to you. It's Ophelia and you were at my party a few weeks ago. I wanted to say thank you for helping me when I was upset. I don't know what you told my mum but we don't see the Stantons any more so something you did worked. Thank you for showing me how a princess should be and giving me all your good advice and a bit of your lip gloss. I think you're awesome.

Ophelia xx

'I wonder what advice I gave her,' I say, looking down at the message, admiring the penmanship.

'You probably told her to punch a boy.'

'I hope I did.'

At that point, Emma enters the room, looking flustered and possibly a little angry.

'Do you know the waiting list that Igor has? He is one of the best in the business. You could at least try and be amiable in some capacity. I pulled so many strings to ensure you got to work with him.'

I glare back at her. 'He's evil. I don't like him.'

'His methods work.'

'But I have to look at his awful mullet hair and I would argue that is impeding my recovery time.'

Meg comes over to put an arm around Emma to calm her down, which I resent immediately. I was the one hit by the bus.

'Was she always this argumentative?' Meg says, studying my face.

They stand there already knowing the answer. 'I'm a delight and you know it.'

'Igor is coming back tomorrow before we discharge you and I've booked him in for home visits for three months. You can grow to love him.'

'I hate you, too.'

'I know. It's going to be a dream living with you again.'

I look over at them as she says that. The one thing I've learnt is that Emma has a big old pad now she's a doctor. I lived there once apparently when she was going through her divorce but I thought the agreement was that I was going to live with Mum and Dad. I mean, I'll move in with her if she has the better TV packages. Meg reads the confusion on my face.

'So, we were chatting to your doctors and a few consultants who've suggested that we should try and surround you with as much familiarity as possible. It's why we suggested you don't go back to your commune, house share place,' Emma explains. 'I went there to suss it out. There are no stairs in the place, Lucy. You have to access some floors by ladder. I counted five doors that were batik curtains hammered into the wall. I'm not sure it's safe.'

I shrug as none of that computes in my head anyway. 'What are you saying then?'

'We're all going to move in with you. Back to Elm Road, all five of us and Mum and Dad, like the old days, and see if that works in jogging your memory. It won't be for long because kids and work and stuff but we will be one unit together again,' Emma explains, albeit with not a lot of enthusiasm.

I, however, grin to hear it. It feels like what I need to dig me out of this. My sisters are the four people in the world that I love and trust the most. To have their collective knowledge at my feet feels like I can at least fill in major gaps from the last ten years. 'Really?'

Meg nods, a small furrow to her brow.

'It'll be kinda awesome. Like a giant sleepover,' I say.

'It'll be a group of thirty-something women living at home again, having Mum wash our pants and arguing over hairballs in the bath,' Meg replies.

'But you'd do it for me?' I ask them.

They both nod. It's a reluctant nod. One I'm familiar with.

Can you stay in tonight, girls, and help us look after Lucy?

Do we have to?

Yes, she's your sister and it's what sisters do.

But she's so annoying and I have a life, you know?

And she's a part of that life too. You'll need her too, one day. Trust me.

6

'THAT BLOODY CAT HAS JUST PISSED ON THE BED!
CAN SOMEONE PUT THE CAT OUTSIDE?! I DON'T
CARE! WHAT SORT OF CAT PISSES ON A BED?!'

Oh, the sounds of being at home. It's like music and it's not
just Mum screeching about how things should be done and how
someone has left a yoghurt pot on the front bay window and
accused us of being animals. It's the sound of the second step
from the top that still creaks, the gurgle of the central heating
and knowing exactly when someone has entered or left the
downstairs bathroom.

I've been sitting here for two hours on the sofa, just stroking
it and letting its big oversized corduroy cushions envelop me. I
remember this sofa. I remember I invited Josh Reid back here
and kissed him on this sofa. We shared some salt and vinegar
Twisties that he'd bought for me as a gift and I thought that sort
of gift was unparalleled. We also did other inappropriate things
on this sofa but we don't talk about that to anyone else who sits
here on a daily basis.

Some things in here have changed. There are new photos
on the walls and I don't remember that floral wallpaper on the

chimney breast but this sofa, this carpet in between my toes, the piles of Mum's books that she stacks in columns, still remain. I close my eyes for a second. A psychologist I saw before I left the hospital told me to use all of my Spidey senses to access my memories. I put my hands down on the sofa and remember Josh and me sinking into the fabric. He was decent at kissing and knew how to work a bra. But he was surprised I had more than one hole down there, which made me worry about the standards of sex education in his school.

'Are you tired, Luce? Do you need to nap?'

Grace enters the room with a cup of tea. This is a child-free zone and, to ensure the dads of the family can handle the child-care, the majority of nieces and nephews are holed up at Emma's house. Grace hasn't seemed to mind moving back here but she's an amenable sort, cut from the same cloth as my mother in terms of her organisational skills. She's even brought house slippers with her.

I take the tea from her. 'I'm good. I'm just taking it all in.'

'Mum may fillet your cat for dinner, just saying...'

'She doesn't seem to like me or remember me,' I mention.

'She's a scrappy feral cat, Lucy. But that was probably part of the appeal. So have all your memories come flooding back yet from sitting on the family sofa?'

I shake my head. 'Nope. I like how Mum and Dad still have a turntable though.'

'Oh, vinyl made a comeback so they're not even old-fashioned any more, just retro, even cool.'

Upstairs, the sound of tools and air pumps echoes through the walls. Naturally, when the last child had left this place, Mum and Dad transformed my old bedroom into an office and so they're shifting around furniture and beds to accommodate everyone. *I'll sleep on the sofa before I sleep on that. It's not even retaining air. There's a leak. Can you put all your crafting stuff in the loft? Why have you brought so many shoes with you?*

I put my head on Grace's shoulder.

'You guys really don't mind doing this?'

Grace shrugs. 'If it'll help. I have no doubt it will end in the occasional fight and I don't like the idea of waiting for the toilet again in the morning. But this is just for a few weeks...'

'Tell me about you then. Not the sad stuff if you don't want to. This new fella of yours, Max. What does he do?'

'We can talk about it all. You loved Tom, we all did.'

I don't know how to broach that quite yet. In the last ten years, Grace gained and lost a husband, Tom, who I can't remember. Beth has shown me the pictures and fed me the details but my heart breaks to think that happened before Grace even turned thirty. How did she do it? How did I help? I hope I helped.

'Tom was a fitty at least,' I reply. 'Out of all of us, I think you did very well. I know Meg loves her Danny but the appeal is still very much lost on me.'

She laughs. 'The girls and I have made pacts to travel and explore like he did. And Max might start coming with us.'

'Max... with the ponytail.'

'I've got used to that,' she says, smiling. 'I like this new side to you by the way, the one that asks pertinent questions. Old Lucy would have just asked about his skills in bed and the size of his dong.'

I try and summon up a laugh. The sisters talk about this new Lucy a lot. She still has remnants of some sweary bird I used to be but hasn't been ruined yet by the last ten years. They keep reminding me of the old Lucy though. I like her gumption. It sounds like she was a character, bravery seeped out of her pores, she seemed to be scared of nothing. I can imagine her riding across a bridge and trying to take on a bus. Would new Lucy be able to take on that bus? Maybe after a good nap.

'My hoodie looks good on you,' Grace says, punching my arm.

'Thanks. I went through my clothes and everything was a little...'

'Brief and see-through?'

'Cropped. Cold.'

'Well, I have many hoodies.'

'Me too,' Beth says, entering the room, clutching a cup of tea. 'Uniform of choice these days: hoodies, leggings and trainers.' She kisses the top of my head and then comes to sit down next to me.

'Gracie... Emma's going to come in here in a minute with a sketch of how the bathroom shelves will now be arranged. Emma needs a whole shelf for her skincare crap.'

'It's not crap, B. It's organic,' Grace informs her in accentuated tones.

'I literally wash my face in shower gel so I am the wrong person to ask. She's even sorting my sanitary pads into rows. Marie Kondo has turned her into a militant organiser of sorts. All her pants are rolled into tennis balls.'

Beth realises I have no idea who this Kondo woman is. 'She's on Netflix – she's Japanese and adorable. It's a show about tidying your house, decluttering and finding joy in your belongings. It's nice to watch but one of those things you know is impossible in practice.'

I still look confused. 'What is the Netflix?'

Grace and Beth sit there for a moment, cups paused to their mouths.

'Geez... really? Oh, so it's, like, this magical place where you can watch stuff. TV, films, it all gets streamed to your house or phone, and man, it got me through 2020,' Beth explains, taking out her phone. 'And you don't have to wait for episodes weekly, you just binge-watch everything in one. It's a beautiful thing.'

She hands me her phone. This touch-screen technology is new, fiddly. Like I'm buying train tickets but it's just lists of films and TV shows.

'And is it expensive?'

'Less than a tenner a month. Though you spend most of the time just choosing something to watch. You and I used to watch stuff together all the time, we had a whole thread of conversation going on about a show called *Sex Education*.'

'That I have no recollection of...'

Both of them go a little quiet to think about what I've missed and what they need to tell me about. A simple thing like watching the television is new, it's bigger and brighter and there's infinite choice. Next they'll tell me toilets have changed, we don't cook any more, you can teleport and they've made aeroplanes obsolete.

'Oh, by the way, I got you a new iPhone because your last one got squished by the bus,' Grace explains to me, reaching over to a box on the table. 'We'll walk you through it but you were really good at backing up your stuff so we retrieved lots of it off the Cloud. Notes, photos. There were a lot of photos. I organised some of them for you,' she explains, with a hint of hesitation.

Beth tries her best not to laugh too hard. I want to know when we started storing stuff in Clouds.

'Explain...' I say.

'I mean, it wasn't a surprise, but the one thing phones have been good for is that they become a conduit by which you can engage in relations without having to be in the same room,' she explains.

'It's called sexting,' Beth utters plainly.

'People don't even have sex any more?' I ask, wide-eyed.

'Oh, they do but people are also lazy and we explained the Tinder thing to you. So people use that to find their long-term loves but they also now use it for hook-ups and things. They use all sorts... Instagram, Snapchat... They're all ways to just swap photos and videos and chat...'

'And I take it I was active on those things...'

Grace takes my new slimline fancy phone and goes to a photo icon and clicks on it. There is an album there called Hidden and she clicks on it. She puts a tongue to the inside of her mouth and then shows it to me. I'm not a prude, I never was, but it's basically a wall of genitalia before my eyes. Female bits, man bits, piercings and tattoos, boobies, chipolatas and one man who seems to be wielding a baseball bat of flesh between his legs. How? More importantly, who?

'That penis is obscene, that can't be real?' says Beth, huddling into me.

'Are we saying I may have shagged that man?' I ask.

I wasn't an angel at eighteen. I'd slept with four boys before I went to university but to approach that penis looks physically impossible. I look at all the photos. That's me. And *that's* what my pierced nipple looked like. I have nice boobs and I seem to have no problem in showing them to people via the medium of photo in a variety of poses. I also seem to have no problem showing them other parts of me too.

'I don't have pubic hair. Did it not grow past my teens? Did it fall out?'

'Oh no, you liked to wax down there.'

I click on a photo with a white triangle to the bottom. It's moving. He's holding his penis. He's moving. Oh my... We all let out a collective screaming laugh and I drop the phone into my lap.

'The pictures also move?'

'Yes,' Beth tells me.

I pick the phone up tentatively again.

'Hold up, these aren't my boobs?' I say, my finger hovering over one picture.

Beth pulls a face, trying to understand how to broach that subject next. 'So, you were bisexual. You are bisexual. It was something you discovered about yourself in your twenties. You dated a woman you met at uni for a while.'

I stare into space for a moment. Wasn't this more important information to reveal to me compared to the workings of the Netflix? Old Lucy had some redefined sexuality, she was on a different part of her journey, setting sail, discovering new lands. I'm still in the docks. Christ, I don't even know how to drive a boat at this point.

'We should have told you sooner,' says Grace. 'God, this is hard, Luce. We just don't know what you know and what you don't. Can you even forget your sexuality?'

I sit here soaking it all in, this wall of genitalia staring at me. And I'm not aroused, just immensely confused.

'How did you guys know?' I ask.

'You announced it on the sisters group. I think we laughed it off to start. Like when you said you were going to join a circus and have an act involving steel knickers and an angle grinder,' Beth explains.

'We just let you do you,' Grace explains.

'These penises don't even have faces or names. I don't even know who these people are, whether I've been intimate with them. Do you do this with Max and Will?' I ask.

Both of them look at each other, shrugging.

'Yeah, maybe not to this degree of detail. I know you were safe and you got yourself tested a lot. That was one thing Emma drummed into you. She used to show you lots of medical journals on genital disease.'

My fingers jab at random buttons on the phone and Beth reaches over to show me how it all works, trying to encourage me to be a bit gentler. This thing tells the fricking weather. The screensaver is a photo, of all the sisters, on a night out somewhere. It looks like a picture I'd recognise because I look like the me I remember. I press an icon that says Contacts and scroll through the names.

'So I know all these people?' I ask.

The names go on for days. I seem to know four Lauras that I

differentiate in a multitude of ways. Laura the Bitch. Old Housemate Laura. Laura Hair. Laura Paul's GF. And people who don't even have names. They seem to be represented by pictures. I like aubergines for a reason. Do I like aubergine? I don't remember that being a favourite vegetable. Grace looks over my shoulder.

'Well, maybe we can put some names to faces? We can assume that Adam with the three aubergines is maybe the man with the big appendage in your photo roll?'

'We can?'

'Aubergine is like the secret emoji for a penis,' Beth informs me.

I close my eyes, exasperated. There is SO MUCH TO LEARN. And people have not made it simple. What happened to the classic winky face? How do I type out an aubergine? And why an aubergine? It's purple. No penis is that colour unless it's very unwell. They look more like courgettes? Cucumbers? Carrots?

And there are so many names, so many pieces to fill in this very colourful jigsaw puzzle. Do I text each one independently? *Hey, it's Lucy here. I'm texting as last month I suffered a traumatic head injury that resulted in amnesia. Please can you remind me who you are and whether we may have slept together. Thanks and best.*

'I mean, this all can wait, Luce. You're here now with us to just try and piece together the little things, to get your strength back. It'll come back in time,' Beth tells me, slipping her hand in mine.

I click on notes. It's a jumble of things but one thing seems to be pinned to the top which I will assume is there because of its importance. I open it. It's a name and a date.

Oscar, 9th February.

I look over at Grace.

'Maybe he was a kid whose party you did? I really don't know, babe,' she replies. 'I've also accessed your social media accounts. You can have a scroll through those. That could be useful. It would seem your password has not changed since you were eighteen so that made things easier.'

'Passwords_suck_balls?'

'Yeah. And we're having fish and chips for dinner,' Beth explains.

'My favourite?'

Beth nods. 'Some things didn't change, Luce. Don't worry.'

I put my magic phone on my lap and allow the sisters to envelop me from both sides, sitting here in silence. I hope in the last ten years we did this a lot. I'm glad they're here. I'm glad this still feels familiar.

'Can we just sit here all day and stalk people on Facebook? Josh, I wouldn't mind seeing what he looks like now?'

Beth's eyes light up, like this might be one of her favourite pastimes.

'LUCY, THE CAT! THE CAT! THERE'S A REASON I NEVER HAD A CAT! SHE'S EATING A BOX OF PANTYLINERS! SHE'S A FUCKING ANIMAL!' Mum's shrieking rings through the house, and we all laugh. I remember this too.

7

I am trying to think about the last time we were all together like this. It may have been Christmas, it has to be. Being here in this living room, sitting around watching shite on the television covered in fleece blankets and throwing popcorn at each other, feels like a memory from way before Meg got married and settled. She used to come back home and bring bin bags full of her laundry because the washing machine in her flat share was a 'shower of shit' and then spend most of her time eating the contents of the fridge and using us as some sort of detox facility because she felt her liver was failing her and/or her heart had been broken. I remember one time she stole our kettle because some artsy knob she'd been dating had taken hers. If the stars aligned then Emma would be here too and we'd all be in some shared uniform of trackies and big socks, hair nested on top of our heads. We'd share blankets and chocolate on the sofa and watch *Gossip Girl*. Someone would fart halfway and stink out the room and we'd all shriek like harpies but that memory is a comfort blanket to me. There are moments now when I feel completely lost and I zoom in on that like some magnetic north, hiding under that blanket, even enduring the smell of Grace's farts. We always knew it was her.

The only thing about now is that things are a bit different. Mum and Dad are having a night out today, away from us kids, so they've left us to fend for ourselves. They did this a lot when we were teens, it was necessary for Dad to escape the faint radioactive glow of hormones in the air, but they used to buy us pizzas and bottles of Coke and remind us to lock the French doors because Mum was always paranoid (having watched too much crime drama from the nineties) that someone was going to kidnap one of us. I mean, that's a brave bloody kidnapper who'd try that. Can you imagine that poor criminal? He'd leave this house without an abductee and most likely without a face.

Those nights would sing with joy, fun and laughter. Tonight though, they sing with the sound of Beth snoring. Like drooling levels. I swear if we turned off the TV then we'd hear the walls rattle lightly. Someone close that girl's mouth. I guess she's allowed because she's a new mum. Emma hasn't changed. We're watching a quiz show and she still answers all the questions on the edge of her seat, competing with no one else but herself.

What has changed are the snacks. It used to be all about the pick 'n' mix but now we drink wine and eat olives and posh crispbreads with dip that has pecorino in it. My sisters ask what they marinade the olives in. *Is that thyme? It tastes woody. Are these Greek? They're so plump.* It's oil and herbs, girls. Grace, you used to pick the olives off your pizza and say they were the devil's grapes.

'Who the hell doesn't know who Anne Boleyn is? They've made about six BBC dramas about the bitch,' screams Meg into the telly.

Meg's animated critique of people on the television is a thing of legend. *What the hell has he done to his house? I could sew a better dress like that if I was drunk and didn't have hands.*

That chicken isn't cooked, it's so not cooked. He's going home!
Except back then it was just a loud young opinion. Now she's
drunk on the wine, it's a bit lairy. If we were in public, she'd
start on someone outside a kebab shop. I like that Meg so I won't
discourage her. It's excellent value Meg.

'I don't get this show. They have to catch the things and
then they win the money?' I ask, my hand straight into the
crisps.

'But if he catches both balls then he wins the lot. If he drops
it then he's going home with nothing...'

I pretend to feign interest. For some reason, it seems to be
essential primetime viewing to at least three people in this
room, except for my girl, Beth. In fact, I lie. There is also
another being in the room. Pussy graces us with her presence
tonight. Pussy still has yet to endear herself to anyone in this
house. She slept on Meg's head the other night, attacks the
washing machine when it's on and smells like egg. There is a
look about her that one would liken to some old lady who just
wants to sit in her house, eat tinned goods all day and be left the
hell alone. *Don't touch me, or I will seriously have your eyes.*
How did I pick her to be my pet companion in life?

'I can't believe he went for that answer. He'll regret that...
Use your lifeline,' Grace yells, studying the screen and talking
to Matt, Essex, like she knows him. Grace and I used to sneak
down here at night with our duvets, camp on the floor when
Mum and Dad had gone to bed and watch Channel 5 documentaries about sex toys and then laugh so much we wet
ourselves.

The only thing that hasn't changed here is the crisps. Thank
you, Doritos, for still staying triangular and crispy and coated in
good flavours that still stick to the roof of my mouth. I rake
through the bowl with my hands.

'You want some dip?' Emma asks, handing over her posh
cheesy stuff.

'I'm good.'

She senses the sullen version of myself in the room. 'You OK? You love cheesy dip.'

'I do?'

We never had posh cheesy dip growing up. We had houmous and salsa out of a jar. Snacks in front of the television were microwave popcorn and big tubs of chocolates, which we'd physically wrestle each other for and pull hair over the toffee fingers. It was cheap crisps that felt like polystyrene in your mouth. Big mugs of tea. But my sisters all became posh grown-up bitches in the last decade with their wine and olives.

'And the answer is Reese Witherspoon, not Judi Dench,' I say.

They all turn to the television where Matt from Essex has lost his money. Bye, Matt. Have a good trip home with your zero pounds. Had I been in that studio, I'd have won £350,000. Grace slaps my arm.

'How did you know that?' she asks in disbelief.

'Because that was in 2006 which to me was only a few years ago. I can't remember who I've shagged in the past decade but I can tell you anyone who's won an Oscar in the noughties.'

The sisters all go deathly quiet, bar Beth, who may as well be in a coma anyway.

'Should we get a board game out?' Emma asks.

'Operation?' I joke feebly. The sisters all side-eye each other, so much so that I feel I need to comment. 'Like, when did you guys get so grown-up?'

Meg and Emma look at me, insulted. *Yes, I'm calling you hags old.*

'Because we *are* grown-ups,' Emma protests. 'We have families now.'

'Yeah, but that doesn't mean you had to get boring. Is this what you do on Saturdays now?'

The way they all shift looks to each other and then to the ceiling tells me yes.

'And what is wrong with that?' Grace asks. 'We're not party girls like you. I can't do those sorts of nights any more. The last time we had a big night out, you jumped off a pirate ship.'

I sincerely hope I was dressed for the part.

'Christ, it takes me a weekend to get over a hangover these days,' Meg adds.

'This is just not what I remember. What I remember was...'

They all wait with anticipation to see what I say next. It seems they're hoping for some breakthrough moment when I'll be eating roast chicken and then the memories will flood back to me. Unfortunately, my mother's roast chicken is far too dry for that.

'I remember we'd sit here and watch a crap DVD or an episode of *Dawson's Creek* and hear all the stories you guys had. Meg and Beth talking about their nights out, men and sex. You made it sound so fun. I worshipped the tits off you all. All that freedom and fun. The way we'd laugh for hours till our stomachs hurt. Now you're talking about herbs.'

Emma laughs under her breath, 'I never had sex stories.'

'True, you just stayed dull.'

'You can watch all of *Dawson's Creek* on Netflix,' Meg informs me. My eyes widen with excitement. 'I watched it all again recently and still crushed over Pacey Witter.'

We all sigh. God, we loved that boy. He's the only man I'd fight this lot over.

'But what other stories are you talking about?' Meg asks, curious. 'We had sex stories?'

I sit up for a moment to prepare myself. 'You once told us about some Dutch man you met on a night out. You brought him back to yours and shagged him in the kitchen and you said you didn't even know his name.'

Meg flares her nostrils. In fact, she rolls her eyes back in her head to have to think back that far.

'I did do that. Once. Don't tell my daughters I did that, please. That is everything I'm trying to tell them not to do.'

'But you gave us every detail. You said he had abs like a draining board and you both lay naked on your kitchen table and swigged at a vodka bottle in the moonlight.'

Grace and Emma look at each other almost in worry at my corny recalling of these events.

'You remember more than I do and you weren't even there,' Meg adds.

'I was thirteen, fourteen? When you came back and told me that story I thought you were a goddess.'

Meg sits there, pensive to hear those words in her trackies and bed socks. She slowly sips at her wine, as if hoping it will help her work out where those goddess years went to and where she did indeed meet that Dutch man. Did he have a name? What happened to him? Why didn't she lock that down?

'Luce, it was just a one-night stand. Something to do in my twenties, some rite of passage. I'd almost forgotten about him...'

'Because you married your grumpy man Northerner? Does he do the sad woodsman thing in bed too?' I ask, giggling.

'No, but the man has timber,' she retorts, opening her eyes widely. 'Hun, I'd be lying if I said I don't think about Dutchman occasionally... once a year at most... but those days are behind me now, unless you want to hear about the time Danny and I—'

'NO...' Emma intervenes. 'I don't want to hear sex stories about a man I'm going to be sitting across the table eating roast potatoes with tomorrow.'

I flap my hand around to quieten Emma. 'Tell me...'

'He once dropped me during sex?' she bursts out. Is this the most interesting sex story she has of late?

'Oh, we knew this already... You may proceed...' Emma says, going back to her dip.

'He dropped me, I twisted my ankle. We broke some drawers.'

I search her face. This is not the same as her telling us how a Dutchman took her knickers off with a spaghetti server and I think she kinda knows it.

'Or I could tell you about the time we had sex in our Volvo and got caught by the police?' she says, a cheeky glint in her eye.

'Noooo...' Emma protests. 'I've sat in that car. I don't want to hear this story.'

'Tell me more...'

'I thought the policeman was going to shoot us so I hopped off too quickly and then Danny opened the door in his face and made his nose bleed.'

Grace cocks her head to the side. 'You did the what now? Did you get arrested for dogging?'

'It was not dogging. It was two married people having consensual sex.'

'Outside,' Grace says.

'We are all judging me but Emma over there had sex with Stuart,' Meg exclaims.

'STUART?' I squeal, glaring at my straight-laced sister. 'YOU HAD SEX WITH STUART? SO HAVE I!'

Stuart is Meg's brother-in-law and the urban legend is that he's the only man on this planet to have had relations with at least two of the Callaghan sisters, now apparently three. He snogged Beth in a taxi. I slept with him at Meg's wedding – if you could call it that, we were both quite merry, and I believe he spent most of the time half-mast talking to his penis, willing it to work.

'Emma had outdoor sex in that instance too...' Meg informs me.

'I hate you all,' she says, pouring herself another glass of wine.

'Beth gave Will a handjob at a gig once,' Grace casually

says, trying to add to the conversation. We all look over at Beth, still asleep. I can literally see the scars from when they removed her tonsils.

'I did. I had to wipe my hand down on my coat and the stain never came off,' she mumbles before curling up into a different position and falling asleep again.

Grace looks over at her calmly. 'I'm sleeping with a man with a ponytail, sometimes he ties it back with a scrunchie.'

Grace is dryer than a dry Martini served in a sand box. She and Emma won't play these games but I hope ponytail man makes her happy. She deserves happy.

'We do have fun. The fun just changed. It's kids and relationships and work, it's all just evolved,' Meg explains. 'Different things make us happy.'

'Then I have a question?' I ask, staring at the quiz show in the background. They have a new contestant on who thinks Asia is a country. He deserves nothing. 'Why didn't I evolve? Why didn't I seek out these same things? I'm looking at Facebook and I just see someone who refused to settle down, some perpetual party girl. Was I allergic to love? Commitment? Men?'

'That may have been my fault,' Emma discloses. 'You saw a lot of what happened there with my divorce with Simon, all the times he'd cheated on me. Beth and Will had a relationship hiccup when Joe was born too. They couldn't work out parenthood. It was a bit messy.'

'And then Tom and I had this big rollercoaster relationship, got married and then he died...' Grace says. 'So I always felt all of this made you see relationships a little differently. Being some free agent always kept you safe from hurt. I don't think you trusted love.'

'Though you did sleep with that one fella who gave you hives so maybe you were allergic to something in that case?' Emma jokes.

'Where were the hives?' I ask, aghast.

All the sisters look mildly hurt that they have to think about this story again.

'You're allergic to walnuts, no other nuts, and you two were doing things with a carrot cake. Luce, you made me look at your labia. You made me apply antihistamine cream to it.'

Beth wakes up giggling to hear that story. She shouldn't be laughing but, secretly, I like that sound.

'And being this free agent made me happy?' I ask.

'The happiest,' Grace says warmly. The older sisters look like they don't disagree but seventeen-year-old me feels mildly disappointed that I didn't strive for something grander. Back then, with Josh, I had plans. I thought about growing old with him and what our kids would look like. I thought about a version of my wedding. It would have involved an open-top bus of some sort, me being a slightly inappropriate bride. We would have danced into the night. It's a sobering thought to think I leant away from this. I went down another path. This path that seems to be lined with shot glasses and bright glittering lights. I was always easily lured by shiny things but now I worry all of that was just an attempt to not grow old, to be forever young, forever sitting in this living room with my girls and refusing to adult in the real world.

'Annoyingly happy,' Meg tells me. 'The beauty of you was that you didn't want to fit in a box. So many things define women and you didn't want that at all. You didn't want to be a mother, a wife...'

'You are amazing in that respect,' Beth adds. 'I was torn about being a working mum and you always told me to have it all, to not have guilt for doing that either...' she tells me with a touch of emotion in her voice. 'And that was everything because I think it makes me happier, a more complete version of myself to have both in my life.'

Deep down, I applaud this version of myself – life guru, Lucy.

'And you're universally loved for who you are. You ask any of our girls who their favourite aunt is and we don't even come close. We don't even resent you for it,' Meg adds.

'Well, I could have predicted that even at seventeen. Do I teach them dance routines?'

'The worst sort,' Emma says despairingly.

'Did I teach them the TLC one?'

'No, I don't believe you have,' Grace says.

Meg expels a laugh in exasperation. 'You don't remember anything but you remember that routine?'

We used to do that here, in this living room, all lined up like we were the best girl band you'd ever seen. We'd tie knots in the bases of our T-shirts and tuck them up and over the necklines, wearing big baggy combats and jeans perched on our hips. I was nine years old and Meg was eighteen and there's an image so sharp in my brain of me perched on the edge of the sofa and her asking me to purse my lips so she could apply some of her Rimmel Heather Shimmer lipstick. There was a point where Grace released a limb into Beth and they both threw cushions at each other and broke a picture frame that we hid to escape our mother's wrath.

'I remember that routine...' whispers Sleepy in the corner, rousing from her slumber. That's what music does to Beth, it speaks to her soul; everything has a theme and a melody. With one eye open, she accesses some magic on her phone and the TV stops and starts playing the song. The technology still blows my mind. Meg is shaking her head as both my fingers are pointed at her.

'You made up the routine,' I say. 'You loved TLC. You wore an eye patch for a while.'

'Shush now, I am not dancing. I will pull something...'

'You used to pull fellas with those moves.'

'No, I pulled them because of my sparkling wit and great boobs.'

I jump to my feet, as does Beth, who starts with some gentle swaying. 'It's a banger, ladies. Remember when Emma didn't understand why you'd call a man a duster.'

Instantly insulted, Emma rises to her feet, looking over at Grace. Lucy got hit by a bus. Maybe the music and the attempts to dance will mean she gets better, it will access something within the labyrinth that's her brain and she'll be Lucy again. Grace removes the old lady blanket from her knees. She may be lunging. Meg is still the one who remains seated, watching me closely as I go through the moves. Left to right shuffle, knee up and down, hanging out the passenger side, lean with attitude and booty pop. The accuracy with which I deliver the moves makes it seem like I've been practising them every day since 2001.

Grace shakes her head. 'I'm pretty sure it was lean and click and then the thing with the head.' Beth cheers as we both booty pop together.

Emma glances at both her hands to try and work out what to do with her arms. *C'mon, Ems, you're a surgeon. Co-ordination is key.* She senses I'm looking at her. 'You forget you trained as a dancer, it's all in your muscle memory,' she lectures me, whilst also mouthing all the words.

Meg suddenly stands to attention. 'It's like you cows can't do anything right without me. It's like in the video. But the arms – NO – SCRUBS. Cross the arms.'

Grace does her best not to stifle her giggles to see Meg spring into action and Meg throws one of those woody olives at her.

'Come on then, line up properly. And phones down, I don't want this on TikTok. Beth, don't freestyle.'

I can't stop smiling and that's because this is what I'm here for. This is what's familiar. Let's dance this out, bitches, but maybe not do that thing with our T-shirts any more mainly because I think Meg isn't wearing a bra.

'This better make your memory come back,' Grace adds, grinning. She's loving it too.

We all know the words, all of them. Every inflection and scaling of the notes, the little rap parts, the echoes of Lisa 'Left Eye' Lopes. Pussy the cat looks over but her face creases into shock as Meg tries to hit a high note, belting out the lyrics. And all of us descend into giggles but sing right back to her. It's a girl band of sorts but one that looks like they took advantage of the free alcohol before they went on stage and maybe forgot their costumes, and their make-up, and their goddamn minds. Meg puts a knee up and I hear a click of something, Emma hits Grace in the face with a hand. Beth looks at me and we sing the lyrics to each other, bodies rolling in opposite directions. We danced to this song like this before. Somewhere else? I'm sure of it. In a club, or was it at a wedding? I stop for a moment to try and remember. I was in a bandeau top. I was wearing a badge.

'You'll hurt yourself, Meg,' says a voice from the hallway.

Mum stands there leaning against the doorframe. There's a look there I can't quite put my finger on. I don't know if she's reminiscing or grateful that the years of us trashing her front room and creating this wall of noise are gone. I'd hope somewhere she might miss it, just a fraction.

'Why is there an olive on my rug?' she asks.

'IT WAS MEG!' Grace squeals, regressing to her ten-year-old self.

'YOU MADE ME DO IT!' Meg throws another and it bounces off Beth's forehead.

'GIRLS! Pick it up. Are you all having fun?' Mum asks. I'm not sure if anyone answers as the scene has descended into raucous madness. To my left, Grace and Beth cradle each other in laughter trying to prop each other up. This is what I remember, so very well.

'Nice night out, Mum?' I ask her.

'Very nice. We went for a Greek meal. Are you OK?' she asks me, catching my gaze. She does this a lot now and I suspect she did it less before. She gives me long lingering looks as if she has a world of things to say to me but also wants to check that I'm just alive, functioning. *This girl band wouldn't work without you, Lucy.* Look at what happened when Geri left. It was never quite the same, eh?

'Well, your father and I are off to bed, now,' she announces to the room. 'Lucy, tell them to stop throwing olives.'

'Make sure you tell Dad to use a condom,' I joke.

She pauses. Old Mother would have hated the crudeness. She'd have answered with a tut and a scowl. But instead she smiles, which makes me think they had the good wine with dinner.

'Ever since you were born, I don't let him near me without one.'

The sisters didn't hear that but I did. Mum made a joke. It was almost funny. How did you miss it?

'Keep the noise down or you'll scare that cat and it'll piss everywhere again,' she says, studying the room, the noise, the song she's heard a thousand times or more. She looks at my face beaming over at Meg, who's doing the robot.

'You girls just carry on. Tell Meg she really is too old not to be wearing a bra though. That's just obscene.'

8

Tables. They carry a lot of memories, don't they? I feel I've known this kitchen table for an age. At Christmas, we used to put the extra leaf in for guests, which Dad had to get out of the garage, and someone always got the dubious task of wiping the cobwebs off it. There's the mark where Meg spilt nail polish and Mum tried to remove it, taking off the lacquer. There's the one where Beth went through her jewellery-making phase and scratched the surface with her craft knives. That time Dad put down a hot pan without a placemat. Oh, there were fights that day. I still remember the feeling of hearing my parents scream at each other. That fear and worry it sends down your spine at such a young age to see two people you love the most rage at each other. I clung to the sister next to me. Emma. *It's all right*, she said. *It's just what grown-ups do sometimes. Love doesn't mean liking someone all of the time.* Now, I trace my fingers along the burn marks and bend down to look at the underside of the table. Mum never found this one. I was angry with her when I was fourteen and she told me off for piercing my upper ear. I wrote I HATE THIS CRAP HOUSE in red biro. Still there, still raging with all that anger. The lounge light goes on and I jolt on the floor.

'Crapping hell, Lucy. You almost scared me witless. What are you doing up, love? Why are you under the table? Do you need anything? Are you in pain?'

Dad. There are so many things to love about Dad. He's a crier, which remains endearing, but I love how he lets his guard down and makes himself vulnerable to show all these women he lives with that it's not a personality flaw. He cries when we're watching *The X Factor* and someone says they're singing for their dead gran and he cries at weddings, exam results and when his youngest is run over on London bridges. Since I've been back – well, since we've all been back – he hugs us all randomly and I've caught him arranging the shoes by the front door and smiling when we're all clattering over dinner and bantering back and forth like he's missed this soundtrack. Right now, he comes over, kisses me on the forehead and pulls me to my feet, encouraging me to sit on a chair. I look at the carriage clock on the mantlepiece: 6.45 a.m.

'I actually woke up and thought I had a shift at work. It's Thursday, right? I usually did the breakfast shift on Thursdays. And I got up and went to the loo and then looked at myself in the mirror and realised that was twelve years ago.'

Dad comes to sit in a neighbouring chair and puts an arm around me. I'm still in one of Grace's hoodies and some brief watermelon print jersey shorts that I found in my belongings. My legs are curled up into me. I couldn't go back to sleep after that so I came down to stare at this table, to indulge in my daily ritual of trying to rack my brains for something, anything.

'Have you had breakfast? A cup of tea?'

I shake my head.

'Then let's get the kettle on at least.'

I love how Dad can sense my confusion but wants to solve it all with tea. He gets up and bumbles through to the kitchen to retrieve some mugs. Three mugs. One for me no doubt but the other's for Mum and he'll bring her tea in bed like he always does. This still feels like the one way to show someone you love them dearly, the pre-emptive strike of a hot beverage brought to someone before they're even conscious is the biggest show of emotion I can think of.

'That gastro-café-pub place you worked in isn't there any more, you know? They turned it into one-bed flats,' he says.

'Really?'

'£450K for one bed. I had a look, too. Couldn't swing a cat in them.'

'You looked?'

'Semi-retirement gives me time to be nosey. Speaking of cats... I think your one's been licking the apples in the fruit bowl...'

'Oh...'

Pussy and I still have yet to bond. I don't know how I'd tell her to stop licking the fruit. Going through my belongings, I also found Pussy's adoption certificate. I got her from a shelter. Apparently, she'd been the longest serving occupant of that place. No one wanted her.

'I do think it's mildly amusing to see your mother so riled though so don't get rid of the thing whatever you do.'

The other thing about Dad is that I am not sure he knows how to deal with any of this. For years, he's always been a silent observer in this family. It's like he knows his limits and he's happy to just offer his help when approached, as opposed to Mum, who bulldozes in there regardless. He's a quiet and reflective gent who we all value for the constancy, the resilience of having lived through all the bedlam.

The front door opens and I arch my head to see Emma come in, returning from a night shift at the hospital. She senses action at the back of the house and comes in to find us. Dad gets another cup out of the cupboard.

'You're up?' she asks me. 'Are you feeling OK?'

I nod. 'I just got up a bit confused.'

'She got up to get ready for work,' Dad explains. 'Her old job at the pub.'

Emma comes and pulls a stool to sit in front of me. 'Any dizziness or pain?'

'Only because I'm up at six bloody forty-five,' I say.

She smiles and takes off her hospital badge, leaving it on the kitchen table.

'Emma Callaghan-Kohli. That's a classy name, sis.'

'You told me that once. You said it made me sound worldly and global.'

'I was right. Did you do good doctoring today?'

'It was pretty eventful. A teen got stabbed and brought in to us. Right through the lung. He's lucky to still be here.'

I pause for a moment to think of Emma at the heart of something so critical. I only knew her as a medical student who I felt didn't make the most of her university experience. Medics seem to be part of this clique who study together, and drink in fancy dress and in moderation but do little else. She used to come back here regularly during her degree as some sort of base camp. To sleep and eat, to allow Beth to stroke her hair on the sofa while she complained to us about Simon, her new boyfriend, who looked like George Clooney but flirted so heavily with everyone that she didn't know whether to trust him. The answer was no but she married him anyway. Apparently, Mum broke his nose some years later and that is something I wish I could recollect.

'He was lucky to have you as his doctor,' I tell her and kiss the top of her head. She studies my face, I guess to see if my recent brain fart is a result of blown pupils or facial paralysis but it's not. She then looks down to my leg. That was something else that was split open when I went flying across Waterloo Bridge, and she checks the scar regularly. It's her way of helping, coping, to pour all her doctorly knowledge on me. I catch her reading articles, looking up brain and memory specialists on her laptop, printing out things of interest for me. I read them on the toilet.

'So let's run through what you would normally do on a Thursday. You'd go to work. Then what? Go on, try and remember...'

Dad brings over mugs of tea and sits down at the table, watching this little exercise.

'I'd finish at three. I'd have done lunch and breakfast service so I'd be knackered but I'd have made myself a lot of espresso to fuel me so by the time I finished I'd be buzzing. I'd take party clothes with me to work and then go get dressed at Farah's and we'd start drinking early. Thursdays were dead in most places so we usually rang people and ended up in Hammersmith or Richmond, except they were full of people in rugby shirts and posh accents, or Kingston...'

For some reason, my words trail off as I say Kingston, and Emma smiles at me.

'But you still don't remember coming to my first wedding, dancing on a table, falling off and Meg having to pick splinters and rose thorns out of your arse?'

'I do not... Was it a complete rager?'

'It was a good band. They were a swing band from Hampshire. Their singer was like a young Dean Martin,' she says, looking into the distance. I know when I have to change the subject.

'Before the summer came, I also used to go to sixth form on a Thursday. Whole day of lessons that day. Compulsory PE in the morning, double English Lit, then I'd spend two periods in the library, drama workshops till home.'

Emma laughs. 'I think I could tell you my timetables too. They seem to be etched into me.'

The five of us all went to the same school, a bus ride away

from here, called King Charles' Grammar, affectionately known as King Charlie's. It's one of London's best, which I always thought hilarious as it's named after one of our worst kings, but if you want to know about a place that laid foundations for all us girls then this is the one. Those walls hold our secrets, they saw us succeed, fail and blossom or, in my case, walk them corridors with enough notoriety to be remembered for the next five years at least.

'School is probably what's freshest in my mind. I found all my study notes in my room yesterday. They're old and yellowing but I could still recite bits of *Henry V* to you. I remember all my lines from my soliloquy for my drama practicals.'

Dad chuckles. 'I remember that. Your mum and I went to watch. You never heard this from me but she may have shed a tear that evening. You were very good.'

'Grade A, thank you very much. *Superbly moving, pace of delivery was sublime,*' I remind them of my moderator's comments.

I pause for a moment. The memory of that night sears through my brain, the anticipation, the energy and time I spent preparing for those ten minutes. Adrenalin bubbled through my veins to be on the stage, some deep sense of belonging, wanting to perform forever. But look where it got me. There is something slightly painful to know that love never came to anything.

'How do you drink tea so fast?' mutters Dad, watching Emma as she downs the cup next to her.

'Asbestos tongue.' She shifts a look over at me, almost worried to see me so pensive, out of the default settings she's used to. 'So, I was going to catch some shut-eye but maybe you and me should go on a little drive first.'

'At this time of day?' I ask her.

'Before the roads clog up. Maybe we should go back to school.'

'Really?'

'It might bring some things back.'

'It might make me want to defecate on the doorstep.'

'Please don't do that.'

* * *

The one thing I've noticed about Emma that has not changed is that she's still very into her porridge. She needs fuel and fibre to keep her going. Even now, she's come back from her shift and she's there with her porridge but it's jazzy porridge now with rice milk and seeds and fruits on top. I don't do porridge. Porridge is for bears and it sits in my stomach like cement. My breakfast of choice was a Twix that was dipped into a cappuccino from the school vending machine. Sometimes I had a weekly banana for health.

We were different students, much to Emma's chagrin. She was the brightest of stars. They would have made plaques for her if they could. *Emma Callaghan (who is now a doctor and got the highest Biology A-Level marks in the country) once sat on this bench and walked these halls as head girl.* My name would be in small print, somewhere. *Lucy Callaghan (who is superbly moving and got four As in her A-Levels, which was a bloody surprise to everyone including her parents as she spent most of her teens fighting the system in a skirt that wasn't regulation length) once attended this school. She once entered the school elections and named her party the Old El Paso Party in which she gave a rousing speech that every Tuesday would be Taco Tuesday and she'd force all the staff to wear sombreros because in her own words 'some of them are dull as balls and need the help'. She won that election but was promptly taken out of contention by the head teacher, who gave an assembly berating the whole school community for not taking the issue of politics seriously enough. Natalia de Vante ended up winning*

for the Liberal Democrats, whose manifesto included the
mundane like recycling bins and bus monitors. Lucy may have
lost her shit at the whole debacle. She made placards. She
protested, goddamn it, that it was an infringement of election
by-laws and shat all over true democracy. Her mother was
called.

It feels like I was only at this school a matter of months ago but, as we drive up now, it already looks different; there are fancy glass extensions to the foyer, new windows and what look like solar panels on the languages block. Some things still feel the same. The field to the front where we'd haul our asses round for the 1500m in the summer, the red brick of the main building where you can peek into the science labs. A skeleton stands at the window who some lab tech has kept there for the longest time, all dressed up. He had a name. Spud. You're still here. I mean, you weren't going anywhere, but still.

'If you do a doughnut on the field, I'll give you a tenner,' I tell Emma as she drives through the school gates.

'I have new tyres on,' she says, edging her car into the most sacred of spaces, the staff car park. 'Shall we park in the deputy head's space instead?'

I laugh and don't discourage her. Through our whole schooling career, there was a deputy head called Mrs Willett who carried an incredible dislike for all us Callaghan girls because when Meg started school there, was bullied and had her lunch money taken in the first week, Mum stormed in (a teacher herself with many years' experience) and called her an 'absolute amateur'. After that, our name was like mud to her.

'I haven't been back here for years,' Emma says, peering out the car window. 'How does it feel? To see it? To be back?'

'It's had a facelift.'

'Oh, someone tried to burn it down a few years back so it was necessary. I say someone. They blamed an electrical fault but the rumour was it was arson. Mum actually double-checked where you were that night...' I widen my eyes at the revelation. 'You were in Edinburgh, touring with a show, don't worry...'

'How do *you* feel to be back?' I ask her.

Emma shrugs. 'My memories are mixed. It was a high-pressure, high-achieving place but I don't think they looked after us very well.'

It's strange to hear Emma talk like that about a place where I'd always assumed she'd thrived. She opens the car door and I follow, linking arms with her, walking around the car park, gazing into windows of empty classrooms. Is this trespassing? Perhaps but it's a thrill to be doing it with the goody-two-shoes sister. Emma pushes against a front door that seems to swing open. She stares at it, knowing we can't go in, but hey, she's with me. I walk straight in and pull her hand.

'Lucy...'

'Emma, live a little,' I reply, winking.

The foyer is as I remember. I sat here a lot on the blue polyester chairs by the office, usually waiting while they rang our mother for crimes I may or may not have committed. There still remains a bronze bust of King Charles that sits on a pedestal and I go over and study his gormless expression and take out my phone.

'Here, let's take a photo of us and Charlie, we'll send it to the sisters.'

Emma's eyes dart in five thousand different directions for fear of being caught. I push her into position and work out my phone camera, styling out the photo so I've got my tongue out trying to lick old Charlie's cheek. I take the shot and cackle at Emma's panicked face.

'We shouldn't be here...' she whispers.

'Why? It's not like we're going to steal anything. There are no kids about. Chill.'

'I don't chill. What if an alarm goes off? The police show up?'

'Then we will run from the police and move to the south of Spain and change our names. You never got into any trouble here, did you?'

She shakes her head at me. 'You made up for that though.'

'It wasn't just me. Beth got caught smoking by the long-jump pitch once. I'm pretty sure Grace has told me she gave a handy to one of the German exchange lads in the art rooms too.'

Emma rolls her eyes for all of our misdemeanours and peers into the school hall that opens up from the foyer, the parquet floor still glaringly bright. She pushes the door of the hall and it squeaks eerily.

'Weren't you forcibly removed from an assembly?' Emma asks me as we walk in.

'I was – it was a thing of legend. You can't sit there and preach about God. It was very disrespectful to the other religions and beliefs that make up the school and I took a stand.'

'The way Grace tells that story, you flashed the school.'

'Because the teacher who manhandled me off the stage picked me up and showed everyone my knickers.'

I take her hand and try to spin her under my arm. Look at all the space we have, Ems. We used to be squashed in here like sardines, all suffering the collective indignity of having to sit on the floor and belt out the school song like we meant it.

'Audete Magnus and forever more...' I belt out at the top of my lungs, a hand reaching to the ceiling.

Emma spins around immediately. 'Shush yourself! It's like you want to be caught.'

'It's the school song. Come on, be game, join in...' I jest.

She gives me a look. You don't remember my daughters but you remember the words to that wretched anthem of our youth?

'Excuse me, are you here for the day camps? They're not in here,' a voice suddenly booms across the parquet, making us both jump. A figure is standing by the doors, peering over at us. Emma still has her smart workwear on but I literally threw on some cycling shorts and have a three-day-old hoodie hanging over my frame with a T-shirt I slept in underneath, no bra, sliders on my feet, and a baseball cap on my head to cover the mess of my post-op scars and shorn head.

'I'm sorry. We were just having a look round. We used to be pupils here,' Emma says, flustered. 'It was a spur-of-the-moment thing, I'm sorry... we should have called ahead. My name is...' But as she goes to shake the woman's hand, she stops for a moment. 'Gemma Chadwick and this is my sister, Victoria.'

The teacher has a harsh silver bob, tinted glasses and wears a boring navy skirt suit with in-between nude heels. She studies our faces closely. *Please don't recognise us, please don't recognise us.*

'It's lovely to see you again after all this time, Mrs Willett,' Emma says. 'I can't believe you're still here.'

'They'll have to prise me out of here...' she says, laughing, still trying to place us. 'I stayed so long, they made me head teacher too...'

Please don't look at my flared nostrils. Please don't. She narrows her eyes at me, her eyes drawn to the tattoos on my ankles, obviously making assumptions about me.

'You were pupils, here?' she asks.

Emma's eyes climb to the top of the building. 'Yes, I was here a few years ago for the centenary celebrations actually. I made a donation to the funds for the new sports hall.'

Mrs Willett seems less suspicious now, like we're not here to rob the place of whiteboard markers and benches. 'Well, do come in and I can give you a brief tour perhaps.' She turns for a moment and Emma/Gemma upturns her palms at me in confusion. We're going in? After this bitchface? To shank her? I mean, I could do the shanking and Emma could sew her up afterwards. I guess we're going in.

'Remind me, what years were you here again?' she asks. I'm

glad I came with the sister who's decent in maths and can help us fake this.

'I left in 2002, Vic left in 2011.' I nod. I'm Vic now, we got casual real quick. I know it's my middle name and it was an easy go-to but if we're reinventing ourselves then at least give me a more exotic name like Magdalena or Emmanuelle. That said, it's mildly hilarious to see Emma doing this. Emma doesn't fib, she's as straight as they come. Has this more mischievous side emerged in the last ten years? I'd like to think so but she's also sweating hard to play along here.

'What line of work are you in?' Mrs Willett asks.

'Oh, Gem became a doctor. She's a paediatric heart surgeon,' I say, on the brag. Mrs Willett looks mildly impressed. She waits to hear what I've done for the last ten years since leaving this place. I don't want to give her the satisfaction so just hope I've retained all my skills as a convincing actress.

'I, too, went into medicine but I went to live abroad. Médecins Sans Frontières. I've just spent the last years working in different refugee camps.'

'Oh yes,' she exclaims. 'I remember you both. Such talent in the sciences.' You old lying goat. 'You are both a credit to this school, we obviously did right by you then.'

We nod. Seriously? I was rubbish at science. It was something that never really computed and I once burnt off part of my fringe on a Bunsen burner. I wouldn't let me near a sick person. I smile though, glad I can dispel her initial assumptions of me. She's still full of her own self-importance and prejudices then. She was the teacher who used to have the biggest go at me about my skirt. She'd follow us around with a thirty-centimetre ruler and tell us short skirts meant we were looking for trouble. I think I once retorted that it went against my rights as a woman not to wear what I want. I got a term's worth of weekend detentions for that.

'So, I heard you built a new drama block here a few years ago?' Emma asks.

'Oh, we did. The old drama studio was literally a room and a broom cupboard full of props. It was time to develop the department as a whole. The productions we put on now are really quite tremendous and the girls' grades really reflect that. Let me show you.'

Emma eyeballs me. It really feels like we're being led deeper into the dragon's lair and I'm literally only in sliders and bare legs.

'Are you all right?' Emma asks me. 'With the walking. Tell me and we can head back.'

'It's all good. Just remember to log this with Igor in case he tells me I've not been doing the work.'

I link my arm into hers tightly, encouraging her to keep close, but Mrs Willett hears the conversation.

'Are you ill?'

'She's just had an operation.'

'Cancer?' she asks, a little too brazenly.

'No.'

'Oh, I assumed with the shaved head.'

'You assumed wrong...' Emma adds, holding me even closer.

'It's not a contagious illness, is it?' Mrs Willett asks, taking a step back, her face scrunched up. I should cough in her general direction now, shouldn't I?

'It was a very aggressive type of malaria, I was lucky my constitution was strong enough to recover.'

'Obviously, something you got from being a King Charlie's girl,' she states.

Yes, a constitution I developed from having to deal with virulent people like yourself. We continue to take a slow walk through the school. The air. The air hasn't changed: this heavy air of expectation in its foundations. We wind around the corners past the school gyms until she heads out to where the old sports blocks used to be. I scan my eyes up its super-white walls and light wood exterior. Sod's law that I would leave and they finally realised the worth of the arts, how drama ignited something in some of us.

'Come in and have a look... we are running some workshops over the summer and sports camps over on the astro pitch so there are some children around.'

We walk in and I'm immediately drawn to the high ceiling, knocking my head back. It doesn't look like the old room. The old room smelt like face paint and feet but I think Mrs Willett wants us to fake some admiration and surprise. I'm not so easily impressed. Inside, a group of girls are in a white T-shirts and leggings working on some sort of warm-up and I smile to see their bare feet, to feel the vibrations as they stamp across the floor. Their teacher comes over to introduce herself, her face completely unfamiliar to me.

'Mrs Willett. Is everything OK?'

'Oh, I was just giving a tour to these ex-alumni. Both doctors.'

The teacher smiles but studies my face closely. 'Lucy?'

'No, her name is Victoria.'

Her eyes bounce towards Emma and I.

'No, this is Lucy Callaghan.' She turns to me. 'I was three years younger than you but you were here. You were a legend. You were the reason I went into drama. I saw a performance with you in *As You Like It* and you were breathtaking. Your last monologue was a masterclass. You had sisters, lots of sisters, right? I'm Maisie Henderson.'

If Emma wasn't sweating before, she now looks like she's run a marathon, a panicked look in her eyes like we need to escape and evade capture. *You can't run, you're an invalid. I'll have to carry you. On my back.* Mrs Willett stops in her tracks and looks me straight in the eye. *Yes, it is I. Where's your ruler now, bitch?*

'Callaghan!' she says in a slightly sinister *Scooby-Doo* villain voice. 'You lied!'

'Kind of but mostly out of fear,' Emma tells her, putting her body in between mine and hers to try and defend me in some way. 'And she didn't lie. I am a surgeon.'

'I will expect that your sister is not though,' Mrs Willett replies, her tone sarcastic and bitter.

'She's an actress. A bloody fine one too,' Emma retorts. The girls in the middle of the room stop to take in the minor drama.

'I feel very uncomfortable that you tried to dupe me into giving you a tour. I think you need to leave my school...'

'I'm sorry... this is my fault,' Miss Henderson says, trying to interject.

'No, it's ours. We did lie and I'm sorry... we will leave,' Emma says, trying to pull me away.

'Just a quick question though before we do...' Emma's fingers literally tense into wire in my hand. *Not now Lucy. Not when you're literally wearing pyjamas.* But old habits die hard.

'It's not *your* school. You never realised that, did you? It belonged to us, it belonged to all these girls.'

Mrs Willett glares at me, like she's getting all her ammunition ready.

'You're saying I should have let the likes of you run riot in this place?'

'The likes of *me*? I think that would have been a fine idea. Why did you hate us Callaghans so much? Myself and my sisters?'

'I am not sure where you got that impression... Lucy... Callaghan...' she says, accentuating my name. And just like that, it's clear that I am still on this woman's radar, she still knows the name, she still knows to fear it. That is bloody excellent.

'Was it because my mum called you an amateur? Did that sting?'

Mrs Willett's eyes widen at the thought and Miss Henderson has to take a step back to bite her lip.

'It's a shame you decided to hold a grudge like some bitter old cod because we're bloody awesome. I wish you'd got to know us rather than thinking we were the problem.'

Emma coughs, actually she looks like she might throw up on the spot from the confrontation.

'But you were. You were one of the most forthright and defiant young ladies we ever had in this school. You questioned everything we put in front of you,' Mrs Willett continues. I smile wryly, pleased I left a mark.

'You say that like it's a bad thing,' I state.

'The apple did not fall far from the tree, let's just say that.'

'Hold up now,' Emma suddenly interjects, her fight-or-flight response clearly kicking in. *We're not leaving now, Lucy.* 'That's my tree you're talking about.'

'Well, some of the apples came out beautifully... others...' Her eyes turn to me. But before I have a chance to reply, Emma chips in.

'Others grew exactly how they needed to. They had to rename the fruit because she was so different, so superbly unique to all the other apples in that tree.' Emma grabs my hand tightly.

'If that's how you want to put it. I found your sister in a storage cupboard once with a groundsman. She made a French teacher cry.'

She's not half wrong. The French teacher was a pervy old tosser though.

'We all had bets where you'd end up. I put my money on prison myself.'

Emma's face contorts in shock. I suddenly think about something Mrs Willett said to me when I was in my last year of sixth form, causing havoc, questioning the status quo. It may have been at the time of my Old El Paso antics. *You'll never amount to anything.* Those words are still fresh in my mind and maybe carry even more gravity after everything that's happened. What am I remembered for? A decent monologue? The fact I was gobby and caused these teachers a fair bit of trouble? That's not something you put on plaques. Christ, was she right? Emma sees that I've run out of steam. My back hurts but she's not done, the purpose of coming over here wasn't to have some old battleaxe lay into me, especially when my memory of her is a lot fresher than she thinks.

'When we came in, Mrs Willett? The first thing you asked was what we became. All you are interested in are labels. But you never asked about the human sides of us – the mothers we grew into, the people we married, the places we've been,' Emma explains.

I don't think I want to answer that either though, Ems. *Yeah, Mrs Willett – I got my vajayjay pierced, am wildly promiscuous and all I seem to own is a cat who eats sanitary wear.* But the big sister has a point. Even when we were just children, this woman weaponised her authority.

'Girls!' Emma shouts, gesturing to the drama crowd in the corner. 'Don't be one of her apples. You grow exactly like you want to. Don't let this one farm you to look like all the others. Bloody shine however you want...'

Of course, this comment has no context so they look at Emma a little confused but I like seeing my sister making a fuss, releasing something into the air that has obviously been bugging her for a decade and more. *You tell them.* I hear angered voices float in and out of my consciousness. A disagreement of sorts. Emma says she'd never send her daughters to this hellhole. I think Willett is threatening to call the police on us. The girls in the corner congregate and watch. Their faces are all shiny and young. That was me, literally a few months ago. Feel the floor under your feet, girls. Let it ground you. You're all shiny young apples.

The words of that final epilogue of *As You Like It* suddenly come to me. I adored the energy, the message for all to love who they wanted, to defy convention and embrace the complexity and wonder of real life. There was a line there about conjuring the audience, about kissing as many people out there that pleased me. The speech is embedded in my brain, it felt like the beginning of something, not an epilogue. I mumble the words under my breath. I remember every word. God, I'm good. They were so bright, the lights in that studio. I couldn't see the faces of the crowd, only hear their applause. And suddenly, my legs just go from under me. Emma catches me.

'Shit! Lucy! LUCY! Call 999, tell them we have a person who's collapsed suffering from a traumatic brain injury. Lucy! Lucy!'

9

'So you're telling me that you, the doctor, let your sister leave this house wearing next to nothing, and went to your old school and took on the headteacher?' Mum says, as she stands over me in bed having actually tucked me in. There's a towel in a plastic basin on the dresser which is Mum's default go-to bowl when someone needs to throw up. That bowl has seen things. That bowl should be in therapy.

'We weren't meant to go in but we did. I thought she was fine. We took her blood sugar in the ambulance, it's just low. She's fine.'

'So you took her on this adventure and didn't even feed her?' Mum adds.

'I will take full responsibility for this,' Emma says, still sweating slightly at the events of the last hour when she cried on the floor of the school's new drama studio thinking I'd stroked out. Of all the places to die, Ems. But hell, maybe this is how I'll get my plaque and it'll be the perfect way to oust Willett from the place: the teacher who'd literally argued one of her ex-students to death.

'Mum, go easy on her. Had she not been there I'd probably

still be on the floor. We've called Mr Gomes, the brain man, and he'll see us tomorrow. Please don't worry,' I say, grabbing onto her hand.

'Well, you're not to move. Only for the toilet. We will bring food to you. I don't want you anywhere near the stairs and a sister is to bathe with you.'

'Bathe with me? We won't fit in the bath. Meg's pubes would float around the bath like seaweed.'

'As in I want them supervising you. Sitting in there with you so you don't fall or anything.'

'Really?' I ask. 'It's got an air of *Little Women* about it. Please assemble around my bed, tell me your tales and plans of the world, we can quilt while I recover from my fevers.' I break open my American accent for that. This does not amuse my mother in the way that it should.

'Please don't joke, Lucy.'

'It's all I have, Mother.'

She comes to arrange the pillows around my back and I catch her eyes examining my scar. It wigs her out, I know. Whereas Meg is fascinated by the grotesque nature of it and Emma cleans it daily, it serves as a reminder to my mum at how easily humans can break. How her daughter broke and they had to put her back together again like Humpty Dumpty. I want to say Mum is stoic but the truth is I don't know how she's dealing with any of this. Every time I see her, by my bedside or over a plate of pasta, she's quiet for once. She shrieks about the cat but she doesn't break into random sobbing like Dad. She doesn't engage with me like she normally does, which is to criticise and for our banter to go back and forth like rocketing tennis balls. Instead, she remains like some wall of strength, her eyes willing me to get better, to get through this. This is her Lucy. She gets herself out of scraps, this daughter of mine; this is just another scrap.

'All that hair gone,' she says, her eyes tracing my fuzzy scalp.

'Hair grows,' I tell her.

'Did you both at least give that Willett woman what for?' Mum asks.

'You raised us to do nothing less, Mum,' I say. 'Is it true you called her an amateur?'

'I called her far worse. It was my greatest pleasure sending all five of my daughters to her over the years. To haunt her with my presence.' Mum says it so coolly and I secretly admire her for it. 'There really isn't anything else wrong here, Emma? You are sure? Do I need to call the GP?'

Emma looks at me, smiling. She's only a surgeon. 'Look, I'll be around all day, I'll check her every hour. I promise.'

There is still some residual anger and blame there but essentially this was no one's fault. The only thing I can blame them for is ineptitude as, when we returned, all the sisters emerged from the house and tried to carry me inside in the same way you might see a Neanderthal man drag back a deer to his cave. They're my bitches but, geez, we need to work on their upper arm strength.

'I'm doing eggs for lunch to get your energy up.'

'Can you feed it to me, Marmee? I may not have the strength to lift the spoon, what with my malaise...' I say, falling back into my accent, putting my hand to my forehead.

'And I've sent Meg and your father to Costco to bulk-buy your favourite things. It's obvious we need to look after you better. We can't have you living off chips and Hobnobs any more.'

'Spoilsport...'

She shakes her head at me, leaving the room. Emma comes to sit down next to me, trying to wipe the sweat from her brow without me looking. Emma doesn't like to fail, for things to go wrong, and she's very much like Mum in how she lets all those feelings swim about inside her soul instead of expressing them.

'I never knew you felt that way about school...' I tell her. 'I always thought you were Little Miss Perfect, that it was your thing.'

'Well, you haven't seen my last decade, Luce. My marriage to Simon would have disproved that completely. And I think the way we were educated contributed to that. I always thought you weren't supposed to challenge anything or rock the boat. You keep your head down and get the work done, your feelings don't matter...'

As she says it, my heart breaks completely. Two of my sisters went through something so awful and painful and I can't recollect any of it.

'Was Simon a complete shit then? I'm sorry. I hope you're OK? Did you see a therapist or anything after it finished?'

'Almost. You moved in with me. You were the therapy. You used all my good shampoo and you had sex in my utility room with a man dressed as Batman but you loved my girls so joyously. You had all the fight in you when mine had run out.'

My heart sings to hear that I was useful during that time at least.

'Batman?'

'He was a school-run dad. His name was Leo.'

'Were we dating? What was it?'

'It was something. He's still a good friend. Maybe you can have a chat with him, it may jog your memory?'

I nod and take her hand. I have Batman questions. Was I dressed up? Was it an event or some kink? Is Leo reasonably good-looking? Like Christian Bale Batman or Michael Keaton? Leo. I don't remember a Leo.

The moment is interrupted by a galloping on the stairs. This sound is not unfamiliar. Our stairs are like the heartbeat of this house. You can tell who's walking up them from the pace and gait on the treads. There's someone rushing to the loo or running away from a fight, someone sitting there taking a phone call thinking none of us can hear. There's the sound of me sitting in the laundry basket asking Grace to push me down because we'd watched too much of the Winter Olympics at Nagano. I still remember the juddering, the big clash at the bottom when I collided with the banister. I remember blood and a giant fat lip and Mum having to write letters to school to explain. There's Dad's slow measured steps and Grace jumping like a gazelle from the third step to the bottom. This is Beth. When she crawls up frantically, using hands and feet. She once admitted to me that she often worries she's being chased because she watched *Halloween* way too young and it left permanent scars. She bursts into the room.

'Hey,' she says, straightening herself up. She looks slightly manic. 'How are you? Why am I out of breath? This is awful. I'm so unfit.' She doubles over and then stands to attention again. 'How was Willett? What a disaster they made her head. Was she awful?'

'Reptilian,' I reply, waiting for her to explain her manic entrance.

'Soooo... Grace is making you dippy eggs with soldiers and I also did a thing. Don't hate me for doing the thing but it's a thing and basically there's someone downstairs?'

'Does he have a mullet? Is he wearing Crocs?' I ask. 'Igor the physio was supposed to come round today.'

'Not quite,' she replies. 'So, when we were on the sofa the other day and we were stalking people, you told me you wanted to see Josh. Well... news of your accident has got round. Not from me. Just the general grapevine and Josh got in touch with me to ask if you were OK and I explained the situation and, well, he's downstairs now with a bouquet of supermarket flowers and, quite interestingly, a box of Maltesers, which to me feels a tad cheap...' she spills out.

I sit there for a moment to take all of Beth's ramble in. I'm having eggs. But Josh? Is here?

'You invited him here? You didn't tell me?' I tell Beth.

'I didn't think you'd be out this morning and I thought we'd have time to prepare, properly. I can send him away?'

Emma nods but I hold a hand to the air. 'No... he's here? He came?'

Beth and I did the full Facebook stalk of him the other day. It turns out we weren't friends on there but it was easy to see from his profile pictures that he married someone when he was about twenty-four and they had two sons together. He's not a footballer any more, he fixes domestic appliances and has his own van, which Beth was angry about because it had the words 'specialises in fridge's' and the apostrophe catastrophe made her bare teeth. It felt awful seeing him. It felt like this was someone I'd spent nearly every minute of every day with. In my mind, we're still together. Back then, he had a souped-up little Vauxhall Corsa, which was his pride and joy and we used to sit in deserted car parks in it and have sex, smoke weed and listen to music until my mum would text in full caps telling me to haul my arse home. My seventeen-year-old self adored his bones, gave herself to him completely and adoringly. That was what I thought love was at that age. It was consuming and full of energy and desire and, even after all my sisters told me about how it finished, I can't quite believe that something so potent just stopped existing.

'Mum won't engage with him and she thinks this is an awful idea after this morning, but it's your call.'

'How do I look?' I ask Emma.

'Pale and bald.'

'You're such a cow. But what if I see him and it all comes flooding back? The memories? He is one of the last people I remember, maybe it will trigger something...' Emma and Beth's faces drop to hear the desperation in my tone. 'Maybe if it's just to say hello, it can't hurt.'

'Five minutes maybe?' Emma suggests.

Beth nods. 'I'll get him up then.'

As soon as she leaves the room, I turn to the dresser next to me. 'Should I wear a hat? How pale am I? Do you have any blusher? Lip balm? Do I look like a fricking zombie?'

'You look like you. The Lucy I know wouldn't care,' she says, putting a hand to my forehead. The footsteps tread heavy on the stairs. Trip, trap, trip, trap. Emma goes to the bedroom door to open it. Oh. Hi. Josh.

In my mind, Josh still wears jeans and Puma sweatshirts and, my days, he had good hair. A group of us dated the lads from the Sheen Lions football team and we'd go to the matches and be indiscreet and cheer every time the boy we were dating had the ball, which didn't go down well with the coach, who eventually barred us. The one thing Josh had in spades was presence. He made us all laugh by taking the piss out of everyone and everything. He was the group alpha and I was drawn to that. However, the man at the door of my room is not that same cocksure guy I once knew. The hair is now gone, shaved, except he's got hints of a dodgy goatee, bags under his eyes, and a questionable tattoo that winds its way around his neck. Is that a name? He's in a zipped-up tracksuit top and there's a hole in the big toe of one of his socks as Mum has obviously asked him to remove his shoes. There's a feeling in the pit of my stomach to see him, I want to call them butterflies but they feel more like old moths just fluttering around in there not really knowing where they're going.

'Lucy. God...'

His face reads horror, maybe relief that he's dodged a bullet. I don't know why. We have matching haircuts. But he has no other words, which is quite unlike him. His voice is deeper, more gravelly. Unfamiliar.

'Josh... hey...' Christ. Say something. 'I'll take it those are for me?' I ask, trying to break the silence.

'Yeah, I didn't know what to bring, you know?'

My first thoughts are that they're not tulips and that he's left the price tag sticker on. He got them at a reduced price. Classy.

'That's kind of you. Thanks. Thank you for coming.'

I await all the memories flooding back but nothing. I sigh and slump my shoulders over. That's a bloody disappointment because I'm going to have to entertain him, aren't I? I wasn't sure what I was going to feel when I saw him. Possibly something like a surge of electricity running through me, I'd jump into his arms like we'd never been apart and we'd have sex in my mum's spare room. Time would not have got in the way of all that love and lust we shared for each other. *The Notebook* really has a lot to answer for. Instead, he stands there with his hands in his pockets, a shadow of the lad I once knew, all grown up.

'Yeah, I heard from a mate what happened and then I got in touch with Beth. She said you thought we were still a thing?' he mutters.

'Well, it's the last thing I remember.'

'Oh, so you've got, like, that ammer-ne-sia thing?'

'Amnesia,' Emma says, correcting him. He looks at her, and takes a step back, almost intimidated.

'Yeah. I mean, don't worry. I know you're married now with kids so maybe I just thought meeting you might bring something back...'

'And?'

'Nothing. Sorry. That's not a reflection on you. So what happened with the football? You had those trials with Fulham. Did that not happen?'

I get a sense that hits a nerve by the change in his expression. 'Did my Achilles in, didn't I? Just wasn't meant to be. Like you with the acting. These things have a million in one chance of turning out.'

'I'm still an actress.'

'Oh. Would I have seen you in stuff? Like on the TV?'

I shake my head.

It used to be all we talked about in his car. How I was going to be his WAG with a respectable sideline in winning BAFTAs while he'd be some England hero who'd score a deciding penalty on the world stage and then have a career in punditry and advertising Paco Rabanne. But I guess that's what you do when you're young and your whole life is in front of you. Everything is soaked in hope and youthful dreams.

'And you fix fridges now?' I ask, hoping I'm not pissing too much on his present endeavours.

'Yeah, I'll leave a card with your mum. Dishwashers, dryers, freezers. Steph is in the beauty biz.'

'And Steph is your wife?'

He nods, a little worry in his face that the news may break me but I get it. He married someone else and I'm cool with that. Now I've seen him in the flesh, I know I haven't missed out on some great love.

'Yep. And we have two boys, Hudson and Hunter.'

'Oh, are they twins?' Emma asks.

'Nah.'

He gets out his phone to show me a screensaver of him and the family on holiday. Steph is preened and skinny and the lashes are a statement. She's not me because I get the sense I'd be drunk on that holiday and unable to stand. This is the moment when I should smile and pour praise on this little foursome outside some restaurant in Spain, looking tanned and happy, the boys in matching outfits to their dad. But unfortunately, along with the picture there is also a text message from someone called Henno.

Still shaggable, mate? Or a complete munter now? Or like a complete veg from the accident? Still would if she's still fit.

Naturally, Josh thinks my shock comes from the picture so looks horrified as he takes his phone away.

'Luce, are you OK?' Emma asks, coming over.

'We broke up in 2010. I'm sorry if you're upset,' Josh adds.

I reach down and take the phone from his hand, turning it to face him. His face drains of colour.

'Oh shit, that's awful. Like, he's not even a good mate. Well, he is but that was a bad joke to make. I didn't come here for that. I came to see you because Beth said what happened...'

Emma glares at the phone, wondering what she should be doing. *What was the joke?* If you can call it that. But the fact is I'm not upset. I'm disgusted, silently fuming. I feel old Lucy would have quicker reactions than the ones I do right now. I heard she once threw someone's phone out of a window. Good for her.

'My sisters tell me what we had ended in Oceana. Farah found me because she saw you all over some girl in the toilets.'

'Well, yeah... you don't remember that? We'd had a proper fight because you were going off to uni.'

'So you just hooked up with the next girl that came along?'

It feels strange to call him to task on this over a decade after the event but the rage simmers in me. If I was full-strength Lucy then I suspect I'd launch myself at him. I hope I did at the time.

'This was a pretty long time ago.' He keeps looking over at Emma, hoping she will intervene, but she stands there, arms folded.

'Why don't you tell Lucy what happened at the time?' Emma says.

'It was your birthday. We were all celebrating that and A-Level results and all your sisters were there, they'd all come down for the night. Are you sure you don't remember this?' he asks tentatively.

I shake my head.

'It was your eldest sister who went for me first. The other

girl involved then went for Beth, they properly had it out and it
was all a bit of a do. We got thrown out and I think you and your
sisters were barred because you went for a bouncer, and then
we never spoke to each other again. No, I lie. I think I did when
I came round accusing you of slashing my tyres and then your
mum chased me down the road and said if I wanted to see real
criminal damage then she'd show me.'

I try to hold in my smile. And suddenly, all these notions of
young love just escape like hot air into nothing. Thank the lord I
did not try and salvage that or flog that relationship for years. It
wasn't love at all, in any shape or form.

'So basically, you were a knob.'

'I was called far worse that night.'

I laugh. 'Well, you can tell your mate, Henno, that I'm still
shaggable, I'm not a vegetable and he should go stick his dick in
a bear trap.' Emma realises what I saw before and her jaw drops
in horror. 'I may now know why we're not mates a decade later.'

I'd like to say he shows an ounce of repentance or guilt but,
instead, his back straightens out. 'Look, I came here to be nice,
to help you access all them lost memories, not to be made to feel
guilty for something I did a long time ago.'

'Tell me, Josh. Did you get run over by a bus?' I say,
completely deadpan.

'That's not the point. I did love you, once. You were a top
girl.'

'I still am.'

There's a moment of silence as he studies my face, knowing
it's time for him to get out. We're done here. Leave the chocolates though. I'm owed that much. In the bedroom next to ours,
I hear hushed whispers through the wall as Beth, Grace and
Mum are obviously vying to hear what's happening. Is that
clapping? It's certainly Beth trying to bargain with Mum to stay
in the room and not get stuck in.

'Well, whatever happens, I do hope you get better, Luce,' he tells me, smiling. That smile hasn't changed. It was cheeky and I would have done anything for it. Once. I might wave back. Au revoir, shithead.

He leaves, Emma following him out and I hear his footsteps on the stairs. Trip-trap-trippity-trap and the front door opens and slams shut. Faces appear at the door. I lie back. Memories that I thought were important are just meaningless or a small little corner piece in a much bigger puzzle. I'm exhausted but glad I didn't end up with him with identi-kids in matching shoes and my name tattooed on his neck.

'Are you OK, Lucy?' Grace asks.

'You're telling me you all had some group brawl in a nightclub?' our mother asks. Mum seems to have not been filled in on some of the detail of that night. 'You told me Meg got that black eye because she fell out of a minicab drunk. She was a mother!'

The sisters' eyes look in different directions of the room.

'And we're not allowed back there?' I enquire.

'Oh, we are. Oceana closed and changed into something else. But you jumped on a bouncer's back after he tried to forcibly remove Meg, threw up on him and broke a table. Apparently, they used to have your face on a poster in the entry booth. But it didn't matter. Weeks later, you went to university,' explains Beth.

It was like Josh never existed. He got removed from memory and replaced by men with aubergines for willies, dressed up as Batman.

'Gracie – go get her eggs on...' Mum tells her, studying my face. I don't know what I need at this precise moment but my mother seems to think it's protein. 'I never liked him. He had that arrogant man energy, he had some sort of garage street name for me that was funny to him but no one else.'

'Madame Fee-Cee,' I suddenly recall.

Beth tries to stifle her laughter.

'I'm glad the pertinent things have stuck, Lucy. It sounded

like faeces. He was basically calling me human waste. He had no respect for this house or you. He was lucky we let him back in,' Mum says, gesturing to Beth, who wonders how productive her intervention really was.

'Well, it's done now. I now know what happened. I know I'm not in love with him. I just have to piece together all those uni years. God, did I really slash his tyres?' I say.

That feels like my sort of energy but I'm glad, for one night only, the sisters were a part of that. That we were all one big gang, taking on the world, getting thrown out of joints. But a face pops up from behind, having skipped up the stairs.

'No, I did,' Emma says, grimacing. 'I used a scalpel too.'

Beth laughs uncontrollably. My mother might shake her hand.

10

'So you collapsed. Yet you're still alive. I don't know why you are moaning at me...'

I really bloody dislike you, Igor. I don't think your mother even liked you if she gave you a name like that. He stands over me in this exercise studio, watching as I balance on one leg trying to stretch out my calves.

'I collapsed because I was walking and my body obviously isn't ready for full exercise.'

'You're so full of crap. That was two weeks ago. You collapsed because you're not eating well – it's in your notes. You don't want to exercise because you hate me and the control I have over you. Now stretch before I tell your sister.'

I lunge to the side, grimacing a little but maybe not as much as before because I think some of this might be working and my body might be coming back to life. I will not admit this much to Igor though. He watches and makes a note on his stupid clipboard, the one I usually imagine smashing into his face.

'Good, Lucy. We'll call it a day there.'

'I think you just paid me a compliment.'

'You think I did.'

Today, they've shipped me into town to some fancy rehab gym with a pool so I can have a full workout and I suspect some of my sisters can spend some time with children and husbands and not have to babysit me. What's it like all living together again? It feels like home. I like these new habits we have of getting into comfy clothes and 'binging' TV shows together, sharing chocolate and wine. Other times, it's Mum questioning who hasn't flushed a toilet and Grace falling out of a bed because Beth rolled over and kicked her out. But unfortunately none of this shared living experience or meeting Josh aka Dick-face in real life after all these years, has brought back any memories so we have to dig further.

After I shower up today, I'm going down the road to meet Tony, an old uni friend who I hear my mother was very sad I didn't end up with. This is a surprise given my mother takes a combative stance with any man who tries to infiltrate her clan but apparently I'll know when I meet him. He's charming, can speak four languages and he once told my mum a dirty Christmas joke about snowmen that she still uses to this day, which is a shock as Mum doesn't really do smut. Or jokes.

'Your sisters tell me you were very into exercise before the accident so I do not know why you are so resistant to work with me,' Igor explains.

I can't say because his mullet offends me, can I? The truth is, I think it's because I don't like him seeing me at my weakest, when my arms are like spaghetti and my legs don't work. I don't want anyone to see me like this because it feels vulnerable and exposing. That doesn't feel like me. This is too deep to tell someone I dislike so much though.

'You are getting there, Lucy. You're walking around, you've regained some strength in your joints. It was good to get you in the pool. You're here today on your own. You're getting to a good place.'

'I'm not on my own. My dad is waiting in the car with a newspaper and a puzzle book.'

He laughs. 'You're funny.'

'I wasn't trying to be.'

'I'll see you at your mum's house in three days.'

'I'll bake a cake.'

'Lemon, please.'

With shards of glass in the icing? He leaves as his next client is outside waiting and I head for the showers. We are lucky to have Emma and all her connections as this place really is high-end, unlike any leisure centre gym that I've been in and that's because of the free towels, which I'm not quite sure if I'm allowed to keep. As I head into the communal showers, I look around and seem to have got the back end of some junior swimming class. I watch as mums and au pairs dance around trying to get their little ones to wash their hair without getting wet themselves. I strip down to my swimming costume and join them, noticing a little girl looking up at me, foam hanging from her curls. She studies the tattoos about my person and the scratches and scars down my legs. I look over at the woman I assume to be her au pair, who is trying to signal at her that it's rude to stare.

'You're Lucy?' she says, surprised.

'I am,' I say, studying the girl before me in her navy and pink Speedo swimming costume, goggles and hat in hand. Are we related? I hope you're not a niece I've forgotten about.

'You did my party once, my name is Ophelia.'

I study her face, remembering the name. 'You wrote me a thank you note.'

She nods and smiles but I can see her examining the top of my head, confused. 'What happened to you?' she asks inquisitively.

The problem with my hair at the moment is that it's a strange in-between stage where it looks like it may be a fashion choice but the scar is still there, plus the other various remnants of my injuries. My inclination is to tell her a whole different story to make things interesting but also to hide the fact I nearly died the day of her party.

'I also work in the circus and I was in an awful accident where I fell off a trapeze.'

Ophelia's eyes widen, as do her au pair's, who's now worried about the tattooed lunatic standing beside her charge in the shower.

'I mean, I'm fine, but they had to cut off all my hair, which actually might be better because now I can just wear wigs and it's much cooler in the summer.'

'And easier after swimming,' she adds.

'This is so true.'

Her au pair hands over some conditioner and I offer to squeeze some into her hair, her hands clawing up to run it through her curls. *I should remember you, I only met you a mere matter of months ago.*

'Was I Elsa at your party?' I ask her.

'No. Cinderella?' she says, disappointed that I wouldn't recall that detail.

'Oh, of course. I remember it well.'

'You do Elsa?' she asks.

I now have a frame of reference for who this Elsa lady is and all I know is that she likes her ice and kids go batshit crazy for her.

'I do. Actually, can you clear something up for me? You said in your thank you note that I said something at your party? I gave you advice?'

She nods. 'You taught me some great phrases and words to use when people aren't being very nice to me.'

I widen my eyes. Which ones, love? There are catalogues of the things.

'You were really kind to me,' she says, twisting her lips about, slightly embarrassed.

'I'm glad. Thank you for your note. You have wonderful handwriting. Did you get good birthday presents?'

'I got a pony.'

'Oh. A real one?'

'Yes,' she says hesitantly. I sense she didn't ask for the pony.

'If I had a pony, I'd call it Tony after one of my best mates.'

She giggles. I wish I remembered you, Ophelia. You seem lovely. I hope I did a good job at your party. Cinderella doesn't really do much except clean and lose her shoes.

'How did you fall off your trapeze?' she asks.

'Well, I have a partner called Igor and he didn't catch me.'

Ophelia feigns shock. 'That's awful. What a terrible trapeze artist. Did they fire him from the circus?' she asks.

'They fed him to the lions.'

'Poor Igor.'

'What about me? He dropped me. I landed like a sack of potatoes,' I say dramatically.

I love that she's still in on the joke but the look on her face changes a little as she catches sight of the scar on my head again.

'I'm glad you're OK, Lucy.'

'So am I. How crazy I get to bump into you, in here of all places as well.'

'I always thought princesses shower in waterfalls with birds and squirrels.'

I nod. 'Only at the weekends though. I come here for the free towels. Now lean back, your fringe is still full of bubbles, lovely.'

* * *

Tony. Tony. Tony. There's a strange anxiety in my stomach as I sit in this pub waiting for Tony and I'm not sure if it's because I have no recollection of him at all or because of what he's going to tell me about my life. I'm not sure of the politically correct way of saying these things but Tony is a dwarf. He's smaller than the average guy. I can imagine that didn't faze me at all, I wouldn't have had any problem with him being my friend, but there was obviously a time when we also were intimate, which intrigues me. Facebook has been my friend here as I've been able to examine all the pictures of us, all the drunken nights out we had, times when we worked together too. The one thing that separates him from Josh perhaps is that we still seem to be friends, we still chat and party together, and any romantic split was amicable at least and didn't involve my sisters and me forming some sort of prison-girl-gang in a nightclub.

I peel the sticker off my beer bottle and watch with curiosity some of the other people in this place. The beginnings of some lads' night involving the football on a television, the after-work drinkers and a man who's sitting on his own, as if he's pondering the value of his life and whether he should go back home now or later when his wife is in bed and he doesn't have to talk to her. He gives me a cursory glance, probably wondering why I'm here on my own too. *Poor love looks like she's been dumped or waiting on a date that's never going to happen.*

'Lucy...' a voice suddenly says from behind my booth.

I turn around. 'Tony?'

He laughs at the question mark at the end of that sentence. 'I seriously did not think it was true.'

He searches my eyes and I don't quite know where to look. He's tattooed and he's wearing a baseball cap but there's a warmth in his demeanour that makes me trust his smile. I'd remember him. I really think I would. I smile back when I realise we're just staring each other out. He puts a bottle of beer down to the table and jumps on the seat next to me. I don't know what I was expecting. The pictures showed me someone who is obviously cooler than most. His Facebook profile is filled with experiences and nights out, holidays and parties, but there's no perceived awkwardness about his differences. He puts his arms out to hug me and give me a kiss on the cheek and I reciprocate. The man sitting across from me now has a reason to stay and watch. The date has appeared and this is not who he was expecting at all.

'I feel like you're slowly taking me in...' Tony jests, tapping my beer bottle and then taking a swig.

'I am. Kinda...'

He sits there, pulling different poses so I can examine him from many different angles. Hand to the chin, blue steel, flexing his arms. I laugh.

'So in your mind, I don't exist. You're just a seventeen-year-old Lucy meeting me for the first time...'

I nod.

'I can't believe it. I'm so sorry I never came to the hospital to visit. I was in Rome. Darren called me to say what had happened.'

I shrug. 'I'd have been none the wiser. I'd probably have thought I was hallucinating you.'

Tony laughs. He's immediately likeable, there's just something behind his blue eyes too that's immensely calming.

'So, you want me to bring it all back for you?' he asks.

'If you could. And I'll get this out the way too. Did we sleep together?'

Tony puts his head down on the table, almost in sadness.

'Well, that tells me all I need to know about the quality of the sex if you've wiped that from your memory.'

It's my turn to laugh now, glad he's been able to turn that into a joke and not be offended.

'We did, Lucy. Many times. I think we were almost dating for a while but you know what university relationships can be like. We promised not to put labels on it. It was like friends with benefits when we were drunk and in the same room.'

Oh. I look down at my beer bottle, now slightly panicked.

That is not what the intention of today is at all. This is an avenue I've not explored. I've not had sex since the accident. Maybe good sex would help? An orgasm and a sudden rush of blood to the head would fix everything. But suddenly I feel quite unprepared. I've forgotten everything so have no skill set, only those I've acquired from having slept with a handful of people at sixth form. I also have not paid much attention to my personal grooming. When you're hit by a bus then your bush doesn't become the priority. I didn't care much when I was in the pool either, the whole world was welcome to gawp if they wanted. Tony senses my panic and puts a hand in mine.

'It's OK. I wasn't going to suggest we do it in the back seat of your dad's car.'

My eyes widen.

'I saw him on the way in. We had a chat. I invited him in but he was mid-sudoku so turned me down,' he says, chuckling.

'So you've met my family? That's pretty serious?' I ask.

'I spent Christmas with you guys. The story starts that we met at university at a club. We both worked there – you were a dancer and I worked the bar and did the odd DJ gig. We used to have dance-offs to entertain the punters. You should see me work a pole.'

I knock my head back in laughter.

'It was a posh club. That job paid off our loans. But what we had was just a meeting of minds of two people who got along and had a laugh. We flirted for weeks then eventually got together and had some fun.'

He shifts his eyes around, trying to lighten the mood. He picks up on the old disco tune in the background and circles his shoulders around. OK, he has some moves. I join in tentatively with this table dance as he uses his hand to beckon me to get more involved. I can sense why there may have been an attraction there, he's charming, cheeky. Old Lucy would have danced and got drunk with that man, for sure. You can picture it. The dancing would not have been subtle but oh my days, the joy, the laughter.

'I was there when you had your first tattoo done. You screamed at me the whole way through and called me a load of swear words then went back and got your next one two weeks later...' he recalls. 'And after that, we just hung out. I liked that you didn't want to label what he had, we were young and just working things out, but, for ages, you were a ride or die. I adored you. Scrap that, I adore you.'

'A ride or die is a good thing?'

'It is. Someone you would show up for, whatever. I met your family after we did a Christmas club gig. For that one, I had to dress up as an elf... don't judge, I'm ashamed I went there myself but the money was off the scale... You were sexy Mrs Claus. We did the Eve shift which meant we got, like, triple pay but it saw us end work at four a.m. so we crawled to your mum and dad's for lunch...'

'My mum likes you...'

'I'm good with mums. I beat her at Scrabble that night, which apparently never happens but that's because I kept topping up her sherry glass. She was wasted by the end. Your dad and Danny had to carry her upstairs... they dropped her and that's why the light fitting at the bottom of your stairs doesn't work any more...'

He speaks about all these people in my life so casually like he knows them all, like he's invested in my life, and, for a moment, I feel guilty not to be able to return that friendship, unable to ask him about his life and family.

'And so Rome? What's the deal?'

'I studied Italian and philosophy at uni. I then went on to do my doctorate and now I live in Rome, I lecture, I drink a lot of very very good wine.'

'Are you married? Kids?'

'No. There are women but I continue to not put a label on

things. Life is good, Luce.'

He reaches for his phone on the table and opens up some photos. 'You visited me about a year ago for a weekend. We went to a gig and hung out.' He clicks on a photo of me on a sun-drenched terrace, wearing a wide-brimmed hat with a pizza as big as the moon in front of me. All these pictures show me someone who is so perfectly happy, so relaxed and carefree. I just wish I could remember where it all came from. I wish I could remember why I didn't want to stay with this lovely man here who's obviously smart, sweet and who I clearly had some form of connection with.

'And did we do the thing?'

'Last year? The sex? I believe we did. Again, slightly offended that's not etched into memory... we did it on a balcony, we gave the neighbours' grandmother a nervous breakdown when she caught sight of us... I had to move.'

I break into hysterics. Am I turned on here? I could be. But that panic sits in my soul again, especially as I know my dad is outside this pub doing his sudoku.

'How much sex did we have?'

'Do I give this to you in exact amounts or...?' he says, waving his fingers around.

I snigger. 'I think I'm just trying to work out the sort of person I was, the sex I was having, with who? The last decade or so sounds...'

'Eventful?'

I nod. 'When I left for university, I'd just broken up with a boyfriend who, in my mind, when I woke up I was still with. And now I'm being told I went to university and became a bit of a...'

'Don't say the word...'

'Was I?' I ask him.

'Lucy, we had some pretty hot sex. You were experimental, you didn't have any hang-ups about yourself, you were just good fun. We laughed so much. We both once streaked naked through a Tube, for a bet. I'm not sure if I'm still allowed to ride the Circle Line.'

My hands cover my mouth and he looks surprised. I guess old Lucy wouldn't be so embarrassed at that revelation, she'd bask in how outrageous it is, but I'm still getting used to this girl's gall, her courage.

'Luce, when I met you, you were so bright but in so many ways. We didn't just get drunk and shag. We talked about books and politics. Your eyes would light up at the novelty of everything. You were so keen and ready to go out in the world and just explore the infinite possibility that lay at your feet. That fearlessness to throw yourself into anything and everything was what made me love you.'

'You loved me?' I gasp, almost in shock.

'I think we loved each other. Maybe not in a romantic sunset kinda way, I don't think either of us believed in that, but enough for me to jump on a plane when you ask me out for a drink.'

What is confusing to me is, somewhere down the line, I obviously stopped looking for my sunsets. When did I come to all these life conclusions?

'When my dad died, you came to the funeral. You sat at the back of the church and afterwards you got me drunk and slept on my sofa for three days to check I was all right. So just in case you thought all we did was get naked together.'

He grabs my hand and, for this small moment, it's everything. To think I had a wonderful soul like this who was my friend. *Can I take you back to Mum and Dad's? They like you. It'd be a break from the board games.*

'I like the new look, by the way. It's very Sigourney Weaver in *Alien*.'

'At last, a cultural reference I get.'

'It's badass.'

'But cold.'

He reaches a hand, stroking the blonde fuzz on my head.

'Thank you for being here. For coming all this way to have a drink with a mate.'

'No blowjob?' he jokes, laughing.

I want to say maybe but hell, this is a moment I don't think I want to spoil. Let's get drunk first. *But it's lovely to meet you, Tony. I'm so very glad you're here.*

'While we're here... Did you know anyone called Oscar? He's a name that's appeared on my phone and I have no idea who he is.'

He shakes his head, with a look that says, with the number of people we obviously had relations with, it could indeed be anyone.

'But look, we know the same people so I'll give you some numbers of people to call, chat to. Start with Jill, Jill Rigby.'

I narrow my eyes at him, asking him to let on but he doesn't. 'That's her story to tell you,' he replies, a cheeky glint in his eye.

But before I have a chance to delve, two people standing by our table get our attention. Both are here to watch the football and are clearly a few pints in. Tony eyes them curiously.

'Nah, mate. You ask them...' They're obviously in on some sort of shared joke that neither I nor Tony understand.

'It's just... are you two together?' says one boldly. Bold because that's some haircut on him. Did his barber have a stroke in the middle of that trim? 'Like, how does that work? What with him being a midget?'

Tony smiles. You can tell this isn't the first time he's heard this and it's not like him to rise to the drunken bullshit of two crapbags. But there's something in me that's riled instantly. Not only because I feel defensive of this man I've literally only just met but because their comments are derogatory and devalue both of us completely. It's only then I realise why Tony is smiling. *Don't rile, Lucy. You really shouldn't, boys.*

'We're married,' I tell them, completely po-faced.

The grins get wiped off their faces pretty quickly as I nestle into Tony and link an arm around his. I think I actually hear one of them physically gulp.

'Look, we was just asking...'

'Nah, you were taking the piss. Because this one, I'll tell you a secret...' I say, pointing to Tony and leaning over the table, 'Some of the best wang I've ever had. I'll be thinking of you needle dicks when he's giving me some later...'

I pause for a moment when I say this. Needle dicks. I don't quite get why. Tony shrugs at the blokes in question. One of them looks like he wants to start something but isn't sure which one he should be taking on.

'All right, calm down, Snow White.'

'Actual dick for brains. Can you believe this one?' I say, turning to Tony, who laughs under his breath.

I hope the actual Snow White does this for her mates. Hell, maybe that should be part of my princess act. Come on then, lads. My teeth are gritted, energy in my veins like I want to punch something.

'Bi—'

But before the man even has a chance to have the word leave his very mouth, Tony gives the table a nudge. It's a brilliant move because it's enough to hit one in the man bits and for my drink to spill and splash the other in the crotch so he looks like he's had an unfortunate accident.

'Tony!' I shriek.

'Lucy!' he replies mockingly.

He laughs but senses the rest of their mates are looking over. Tony pushes me out of our cubicle, urging us to make a quick exit. He leads us around the corner to a darkened stairwell.

'What did you just do? We're going to get beaten up,' I whisper.

'And? We could take them on. I'd challenge them to a

dance-off,' he replies, keeping watch for louty football hooligans.

'Tell me, was I lying? About the wang?'

He smirks and raises an eyebrow. 'Wanna find out?'

11

'You slept with Tony?' Meg asks me, sitting next to me in the car.

'If you mean, did he pleasure me in a pub toilet, then the answer is yes.'

Meg flares her nostrils and I grin back with all my teeth on full show, hoping it will better her big sisterly disapproval.

'Dad was in the car outside that pub, waiting for you...' she answers.

'He also gave him a lift to the train station after...' I say. 'They spoke about the weather, it was so civil.'

Meg shakes her head at me, which is her automatic response to most things these days. But I don't care as the memory of that evening makes me smile. The beer in our systems helped us evade the football muppets but it also gave us the bravado to sneak off to the bathroom. Tony took my hand and led me into a cubicle. I don't feel any shame, any guilt, because it was a nice moment where someone wanted to be intimate with me, who wanted to make me feel good. He didn't push the agenda; I saw the penis. I admired the penis. I didn't touch the penis. We took it as far as I wanted and there seemed to be a need there to protect me more than anything and it was appreciated. It also made me grateful for thongs because, hey, access.

'You two aren't...' Meg asks.

'Dating, no? He's gone back to his corner of the world and I know what happened there now.'

I sense Meg's disappointment as all my family love Tony but to me it was a perfect moment. Since the accident, I haven't felt that way towards anyone, I haven't felt attractive or sexual, so it was beautiful for that to re-emerge in a way, for me to connect to myself again like petals unfurling on a very nervous flower.

'And seeing him brought back nothing?' Meg asks.

'Unfortunately, no... But he gave me some names of people to track down, talk to...'

'Any joy with the Oscar conundrum?'

I shake my head. The Oscar Mystery remains a puzzle in our house that the sisters have all committed time and energy to solving. *Oscar, 9th February.* The pinned note on my phone meant something but there was no Oscar in my contacts or even in my Facebook friends. I followed Instagram people called Oscar but, after some random messages, it turned out that I knew none of them very well. Except one who wanted to change that. *It's all right, love. You still live at home and kiss your dog on the mouth.* The agency confirmed that I'd not done any parties for an Oscar on that date either. So he was either a one-night stand or maybe he was someone else. We all had fun imagining who he might be: maybe he was a sculptor and I'd posed for him on that day (nude obviously), maybe he was a debt collector, maybe he'd done me wrong and I had a plot where I was going to avenge his wrongdoings. The sad fact was he probably wasn't anyone that important at all but, still, the sisters dig, they rake through my browser histories and have made it a fun project. It makes me think that if the inclination was there, we could start our very own Charlie's-Angels-style detective agency and take on the world.

'Well, maybe there will be clues in your bedroom,' Meg says as she takes a turn into a leafy suburban road in South East London, terraces of townhouses reaching into the sky, the street punctuated by 4x4 cars and impeccably kept gardens. Today, Meg and I have come over to my old neck of the woods, my manor in Herne Hill where I used to live a sketchy existence in my commune/shared house. There's the hope that sifting through my room may bring something familiar to mind or indeed give us some key clues to the identity of the mysterious Oscar. As she reverse parks (badly and with much swearing), I'm not horrified at my street. It's quite leafy and normal, I think I hear actual birds chirping and we're parked next to an Audi, which is the hallmark of reliability.

'Have you been here before?' I ask.

'No. I'm almost surprised...' Meg replies, looking around, but then our gaze falls on the house we're searching for. Oh. The one thing that gets my attention is that the house number has been written on a coaster and hammered into the front door with a single nail, but even without that you can tell the place is in some state of disrepair from the makeshift curtains, peeling paint and the old toilet in the front garden. We take a slow, hesitant walk towards it, pangs of teen disappointment that this is the house where I end up as a nearly thirty-year-old woman.

'You!' a voice suddenly pipes up from behind me.

Meg and I turn to see a man in a suit wheeling in a bin, an impeccably numbered bin, as I glance over to ours, which seems to be labelled with a spray can.

'Hello?' I reply tentatively.

I hope I haven't slept with this dipstick. For one, no one does pinstriped suits with a patterned shirt. It's like he deliberately wants to hurt my eyes.

'How many times do I have to tell you lot to stop putting

your bottles in my recycling bin? You don't rinse them. Christ, you don't even empty them sometimes.'

I will assume this man is our kindly neighbour and there may be a reason we gift him our recycling.

'It wasn't me.'

'Of course it is. I can't believe you have the gall to lie about it now!' he continues ranting. I notice his kids and their noses pressed up against a living room window to take in the drama. I can't give your dad a swift kick in the nads with you looking, eh?

'I mean, it wasn't me because I'm not living here at the moment.'

'You've moved out?' he blurts out hopefully.

'She was ill,' Meg pipes in, the man's tone and demeanour obviously riling her too.

'Oh...' he says, not a hint of compassion in his voice. Methinks we didn't quite get on, you were not the sort of neighbour who we borrow sugar from.

'I thought I hadn't seen your demon beast around for a while...'

'Pussy?'

'Excuse me?'

'That's her name.'

Meg now twists her lips around trying to keep in the laughter.

'Well, she used to defecate in my kids' sandpit. We caught her on camera.'

'Then cover your sandpit?' Meg suggests.

'And who sits there and films a cat having a poo?' I ask.

He eyeballs us both, knowing that he will lose this fight but needs the final word.

'Well, tell your "friends" too that band practice and singalongs at three in the morning are not appreciated.'

He turns and drags his bin away. I hope they went super heavy on the bass.

'Nice to see you made a positive impact in your community,' Meg sniggers.

'Glenn got his knackers in a twist again?' a voice says from my front door. It's Cass standing there. I smile to see her and give her a hug. So this is where I lived? I peek my head through the doorway and it's as I imagined, a shelf to the side of the front door that seems to be a display for takeaway menus and ashtrays, and a bizarre collection of items: a cello case, a pub umbrella, a very dead potted plant and the legs of an old mannequin.

'I guess Glenn doesn't like us much then?' I ask, following Cass through the hallway.

Cass remembers that I have no idea who he is. 'Oh god. Him and his wife, Sarah, are City types and, naturally, we don't fit in with their townhouse-Wisteria-Lane vibes so he raises a fuss to try and move us out.'

'Are those your bottles in his recycling?' Meg asks.

'Maybe?' she replies, winking. 'But Maureen the other side of him does it too because he objects to her smoking weed for her glaucoma. Ignore him, we all do.'

Meg links her arm into mine as we walk the corridor, looking up to a naked lightbulb swinging quite precariously. As we enter the kitchen, a smell of melted cheese greets us first but then Meg and I take a step back slightly to see the person standing over the hob. Firstly, the man is a giant, easily six foot eight. I see glimpses of tattoos under a black T-shirt but he's also wearing boxer shorts, sliders and socks. I do like that he has an apron on to protect himself though. I've seen pics of him before but, in person, the man is quite a presence.

'Luce! Mate!'

He has tattooed eyeballs.

'Bill,' he says, coming over to hug me, a stainless steel fish slice still in hand. I hug back, nestling myself into his black beard.

'Bill the housemate?'

'Correct.'

Meg doesn't quite know where to look given the man needs to throw some trousers on but she smiles.

'Sorry, I didn't know we was expecting company.'

This implies Bill went about the place in his boxers on a regular basis, which makes me glad he was that comfortable around me.

'This is my sister, Meg.'

'Pleasure. Well, I'm making a frittata. Your fave... with beetroot and feta. Fancy it?'

Meg looks to me and Cass realises, again, there are gaps in my knowledge.

'Bill is a sous chef,' Cass tells me.

'So you always eat incredibly well under this roof,' he tells me, reaching over for some plates.

Meg shrugs and sits herself down as I take in the room around us. Nah, I don't know this place but there's a wonderfully warm and inviting feel to it. Bill obviously has all his chef equipment, spices and jars about the place, but I like all the mismatched mugs, the photos and flyers stuck to the wall with Blu-Tack, the random Persian rug in the middle of the stone floor.

'So how many of us live here?' I ask, looking out the window to the garden where we seem to have quite the allotment out the back, an assortment of hula hoops and three old BBQs.

'Eight including you,' says Cass. 'I used to waitress with Bill and he told me about this place and we nabbed a couple of rooms. We created a mezzanine level so we could get two extra people in and that helps with the rent.'

'That'll explain the ladders,' Meg says, having heard what a health and safety nightmare this place is from Emma. 'Is it just mega parties every week then?' Her eyes shift to a very impressive wine bottle collection on one of the counters.

'Just every other week,' Bill jokes. 'We all have a range of shifts so the schedules are a nightmare. Most of us start and finish our days quite late. But it's cosy, it's all very like-minded. We've missed you, Lucy.' He sprinkles some pea shoots on a frittata and puts it in front of us with a bowl of bread. Is he the reason I lived here? Because this looks bloody decent.

'We're all mates. You've met my mum. You and her went to one of my gigs together.'

Gigs. This feels more in keeping with his look.

'Remind me of names...' I ask.

'My mum is Gwen, the band is called PissHammer.'

He takes out a photo on his phone. On it is a picture of a woman with a blonde bob, wearing beige pedal pushers. Bill and her bandmates stand around her looking like they're about to sacrifice her to their rock gods. Oh, and that's me. I went leather, knee-highs and eyeliner for the event at least.

'And how is Gwen...?' I ask.

'She's perfect, mate. She says hello. She's glad you're OK.'

I smile and take a mouthful of frittata. It is hot as balls but, damn, this is tasty shit. Bill then pushes a mug in my direction. I pause to see the quote on the mug: *Strong as Tits*. Meg smiles to see it too. It's a family motto of sorts, one I'm glad I put out into the world in my teens.

'This is mine?' I ask.

'One of our housemates is a potter. She got a special set made for your birthday once,' explains Cass.

Bill clinks my mug and smiles broadly. I think his gums may also be tattooed with crucifixes but I say nothing.

'Damn you, Bill,' says a voice from behind us. 'You made frittata and didn't say anything?'

The tone of the voice is posh old man and I turn to introduce myself, but not before Meg shoots a mouthful of egg across the table. The old man is naked. Not a thing on him, sixty-year-old balls out in the kitchen.

'I'm Nigel. I'm a lawyer.'

'And a nudist,' Cass mumbles. We hadn't noticed.

* * *

After we meet the very lovely nudist and eat the frittata, Meg uses the toilet and gets all judgy (*It smells of weed and fruity shampoo, Lucy*) and we finally climb a ladder and get to see my room, which as imagined does look slightly like a modern art installation where bras seem to be hanging off every conceivable door, radiator and chair. What is quite warming is to see the many photos I have all over the walls and a seventies floral duvet on my bed that I had as a teen so some things stayed, the best things. Meg stands in the middle of the room, looking properly mumsy, hands on hips, not knowing whether to gather the dirty laundry or have a go at me.

'Looks like your cat slept in here too,' she says, rolling a toe through the cat hair on the floor but pointing to a cat bed on the window sill. It overlooks the garden next door so I like the idea Pussy watched over the neighbours and possibly laughed about using their sandpit as her toilet. Meg walks over to a makeshift dressing table and picks up stacks of paper on it. 'I see there was a very good filing system in place here.'

I grit my teeth, more distracted by a very nice vintage Reebok zip-up top that I want to take home with me. Meg picks up a receipt that I used to dispose some gum in.

'Grace was going through your accounts by the way. You should keep some of these receipts if you're self-employed, it's all tax-deductible.'

Scrap everything – that is possibly the most grown-up thing a sister has ever said to me. My blank look tells her everything she needs to know there and she sifts through the pieces of paper.

'You spend a lot of money at ASOS,' she tells me before

pausing. 'And you got a distinction in your master's... this is a certificate! Hell, why isn't this in a frame, Luce?'

I shrug, silently impressed by my latent genius though.

'This is also a handwritten letter...' she says, scanning the words. I go over and put my head over her shoulder.

'Is it from the mystery Oscar?' I ask jokingly.

'No, Christ – my eyes... It's a love letter. The boy's grammar is appalling. I'd be the first to object if you wanted to date this... Who refers to their penis as a member...?'

I yank it from her hands as she then opens drawers in the dresser, all stuffed with similar random pieces of paper. She sighs then opens the wardrobe but takes a step back as half of it seems to be human hair.

'For the love of crap, I thought that was filled with cats.'

She pulls one out and it seems to be a wig. It's bright red with shells attached so I will assume this was part of my party princess stash. She shakes it out and puts it on, looking at herself in the mirror.

'I look like Ariel in her baby-weight-and-takeaway years...'

I saunter over and pull out a brown one with a built-in beehive to the top. I put it on and brown tresses fall about my shoulders.

'Belle. *Beauty and the Beast*. The joy of having three daughters is that these things are now my specialist subject,' Meg informs me.

I glare at myself in the mirror. 'I look like Marie Antoinette.'

'The Topshop version.'

I want to laugh but it's a strange thing to see me in hair and my eye is drawn to all the wigs and costumes inside that wardrobe. Reminders that I've spent the last decade just playing dress-up. Meg has a look through all the other costumes until she gets to a leather catsuit.

'I never saw a princess dressed like this.'

'Apparently, I also diversify. The agency told me I did the

occasional superhero party and I'm a very good Black Widow, whoever that is.'

Meg raises her eyebrows. She digs through the cupboards to find more boxes of books and lecture notes, intermingled with receipts and the like. I continue to look at myself in the mirror, holding a sunshine yellow Belle dress up to my frame, swishing the skirt.

'Did you ever see me do the parties, Meg? Was I good?'

She turns from the mess that is my wardrobe to look at me, smiling.

'You came up to do Eve's sixth birthday party as Elsa. You made her year. Kids still go on about that party in her class. They thought I paid hundreds of pounds for a proper impersonator, they didn't realise you did it for a bottle of wine and a tube of Fruit Pastilles. I think you also shagged one of the dads from that party but we don't go there.'

'Was he at least fit?' I enquire.

'Builder, divorced, you told me he had a dick that pointed due north-east when erect, still asks about you at parents' evenings...'

I should cackle loudly at this but Meg senses me staring blankly into the mirror, my mood low.

'Smile, Belle. Remember you end up with the Beast and have a French candlestick as your best mate.'

'Yeah, maybe. Just feels like a slightly shit job to be having at my age. Did I tell you when I was at the posh rehab gym, I bumped into that girl who wrote me the thank you note. Ophelia. Apparently, I was quite the hit at her party too. I taught her some excellent turns of phrase.'

'I can imagine.' We both sit down on the edge of my bed. 'Look, I can't picture being in your line of work is easy but you were very good at what you did. You were born to entertain, to dance and sing. You worked very hard, you did all sorts of rubbish jobs to supplement it, put yourself through courses. All I ever saw was someone who grafted.'

'But what do I have to show for it, Meg? Half a wardrobe of costumes? I can't even remember the songs, the routines. If this is what I was doing to build a career then it feels a bit crappy. And now what do I do, start again? Do this for another ten years? Who wants to see a forty-something princess prancing about?'

'I would. Anyway, by the time you're forty, you're not a princess any more. You're a queen.'

I smile and rest my head on her shoulder. Queen. The best sort though. She rules alone, she takes on many suitors, she throws the best parties and wears killer gowns.

'We'll take some of this paper home and sift through it. It'll give Grace something to do. She can get out her highlighters. Maybe it will give us some clues. To Oscar, to everything. It's not just wigs though, is it? It's a master's hidden on your desk. You were much more than a wig, Lucy Callaghan.'

Only the biggest sister could bolster me in such a way. That said, I may take the wigs home, for the fun, to cover up my in-between hair and annoy our mother. Meg shuffles where she sits and reaches beneath her to pull out something bulky from under my duvet. She reveals a pair of men's pants that must have been lurking there for at least two months, so much so they're stiff like cardboard. She shrieks and throws them in the air then wipes her hands down on my sheets.

'Lucy, who the hell left here without any pants? That's so gross.'

'Maybe they're Nigel's.'

'I really hope not. I feel that naked image is etched onto my retinas now.'

She bends down and also finds a used *Strong as Tits* mug that has an inch of cold tea in the bottom. I like that I have a set of them for every day of the week.

'It's grim that this is still here but this is you, all over. Strong as Tits. It's even yellow. You always said that was your favourite colour...'

'...As the others were far too dull and sad.'

Strong as Tits. Look at how I inspired pottery. Look at all the photos on the wall, all those costumes and joy. I glance down at the mug. Let's take you home too as a reminder of who I was, who I still am. I open the window to my room and throw the remaining tea out of it.

'What the hell... FERAL! ABSOLUTELY FERAL!' I look down and it's our good neighbour again, the tea landing on his laundry drying on an airer outside.

'Time to leave?' Meg asks.

I nod, very very quickly.

12

One of the unfortunate side effects of living at home is that my mum does the laundry, meaning she washes all of our underwear. From Beth's giant comfy maternity knickers, to Meg's llama-print specials, to my thongs. Oh, the thongs. Mum doesn't get the thongs and she doesn't just wash them, she throws them away because, in her own words, *There are no gussets in some of them. I assumed them to be leftover bra straps that didn't seem to match anything. Knickers need gussets. Otherwise, what is the point? There are hygiene matters to consider. Your vulva can't just be hanging out in the wind.* It was a rant that she made over one of her beef casseroles at the dinner table. Beth started giggling at the word 'gusset' and Meg laughed so hard that she spat out a carrot that landed on Pussy (the cat). Once the word 'vulva' was mentioned, Dad excused himself from the dining room table to go eat his beef off the kitchen counter.

Mum has always been very open about these things with us. She was a sixties feminist who encouraged all her girls to go out, conquer the world and make informed choices about our bodies and fight our corners. It was an empowering parenting stance that came with its sharp edges but it meant that from a young age we knew about things like consent, sexual agency and could tell vaginas from vulvas. In any case, this leaves me with no knickers and Mum is on a mission to go through all our drawers (quite literally) and sigh and shriek at the sight of our undergarments. Dad says it gives her a project and takes her mind off the fact I nearly died but she and Meg have knocked heads quite badly over it. *I'm nearly forty, you know who still buys underwear for their kids when they're forty? The mothers of losers and serial killers.*

And so to try and keep the peace, three of us sisters, Grace, Beth and myself, stand here today in the lingerie department of Marks & Spencer, ye old faithful place to buy one's underwear, while our mother sifts through the shelves and pegs looking for suitable solutions for her adult daughters. Oh, Marks. You've not changed much, eh? Still so reliable, still so dull. It's well-lit, well-fitting T-shirts, well-meaning people buying ordinary clothes that wash well and go with anything while an inoffensive acoustic soundtrack plays in the background.

'What about these, Mum?' I say, picking up a thong and flinging it at her like a catapult. It lands on her head and she reaches up and pulls it down, not looking mildly impressed.

'Exactly, what is this? Your bags were full of pants like this, Lucy.' This is a bit trendy for Marks as it's a leopard-print thong with sheer bits. She flings it back at me, on her knees on the floor going through the sizes of some multipack black minis.

'Mum, they're super boring,' I say.

'They're functional, Lucy. They do their job. Have you been going to your physio in your dental-floss knickers? Has Igor seen everything?'

'Most likely, the lucky bastard.'

She shakes her head as I find Beth, who's around the corner sifting through some five-pack multipack shorts.

'Oooh, stripes... get you...' I jest.

'Fancy knickers are wasted on me, thongs get lost in my arse,' she explains.

My mum pops her head around the corner like an angry guard dog. I rake my fingers along some of the knickers on display. Back in my late teens, we all wore cotton minis but I had gone out and bought more modern stuff for myself. We once bought fake designer knickers from the market that spelt out Kalvin Cline on the waistband. We used to wear those with combats and think we were a bit hip hop.

'So was I always about the thongs?' I ask Beth.

'Well, yes. But knickers are a personal comfort thing, aren't they? I like a big pair when I'm on my period or in a fancy dress to hold everything in. I just throw anything else on for the everyday. I'm very bad at replacing mine too. Mum actually threw all my knickers away because they're so old. The elastic had actually gone.'

'I clean my windows with better rags,' Mum's voice says, drifting in.

'And if she's treating me to new Marks knickers then I'm all in...' she whispers. 'Just not thongs though, I just don't get them.'

'What do you mean?'

'Well, I wasn't in your line of work. You waxed and kept that area tidy. My whole situation down there is Amazonian.'

I lean on her as I burst into laughter.

'Would the explorers get lost?'

'Yes, they'd need machetes to hack away at the undergrowth.'

My mum's face appears again. 'Girls, we are in Marks and Spencer,' she mumbles, like we might be in church. These middle-class people won't be able to handle our pube chat. Heads will explode. Naturally, I need to rile my mother up so I grab a pair of supportive-looking Lycra pants and wear them on my head.

'LUCY!'

'Is this a better way to wear knickers? I don't quite know,' I say, striking a pose to model them appropriately, like the mannequin at the end of the aisle.

Beth sniggers quietly but more so at the panic in our mother's face. Lucy, you can't get us banned from Marks & Spencer. Mum will have nothing of value in her life any more if she can't come in here. Mum tries to grab them off my head but I am too quick and wily for her. I may do the running man in them for the laughs. She manages to grab them and puts them in the basket.

'Who are those for?' I ask. 'I've seen ships with smaller sails.'

'Well, you've worn them on your head. I have to buy them now,' she moans.

'It's not like I wore them properly and went lunging around the shop. Christ, Mum...'

'Remember where you are... behave yourselves...'

Beth bites her lip. We should be following Mum around like little nuns on a day out, bowing our heads in reverence to the surroundings and not looking the lingerie directly in the eye.

'She's right, Mum. Those are thirty-pound knickers. It's not like she left them with skid—'

Mum puts her hand in the air before Beth even has time to finish that sentence then points to a place far away from her. We do as we're told though I may have time to grab the bum of a mannequin while she can still see us. I think the look she gives us points to her disowning us officially. Beth pulls me away before I can go do anything worse with the mannequin.

'You did that once when I went maternity bra shopping. You wore the bras on your head to prove to me how big my norks were,' Beth tells me.

I smile to know I run with a theme when shopping for underwear.

'Was it hilarious?' I ask.

'We got told off by a security guard who ended up taking your number. You dated for a month.'

We walk past a section of underwear that is all about the luxury and the matching sets. These are high-class thongs for the more discerning housewife. Mum will certainly not pay for any of these, though it is a surprise to see Grace perusing this section. That's definitely not a floral midi. It's a lace body that is both quite see-through and has attachments for stockings. She runs her hands over it and, like Grace, checks the price tag first.

'Caught you...' I say, sneaking up on her. She jumps back, shaking her head at me. 'Oooh, Gracie, this is fancy. I like this...' I say, stroking it.

She pulls a face. 'I don't know. It seems a waste. People don't wear these every day, do they?'

'I guess it depends on their line of work?' Beth suggests.

'Are you thinking of buying it to add a bit of luxury to the bedroom?' I say, in estate agent tones.

She rolls her eyes at me. 'Maybe? But I'd have to fling it on every time we have sex to make it feel like it's worth the cost,' she says. Spoken like a true accountant. 'I like sex with Max but I don't know if he's worth it.'

'Plus it doesn't have a gusset...' I add.

Both sisters laugh. 'God, I'd look ridiculous in this,' Beth jokes and I sense a bit of self-deprecating wit there as she's carrying a bit of baby weight.

'Don't be a donkey. And who says these types of outfits are for men? Maybe we wear them to feel better about ourselves, to feel sexy as opposed to looking it,' I say, fiddling with the straps.

Beth smiles over at Grace.

'What?' I ask them.

'Nothing,' Grace says. 'That's just a very Lucy thing to say.'

I grin and take down two and throw them into Grace's basket, hiding them under the dressing gown Mum's also forcing me to acquire. It's tartan. It's ugly as balls but Mum is sick of seeing my nipples when she's having her muesli.

'Shall I get some for Meg and Ems too?' I add. 'We can all look like the Pussycat Dolls.'

'Or not,' Beth says.

I try and find one in my size and examine it in more detail. 'Would I have worn something like this?' I ask.

'You'd have worn this out,' Beth tells me. 'With hotpants and trainers and, hopefully, a jacket of some description.'

'Really?'

'Lucy, you had bras with built-in nipple clamps.'

'Not bought from here then?' I jest.

'No, I think you're the only person I knew who had a loyalty card with Love Honey.'

I pull at the suspender straps and let them ping back in my hand.

'To be fair, you went on stage wearing something like this. You toured with *Chicago*. Every night, just on stage in pants,' Grace adds.

I'm only able to recall this because I've seen some pictures. I wear a bowler hat well.

'You were kinda awesome in that. You do the Fosse thing very well,' Grace says.

Having visited the house share, the sketchy evolution of my work history is slowly being fleshed out. I didn't just do princess parties in big wigs. At university, I went to drama and dance classes. I pushed that agenda, I worked my arse off to be noticed, to learn, to grow my CV. I toured with a couple of shows, worked the panto season hard. I like that Lucy plenty.

'Hey, we're in London. Maybe we should have a tour of some of the theatres you performed at?' Grace mentions.

'That's a lovely idea,' says Mum, appearing with a full basket of multipacks.

'Mum, there's about fifty pairs of knickers there. Is that really necessary?' Beth asks.

'Yes. We also need to buy Lucy a nightie.' She points towards a mannequin wearing a white full-length nightdress.

'For when the three ghosts of Christmas come to visit me?' I ask, bent over in laughter.

She doesn't laugh back.

* * *

Knickers bought and lunch acquired in Soho, we're now outside the Garrick Theatre, which stands near Leicester Square currently showing a musical that's winning many awards. I stare up at the imposing Victorian architecture with its blue windows and doors, at the large posters and glittering signs, but I feel nothing.

'Anything?' Mum asks as we all look up at the building.

I shake my head. 'I was on stage there?'

'I saw you in *Chicago* there as an understudy in the ensemble, called in last minute because you knew the show,' Mum says. 'A group of us went.'

'Actually, a group of us nearly got thrown out because we cheered so loud at the end,' Beth adds.

I gaze up at it again and picture it all. I like that show. That would have been fun. I would have rocked up at the stage door, sashayed in, revelled in the build-up to show time getting our hair and make-up ready, and slipping into a costume.

'But never the lead it would seem, always making up the numbers at the back,' I state.

'Maybe but it's the nature of the business. You never let it deflate you though, every small part and knockback just made you stronger, more determined to succeed,' Grace informs me.

'Was I decent though? Or was I flogging a dead horse?' I joke.

'You adored it but, yes, you were very good,' Mum says.

That's high praise from Mum. I'll take that. We continue to walk past the theatre until we notice a door opening and a man starting to put out ropes, to herd the crowds and queues later on. He looks up at me.

'Lucy Callaghan?'

I look the man in the eye. He's short and balding, the human version of a doughball, but his face lights up to see me and he comes over. Mum has a worried expression, perhaps thinking I've either had sex with this man or owe him money.

'How the hell are you?' he says, clearly judging the new hairdo.

'I'm really good, Mario,' I say, spying his name badge. 'How are you?'

'Did someone tell me you were in an accident? I was trying to get hold of you to do a couple of shifts in the bar here and your phone was out of service.'

'Yeah. Bit of a bad one. Phone was in the accident too unfortunately. This is my mum, Fi, and two of my sisters, Beth and Grace. Guys, this is Mario...'

Who I cannot remember at all but I obviously worked for him in some capacity. I hope I didn't have to wear that polyester uniform. Beth looks over at me to see if I'm going to add any more detail about the accident but the truth is I can't bear to. It's getting tiring to see the looks of pity and sadness from people and there are times I want to just slip into that role of old Lucy, this girl who was hard-working, loved and fiery.

'Well, this is a bloody pleasure, can't tell you how much we love your girl.'

Mum side-eyes me, wondering how and why I curried such favour.

'Your daughter used to make me tea, bring me cake, she's a sweetheart and so bloody funny. Does she get that from you, Mum?'

Grace, Beth and I stare at Mum. 'All from me...'

'And when she's on shift, I don't even need to bring the extra security in. Remember that time you tackled that reporter hiding in the bins out the back? You'd have been proud of your girl, Mum. She got him with a broom handle, right in the knackers.'

Mum seems less impressed with this story but not surprised.

'Actually, can I come in and show the guys around? We were just talking about when I was in *Chicago* here,' I tell Mario.

'Of course. Leave your new number at the office too so I can get in touch with you. I can throw you a few shifts here and there. Ashley is backstage too, I think you know each other, go and say hello...' I have no idea who that is but he leans over to hug me and I usher my family through the door.

Theatres. My days, they really are such a wonder and London's West End does them so well. That sense of grandeur and opulence as you walk in across swirling red carpets and ornate cornicing. I'm silent as I study the foyer and my family watch my quiet wandering eyes. Up the grand staircase, we head through some doors where a stage sits, waiting for its evening performance, the sound of a vacuum cleaner in the distance. It's beautiful. Grand columns swathed in gold foliage and red velveteen seats, the lighting rigs all pointed towards the stage. Something in me feels numb though, confused.

'Lucy?' a voice suddenly calls from the stage where a group of dancers seem to be rehearsing a routine. The voice comes from someone who cups her hand over her eyes to see me. I'm going to take a punt that she's Ashley. She stands there in a leotard and tights, dark hair tightly pulled back in a bun, lithe and graceful. Her friends shift me and my posse some haughty looks, hands on hips, obviously angry that we've invaded their space.

'Hi!' I try to say with some animation. 'We're just watching, don't mind us.'

'Come up here!' She gestures. I glance at my mum and sisters before I walk the aisles tentatively, my hands brushing along the seats. I inhale deeply. I find access to the stage and get up to greet them. I'm in a T-shirt, cycling shorts and a baseball cap again, and I've just been knicker-shopping with my mum in my late twenties, so I'll admit to feeling just a bit more than inferior.

'Guys, this is Lucy. We did panto together last year.'

The other girls don't really respond and I will suppose with the way Ashley air kisses me but keeps her distance that we're not the closest of friends either.

'I haven't seen you at any auditions or dance classes recently?' she asks me, scanning me from top to toe in judgement. I know girls like her. I want to say all the words too but, for some reason, I'm mute. I can't tell them what's happened, I won't.

'Oh, I've been trying out different things. You know?' I attempt to reply casually, knowing all of them are confused by my hair.

'Well, that's the nature of the beast, eh? You shouldn't let it get you down. You're a lovely dancer.' From her tone, I will hazard a guess that she's not a friend. A competitor? A frenemy? 'Is that your family?' she asks, looking out at the stalls where my family have sat down, weighed down by knickers, no doubt. She waves to them but they don't wave back. They're well versed in this form of bitchery. There's a sad look to my mum's face. *Give her hell. Remember that much, Lucy.*

'So you're all part of this show now? That's brilliant,' I say.

'Yes. A few months ago I started writing down my intentions and manifesting my true ambitions and it brought me here.'

I want to flick her my middle finger. Manifest this.

'You had a callback for this. I never saw you at the auditions afterwards?' Ashley tells me.

'I did?' I ask her.

'Yeah, they were at the beginning of July.'

When I was in a hospital bed, learning to walk again. My heart sinks into my stomach. Was I close to something brilliant only to have my own stupidity and fate snatch it away from me?

'Oh my god, I have a brilliant story about Lucy,' Ashley continues. 'So she got an ensemble part in *Waitress* when it first opened but then you went out to celebrate your first show, got off your face and then fired. Do you remember?'

One, this doesn't feel like a brilliant story. Two, I don't remember but I laugh, I'm not quite sure why.

'I was in *Waitress*?'

'Well, you were but then you were so drunk that night you sent a picture of your vagina to the cast WhatsApp group by accident.' There's a whole bitchy face smile that comes with that reply. 'They asked you to leave after that. I'm sure it wasn't intentional.'

I have no idea any more but the other girls on stage wince on my behalf as Ashley makes me out to be some sort of deviant.

'It's very you though. Such a joker but always the bridesmaid, Lucy. Never the bride. You really need to start elevating your work and your attitude. You could be so good.'

One of the other girls looks down to my legs, untoned and unmoisturised. She looks less convinced that I'll ever be anywhere near her level.

'Tell me, are you still going out with Adam?' Ashley asks.

'Adam?'

She widens her eyes at me, pouting.

'My Adam? I mean, he was my friend first...'

Oh. That's where the face is coming from. There is also beef about a man here. I went out with an Adam? Who knows any more? There's an Adam in my contacts with the aubergine emojis, is it that one? Given her reaction, I hope he was made to choose between the two of us though and this made her fall to the floor and ugly-cry.

'Ohhh, that Adam! We have some interesting sex at least once a month but it's not serious,' I say, toying with her.

She glares me down. 'Well, we have to get back to rehearsing. I can ask if we can get you an audition here or something but it took us months to get down to the final cast.'

'Oh, that's not why I'm here... We were just in town and we thought we'd drop in,' I reply.

'Of course...' she replies condescendingly.

Oh, wait. She thinks I'm here to try and wrangle my way into this show? Really? I'd have at least worn make-up for that, no? There is beef here, isn't there? I hope I nailed Adam, hard. I hope I did, with the way she stands over me thinking she's better than me.

'I mean, Mario is out front. Maybe he can get you some front-of-house shifts if work is low on the ground.'

I would. If only to break into your dressing room and put Tabasco in your eye make-up. Don't react, Lucy. Not now. Not like this.

'It looks like you're in the middle of something so we'll go...' I gesture, not wanting to draw this out.

'Oh no, stay. Actually, can you tell us what looks better here? We've been doing piqué turns but the choreographer is thinking of changing it to chaîné-chaîné-chaîné-chaîné, ball-change, kick, step-step, leap.'

She showcases an example as the other girls look on. She's peacocking now. Look at me traipsing about on these boards and all my success and slicked-back hair. You're not here, you're not even close. God, I can't even translate half of her jazz dance language. Come on, Lucy. Remember. Fucking remember. But my body and mind aren't playing ball. I look blankly at all of them.

'Or maybe funky chicken, step, turn and jazz hands...?' I say, completing the move in one swift motion. I did that for a panto I was in once, dressed as a mouse. I was fourteen. I even had a tail made out of old tights. The girls on that stage know I may be mocking a serious dance moment or that I may have indeed lost my mind. That wouldn't be too far from the truth.

'OK...' Ashley says in reply, widening her eyes at me. 'Good luck with whatever it is you do next. I guess I'll see you around.' She turns to look at her friends.

Give it back to her, Lucy. Go on. But I have nothing in my arsenal, whatsoever. I stand and look out at all those empty seats bar for three people who are sitting there, watching, hoping. How do you start at the bottom again? I was the lead once, the star of my own show, but I don't know any of the lines, nothing. This feeling of disappointment, embarrassment, is unfamiliar but pierces so very deep and I turn away from the stage, doing all I can to try and hold back my tears.

13

'Farah, there's a quote on the wall. An actual quote about laughing and loving being the key to life. I can literally feel my stomach churning to look at it.'

'Give it a chance.'

'Before I set fire to the place?'

'Lucy...'

Back in the day, Farah was my girl. She also had a streak of wanting to swim against the tide and, together, we were a little raucous. No, a lot raucous, to the point where our mothers had each other's telephone numbers laminated to the fridge so they could check with the other to see if we'd been lying about our whereabouts and to lament at how we were both intent on testing their parental boundaries. In sixth form, we spent a lot of weekends in London 'visiting my sisters' but in fact partying hard at R&B/hip-hop nights wearing very little and having relations with people who were far too old and street for us. For example, C-Boss (twenty-three years old; abs for days; real name actually Clarence). In my memory, we'd made a pact that we'd be friends forever. We'd visit each other at university, call each other, still have mega nights out, getting off our faces in coloured contact lenses, bra straps on show and in skirts so short 'you could see what we had for dinner' (her father, circa 2019).

But Farah is not that girl any more. Farah has a family and she's miles away from here in Amsterdam. That said, she dips in and out to check I'm all right and, today, she and the sisters have conspired to bring me here. After my trip to the theatre and my old home, my mind didn't quite sit right and some deep funk set in. On the one hand, the world of old Lucy presented people like Tony, Darren and Cass to me, new friends and loves, but on the other the last decade has felt so eventful, so full of life and experience, and not being able to recognise any of it is terrifying and frustrating. The sisters knew it was bad when I actually cancelled my thirtieth birthday celebrations and some supposed grand plan I had to hold a music festival party in a field. That wasn't the Lucy they knew. Therefore, they gave Farah a call – someone I know, someone I remember, someone I love.

'You know this hypnotist person?' I ask her over the phone.

'Hypnotherapist, there's a difference. I went to university with him. He's a nice guy. Try it, worst-case scenario it doesn't work but, best-case, your memory comes flooding back and you're healed.' I hear the gurgles of a newborn son over the phone and smile to myself.

'Though if he's wearing a cape, gets me down on all fours and tells me to bark like a dog then I will punch him,' I say.

She knows I'm not even lying.

'Please don't punch him. He's my friend.'

'He's a hypnotist. Maybe he's hypnotised you into thinking that.'

'Behave.'

'Never.'

The baby gurgles again and it's a pacifying sound to me, to hear that my friend is now a mother. I know her wife Astrid too and the idea of their growing family makes me glow.

'How is little Zeke?' I ask.

'He misses his godmother...' she says. 'We all miss you.'

It still feels mad someone has entrusted that privilege and honour to me. 'Hug him hard for me.'

'Obviously.'

'Farah, I have a question... We kept in touch, yeah? We are still good mates?'

She pauses for a moment and I don't know if I've insulted her.

'Luce, I wouldn't call in favours for anyone else. What we have... our love, friendship, is crazy like that. I won't lie, we go months without seeing each other sometimes or even talking and that's mainly because real life, distance, gets in the way. But we're still mates. I should say that's mainly because of you though. You're the one who keeps in touch with all of us. You're a gift of a mate.'

While I like the compliment, there are words there that hurt. That at times we drifted away from each other. She's the sort of person I imagined would be there forever, just on the sidelines, someone I'd see every day, for which I blame nineties sitcoms with their coffee shops and in vogue haircuts. But I guess real life doesn't work like that.

'When we adopted Zeke, you were the first person we rang. You were on a bike at the gym. You literally screamed with happiness and then called us pricks for having kept it all a secret.'

'I screamed at the gym?'

'During a spin class... I believe someone fell off a bike in shock. You then hugged everyone in the room and then got banned from that establishment,' she says, laughing.

'You sound so happy...' I tell her.

'I'm happy because my mate is still alive but in general? I'm good, babe. We're all good.'

'Do you still have a tongue piercing?' I ask her.

I love hearing her laugh. That thing used to clink against

her teeth when she talked and I was there when she had it done. She had to eat soup for a week and her parents freaked out and took away her phone for a month.

'I do. Some things haven't changed. Promise me you'll give this a go, yes?'

'Does this fella wear a waistcoat? I will mock him if he has a waistcoat.'

'He doesn't. I love you, let me know how it goes.'

She hangs up on me and I sit in the reception area, leaning around to see what's happening in this place. It's a therapy centre of sorts and they like them a motivational quote, house plant and primary colour to lift the mood. The room opposite me seems to be dedicated to some sort of arts and crafts. There's some basket weaving, clay sculpture and there's a man painting a canvas in red and black, throwing paint on in quite a haphazard fashion. Crumbs, who hurt you, honey? Someone takes his brushes. I studied this (apparently): therapy through the power of dance. Maybe that is what I need? Maybe we need to go into the deepest recesses of my mind and beckon all of my memories out via a bit of tap dancing. Do we dare go there though? What brilliant horrors lie under my surface?

'Lucy?'

I look up. Christ on a bleeding bike.

'Yes. Are you Cosmo?'

He puts his palms together to bow and acknowledge his name. I don't really know how to describe Cosmo but he's wearing all white, which is always a sign in a person that they lack any practicality but also that they may want you to join their cult. He completes the look with grey felt clogs, a lot of hair, a big Bob Ross bushel to the head and sprouts of it like weeds escaping out the top of his shirt and cuffs. For the love of Etsy hell, that's a dreamcatcher pendant.

'You are most welcome today,' he tells me in a soft melodic accent. 'Farah has told me so much about you.'

'All my best bits, I hope...'

He smiles. That's not a reply though, which makes me think Farah didn't give him the PG version.

'Please come with me,' he says, his hands ushering the way through the centre. I am dubious, I can't lie. Peering into the rooms, it seems like a lot of people sitting in circles, talking, listening, crying, hugging and holding hands as they chant to the ceilings, a wall of tantric whale music, tai chi and positive healing vibes in the very brickwork. The cynic in me wants to run. This is not what Lucy does. I'm led to believe I solve problems with terrible jokes, alcohol and by hitting stuff. Hard. I am starting to wonder what sort of friend Farah actually is that she's led me here.

'So you and Farah went to university together?' I ask him, trying to get more of an idea of Cosmo. I bet he drinks a shed-load of fennel tea and has a pet alpaca whose wool he farms for the socks.

'We did. We lived together for a while in Manchester. Isn't she just the best soul?'

We probably have very different experiences of Farah. The Farah I know and love used to get super drunk with me, entertain people on the night bus with singalongs and flash her boobs out of the bus window.

'She's pretty awesome. And you've worked here long?'

'I set up Sanctum with a friend: it's a combination here of traditional psychotherapies and alternative methods of inner healing.'

I saw a film called *Sanctum* on that Netflix the other day. They took that woman's brain and gave it to aliens. I should have put my phone tracking on before I came here. Don't look at his pendant. Or the fact he has what looks like granola in his hair.

'So Farah filled you in on everything, you got my medical notes?' I ask him.

'I have,' he replies, not giving too much away. *This doesn't make me trust you, Cosmo.* 'How is your physical recovery going?' he asks me, studying my head.

'As good as can be expected. My sister has me working with a physio. He hates me.'

'I doubt it. And have you been seeing any other therapists?'

'They've tried to push them on me. Psychoanalysts, counsellors, but...

'You don't believe in that stuff?' he asks, smiling.

'I have four sisters. It's free therapy.'

I think my problem is that the whole idea of hypnotherapy means I'm easily suggestible or swayed. This goes against my character and I don't want to let my guard down, ever, not least to a stranger. He opens a door and leads me to a room with a yellow velveteen sofa and a chair, moving a metal plate in the door to inform everyone it's occupied. There are still a lot of plants, framed quotes and gauzy white curtains that filter the light in.

'Please take a seat on the sofa,' he instructs me as he heads over to a counter. 'Can I interest you in some matcha? It can sharpen the mind and help relax you before our session.'

I nod, debating whether to warn him that if it's drugged and he tries to get me in his van and drive me to his ranch then I have quite the kick on me.

'So tell me what you know about hypnotherapy, hypnotists, Lucy...' he asks.

'Honestly?' I say, watching him closely as he makes my tea. 'Pseudo magicians, ponytails, "look into my eyes", stage shows where people get tricked into doing chicken dances for other people's amusement...'

He grins. 'Farah did tell me you were funny...'

'I haven't offended you, have I?' I ask.

'You forgot fork-bending and...' He clicks his fingers and waves them around. '... sleep...'

I giggle as he goes over to an incense burner. 'What I practise is hypnotherapy so today we'll be examining your subconscious, filtering through your memories – sorting out your hard drive, if you will.'

I want to tell him we tried that on my laptop. All we found were two hundred saved memes and a selection of very badly organised folders with names like 'University Shite' and 'CV Gubbins'.

'This is lotus and white musk,' he says as he lights the incense, 'this will help you get in touch with your mind's eye.' I inhale deeply to get a whiff. I can't tell him it smells like the Body Shop, can I? 'Now I want you to just relax, slip off your trainers, get as comfortable as you can here.'

He puts my tea down next to me and then does some yoga poses to afford himself the same level of comfort before he sits on his chair. I don't know how to respond so just do as I'm told and shimmy my shoulders, the wrinkles on my forehead most likely signalling my doubt that this will really work.

'So let me talk you through the process. We're just going to get you into a deep state of relaxation, we will work on your breathing, focus your state of mind and visualise some things you can remember. I'll ask you to focus on nothing but my voice to guide you.'

All I can think is that when I'm that relaxed I will most likely break wind. I hope the lotus and white musk will be able to mask that.

'Am I allowed to say, you don't look wholly convinced?' he says.

'I don't know...' I take a sip of green tea to not appear rude. It's bitter, which makes my face wince even more.

'Farah did tell me you were an experimental kinda girl though so it can't hurt to at least try?' he tells me.

Bloody Farah.

'She also said you did yoga – this is akin to that, think of it as guided meditation. If anything, it'll just relax you.'

I smile. Like Igor, there's zero attraction there but there is something calming about him that removes my hesitation about this process. Hell, we've done everything else to try and get my memory back. Let's give it a go. I'll down all this tea, hold your hand and do some macramé next door if it'll help.

'Well, go gentle. You may enter my mind, Cosmo...'

'I'm always gentle when it's someone's first time...' he jokes. 'Now look into my eyes...'

I laugh. He gets my brand of humour at least.

'So firstly, lie back. I'd like you to close your eyes for me.'

I do as I'm told, propping some cushions behind me. He goes quiet for a moment and I flick one eye open to keep watch, like a kid checking to see if their parent is still in the room at bedtime.

'The eyes, Lucy.'

'Sorry, Cosmo.'

He then hits a gong. Don't laugh. I expect ninjas to run in. They don't, which is disappointing.

'Rest your hands beside you, inhale. I want you to tense your body as you do, all the way down to your fingertips, and then release all that tension as you exhale. On my count. One, two, three...'

I do exactly as I'm told but I won't lie, this does feel like the sort of exercise one would teach a pregnant woman. Breaaaattthheee. Puuuuuusssssh. Releeeeeeease. Don't fart, Lucy. I can't say any of this out loud, can I? I need to at least try. For Farah. For me. For all the people who are investing time in trying to help me get better. I pout my lips and exhale. Is he doing the same? I won't open my eyes but I hope he's not reading from a script and checking his Facebook at the same time.

'Clear your mind, I just want you to focus all your energy on your breathing.'

This feels like the very opposite of what we need, right? The mind is already very clear, like a blank page. We need to fill in the gaps? OK. Breathe. I'm glad I wore a comfy bra as my chest is doing a lot of work here. I should have done a wee before I came in here. Breeeeathe. It's actually not awful. Just don't fall asleep, right?

'Can you hear my voice?' Cosmo says gently.

'Uh-huh,' I reply sleepily. It is a lovely voice, a bedtime story kinda voice. Not that I want to be in a bed with him. He can read to me and leave. I'm not sure what I expect now. You see people being hypnotised in crime programmes, everything comes back to them in vivid flashbacks until the moment when they see the killer's face and then they scream and collapse in tears onto the arm of a very attractive TV detective. Nothing is playing back to me like that, just the monochrome fuzz of the insides of my eyelids.

'You're in a safe place, Lucy. Still focus on your breathing and my voice.'

Don't focus on your bladder. I like the way he keeps saying my name. Luuuuuccyy.

'I don't want you to engage in anything new. I don't want you to think about the accident or the present moment but I want you to reconnect to what you can remember. Tell me about you.'

OK. My name is Lucy. That's a good place to start. I'm seventeen. Does he want detail? Does he want to know what I'm wearing? The fact I'm not a huge fan of tomatoes or golf? It's a terrible excuse for a sport. I remember my sisters. Mum, Dad, school, my bedroom.

'I want you to focus on all the senses. Let's home in on a specific memory. Something that's vivid and easy to bring to mind. What can you hear? See? Smell? Taste? Touch?'

Any memory? Cosmo, there are millions of the things. That's like asking me to talk to you about a grain of sand on a beach, to pick it up and tell you all about it. One memory? OK. The sisters, dancing when we were little in our front room. That feels accessible as it's fresh in the old memory banks. I smile inside, not even sure if the emotion registers on my face.

'Are you with me, Lucy?'

'Yep.' Kinda. I'm in my front room. *Don't tell Mum I let you use lipstick, OK?* Meg says. It feels strange, a thick oily layer slick on my lips, and I keep pouting and stretching them so it sits better. And I remember looking at Meg's boobs thinking about when mine are going to come in. I stuffed all sorts in my bras from that point forward to try and create them. Socks. I stuffed socks in my bra. Carpet, I can feel the twists of carpet under my feet. I hear a song and my shoulders moving, the beat of that music like a pulse.

'I'm dancing, Cosmo,' I mumble.

'How do you feel?'

'Happy, free.'

'Those are good emotions, Lucy. Can you think of other times you felt like that?'

When did I last feel happy? When did I feel that swell of emotion in my chest, a smile that lasted for days? Exam results day. Grace drove me to the school in her Nissan Micra. I was wearing a very big belt. Mum said the belt looked ridiculous, like I was a cowgirl and that it didn't actually help holding up my jeans. I was with Farah and we both stood on the grass field out by the front of the school opening our envelopes together. I scanned her face before I reacted. She dropped a grade so I embraced her tightly. *It's still so good, babe. It's just letters on a piece of paper. You can still go to uni.* I felt her body trembling under mine and tears fell from my face to hear her so disappointed. *What did you get, Luce?* she asks me, grabbing my letter. Four As. She squealed. *OH MY GOD, OH MY GOD, OH MY GOD.* There were dogs in the general vicinity who heard that sound. Grace got out of the car across the way and stood there nervously. And she grabbed my hand and we ran across the grass. I looked up and the sun hit my face, the sky was the brightest of blues and her hand around mine was so tight. Farah looked so proud, so happy, and as the air rushed past my face, I felt that happiness, that freedom that this was the starting point of something great. A tear rolls down my temple as I lie here. Ooof.

'Breathe, Lucy. Deeply, in and out.'

OK. Other things that were so good they made me cry with happiness. Tess. Baby Tess when I held her for the first time. She smelt bad though. I'd been handed her after a particularly bad nappy but how she looked, how she felt in my arms, the overwhelming feeling of love was intoxicating. That I felt she was mine, connected to me.

'God, I love that girl.'

'Where are you now, Lucy?'

I'm standing on a stage. I've performed. I am bowing. Clapping. Lots of clapping. I'm so thrilled to be up there, the adrenalin runs through me. That emotion is exhilarating. I want to do it again, forever.

Wait.

TLC are playing again. Why are there so many lights? Why can I taste sambuca? I'm in very high heels. No carpet.

'I don't know where I am...' I mumble.

'Slow down. Breathe. Don't panic. Listen to my voice.'

'I have boobs.'

In my memory. I have boobs because I feel them bobbing up and down as I dance. I'm not using socks to stuff my bra any more.

'I'm happy. I think I'm happy. Josh can cock off though.'

I can't tell if my hypnotherapist is laughing. Why am I telling Josh to cock off? I'm in that nightclub. Am I remembering this? Or just recreating it in my mind? I don't trust this feeling.

'Who can you see?'

'My sisters. I'm still dancing.'

'Why are you dancing?'

'It's my birthday.'

'What date is your birthday?'

'9th February,' I mumble.

There is silence as I say that. That's not my birthday. My birthday is in August, in the summer so I'm always the baby. Why did I say the 9th of February? Whose birthday is the 9th of February? I run through all the sisters. No one is born around then.

'I... No... That's not my birthday...'

'What is that date, 9th February?'

'I'm happy...' I whisper. 'I'm really happy...'

'Why, Lucy?'

'Oscar.'

And just like that, I open my eyes and sit up. Like I've been underwater or had one of those strange dreams where I've been falling. Crikey. That was a fricking trip. What did you put in that tea, Cosmo? I sit there and just look around the room. He senses my shock and puts a hand to my shoulder.

'Are you OK, Lucy?'

'I said a name...'

'Oscar.'

'Did I say who he was?'

'No. You didn't.'

Damn. 'How did you do that?' I ask, staring him in the eye. You're going to take my brain now, aren't you? What strange mind magic was that?

'I didn't do anything... That was all you...'

I feel a little bad I doubted him. I mean, I still want to drugs test the tea though. I remembered something. Oscar. Seriously, who the hell is this dude?

'All me? Really? Then we're doing it again...' I say, lying down and closing my eyes immediately.

'Errr... all right then... just give me a moment. I need to crack a window open...'

'I farted, didn't I?'

He nods.

14

Since my hypnotherapy session, I look at this note on my phone a lot. Who are you, Oscar? Is that the day we met? Is it his birthday? Did we have a good date? It must have been for me to have associated him with such happiness. Some romantic version of myself wonders if it's a date when I'm supposed to return to a certain place to meet him. 9th February next year – maybe that's when we had planned to meet on the concourse of a train station. Under a clock. In my mind, Oscar looks like young Sean Bean. He's sturdy stock with dimples and good forearms. He'd grab me at that train station and say something a bit filthy before a dip, a grope of the arse and the steamiest of kisses.

Beth looks over at me now. 'I went through two hundred and fifty Oscars on Facebook the other night, nothing.'

The sisters and I still dig through this mystery. It gives us something to do when there's nothing on the telly. After I said his name randomly, I didn't recall anything else about him in that session. I was trying too hard to look for him apparently. That said, I'll be back to see Cosmo next week because hypnotherapy randomly helped me remember the PIN number for my credit cards.

I prop myself up on Beth's shoulder as baby Jude sleeps soundly in a sling to her chest. 'In my head, Oscar is the love of my life. The date is marked down as the day I met him.'

'Or, it's most likely the date a debt collector has to be paid. He could just be a window cleaner. A window cleaner you've most likely shagged.'

'Can you say "shagged" in front of a baby?'

'You used to say it all the time in front of Joe. It was a wonder his first word wasn't "jizz".'

She laughs and an old lady sitting opposite us on this train gives us both looks in judgement. All right, Grandma, wind your neck in. Her glances shift between the both of us trying to work out the relationship. Beth and I have never really looked alike so we could be lesbians for all she knows, raising this little baby together. You can tell this doesn't sit well with her so I lean over and give Beth a kiss on the cheek to make her muscles tighten even further.

'Love you, B.'

'Love you too. Stop winding up that old woman.'

'How did you know?'

'Because I know what you're like.'

'She's got issues with just a kiss. It's not like we're scissoring on the train. Sorry, Jude.'

'I love how you're apologising to my baby. You were once holding Joe and told us about a bloke you shagged who had a dick as wide as a beer can.'

'Who was this man?' I enquire, my nostrils flared.

'Lord knows. I didn't keep tabs on names. In fact we used to have nicknames for a lot of them because that helped us pass the time.'

'Like?'

'Jetwash was the one who ejaculated in ludicrous amounts, with some propulsion apparently, you said you nearly drowned. My personal favourite was Sir Lancelot.'

'He sounds polite, well-presented and regal.'

'He was into medieval re-enactment. He referred to his knob as a lance, he wore chainmail and called you his wench. *I shall penetrate your fortress...*' she says, in knightly tones.

I double over in laughter as Beth makes googly eyes at her little infant son. God, this girl I used to be. She really had no limits, did she? There was no line. I am duly in awe of her but intimidated in equal measure. Chainmail sounds like there'd be chafing though.

'Did you ever think it was too much, B? You know, all the sex. Sometimes I hear all these stories back and I'm just sat here in shock.'

Beth shrugs. 'You are too much. But it was kinda the beauty of you too. You always said when fellas do the same, it's labelled differently and you were right to some degree.'

'So I was a feminist too...?'

'You were something else. You had this very strong sense of justice. There was fire in those bones. There still is. You get that from Mum.'

I smile as she says that. Despite Meg and Mum not really seeing eye to eye at all, it's because they're perhaps too similar and I think I'm an offshoot of that. I like Meg's style, how she challenges the status quo. Ems, Beth and Grace have shades of Dad. It is quieter but fully invested in everything, they feel it all, they love others so very hard. It makes me wonder what will become of Jude here. How much of all our family filters into these little people? I hear footsteps thunder down the train carriage. This little one doing the thundering has shades of me in him and I like that very much.

'LUCY!' he squeals, running into my arms. Joe. He's Beth's

eldest, my other nephew. The lad is a force of nature, a super cute one at that but I'm biased. My sisters have introduced me to all these kids and they are truly works of magic. I have formed an immediate love affair with all of them. Behind him is dad, Will, carrying what looks like a camping rucksack.

'Are we having fun, Daddy?' Beth asks.

'There are no toilets so I am going to hope he just did an extraordinary fart and wait until we get off the train,' he explains, kissing Beth on the forehead. Will is new to me but he seems to love Beth and these boys completely and this warms me. She deserves nothing less.

'FART,' Joe announces to the carriage. This boy is great, I like this one.

We're on the train today to go and meet the others at Kew Gardens for a final summer fling with the family but also to celebrate my birthday. I am thirty today. And I should be singing and dancing into my next decade but I've opted out. I just want to spend quality time with my nearest and dearest. Next week, schools go back so Grace must return to Bristol, Meg's kids drive back up North and Emma is going to move back to hers to settle her daughters back into routine. They've done all they can to remedy my amnesia. We've all shared a bathroom, eaten meals together and danced in the front room so hard and with so much passion that Meg pulled something and is now having to use Deep Heat daily. And I've lain there at night, in the grey of our old house, not knowing whether to laugh or cry at the fact my memory is so shockingly absent. Listening to Emma, who still sleep-talks, this warm feeling of a full house in a deep embrace, but none of it works. Ideally, I'd have them just stay here forever but they all grew in the last twelve years, out of that house, expanding the family wings, and it'd be selfish of me to make them stay any longer for my benefit, watching old nineties teen dramas in our jammies.

'Train go brooooom...' Joe tells me, scrunching his face at me.

'It also go choo-choo!' I say, maybe a little too loudly as I seem to wake a man who was asleep in the left corner of the carriage. The sound of Joe's chuckle makes me want to eat him up. Over the way, I notice the old lady staring and I glare back at her as she continues to suss out the arrangement here. Beth and I could still be lesbians. Maybe this is our manny. Maybe we're in one of these new modern three-way relationships. Instead she waves at Joe, who looks back at her with a furrowed brow and sticks out his tongue. *Yes, you are now my favourite.*

* * *

Kew Gardens is around the corner from our house so when we were little it was a go-to day out with five girls because parts of it were free and occasionally Mum said it was important we were aired. There is a very stately magic about it, like any park in London to be fair, and it seems the perfect place to picnic and bring this huge gaggle of children that we've amassed. There are nine cousins altogether: Tess, Eve and Polly belong to Meg, Iris and Violet are Emma's and Grace's girls are Maya and Cleo. Beth broke the cycle with her boys, Joe and Jude.

This is the thing that annoys me the most: that in all of this amnesia drama, I missed out on my sisters becoming mothers. I did see Meg with Tess and it was just such a pivotal moment for her and us as a family: the first niece, grandchild and mother. We all sobbed when we met her, it was phenomenal, heart-breaking, bloody fantastic. But then it happened for all of them and I missed all of it, the birth stories, the cuddles with freshly popped-out bubbas and, most importantly, Grace's story, as her girls are adopted and they found each other in the most beautiful and serendipitous ways. Hell, if I can't remember any of those initial encounters then maybe all I can do now is pick up where I left off, I can still be this wild and crazy aunt that they remember, everyone's favourite. I can give them sugar when I'm not supposed to and inappropriate life advice.

As we walk through the turnstile, it's Maya I see first as she runs towards me with open arms, weighed down by quite a large rucksack and, knowing Grace, a fair bit of sun cream. I bend down to receive the tightest of hugs and a kiss on the cheek for good measure.

'Happy birthday, Aunty Lucy. Your hair is growing back!' she calls out.

'So I don't look like a pumpkin head any more...' I remark. She giggles and I'm bombarded by tiny people who come over to say their hellos. Look all these little faces, just shining bright and gorgeous. They all get gradually bigger and the last one to say hello is Tess. She's almost as tall as me and the hug is ganglier but sincere. Christ, I have a niece with boobs. I hope your mum bought you some nice bras because being the youngest I didn't have that luxury and it's a wonder my breasts survived the trauma of wearing your mother's old crop tops.

'How are you feeling?' she asks me tentatively. There's a feeling that when I first woke up I traumatised this one a little by declaring her some fake imposter of a niece so she seems cautious with me.

'Stronger. Don't tell Aunty Ems but the physio's been working even if the physio is really really not very good-looking at all.'

She laughs and hooks an arm around mine and I don't refuse it as older sisters at the front of the group take charge and start walking to a green space where we can all sit down and eat the many sandwiches Mum seems to have made. A pair of arms appear around my midriff. Eve. Eve is another mini Meg but this one seems to have more of a gob and I like that plenty. They all have these Northern twangs to their accents too, which are bloody adorable.

'Have you remembered anything yet?' Eve asks. Tess glares at her.

'I haven't. Remind me of your name again? Is it Fanny?'

The smiles that response produces are everything. 'Yes, Fanny. That's my name. It's short for Fanjita.'

She's only inherited the best parts of my sister.

'That is a beautiful name. And what is your name again?' I ask Tess.

'Mum named me after the place I was conceived so my full name is Shepherd's Bush but they call me Bushy for short.'

'Bushy and Fanny. She did so well there with the names.'

'And she couldn't think of anything for the youngest so just called her Dave,' Eve says.

I nod and we all giggle, arms linked. The youngest is actually Polly and she sits on her dad's shoulders, blonde curls trailing down her back like mine used to.

'But no, Fanny. I still don't remember a thing. Go on... fill me in. Tell me your best Aunty Lucy story...'

'You came to visit us one summer. We went scrambling and found a lake and you stripped off completely naked and went for a swim. You told Mum to come in and she refused and then you pretended a giant fish was attacking you so she had to go in to save you but it turned out you were faking just to get her in the water,' Eve explains.

'Did you girls come in too?'

'Yes, it's now an annual thing. The girly skinny-dip. Dad isn't allowed to come,' she continues.

'Well, that is a brilliant thing for me to have initiated. The female form is a marvellous thing. You should embrace it.'

Tess studies my face. 'Do you remember I came down to visit you recently? You showed me around some theatres one weekend.'

There seems to be pain in her eyes that I don't remember that weekend; obviously it was special in some capacity.

'I don't. I'm so sorry, lovely. Tell me about it though. I want to know what we did.'

'Well, I live in the Lakes and it's pretty quiet so you showed me all the fun side of London. We saw a couple of theatres where your mates worked and we went to Camden and Borough Market and we ate ramen in Soho. It was really cool,' she says. She gets her phone out and shows me photos. I'm not discreet in any of them. My midriff is out, the jeans are tight and, amidst all that fun, we spent a lot of time taking selfies where I'm either pouting, sticking out my tongue or throwing up peace signs. There's joy in those photos and, from the way I have her in a headlock, a complete love for this girl. Well done, me.

'Did we stay up way past your bedtime?' I ask.

Tess nods. 'You tried to get me in a club, for dancing, not drinking, but apparently that's a secret I need to take to my grave.'

'Well, that's what aunties are supposed to do, no?'

'That's what Aunty Lucy does. Aunty Emma buys us personalised journals and gift cards,' Eve whispers. 'I'm waiting for my weekend. I want to book that in now.'

I laugh, my gaze looking over at all these nieces. God, I want to have mountains of fun with all of you. Line you all up and teach you how to dance to TLC. I need to get to know all of you again, immediately.

'Well, little Fanny... we will book that in when I'm better.'

Both their faces pause for a moment when I say that. I guess, on the outside, I'm nearly there bar my dodgy hair regrowth. I am walking, talking and breathing but there's a look of fear that I will never get better, that they may have lost me if I can't get my mind back, and this angers me more than anything, to be letting these girls down, to have them think they need to mourn me. Goddamn, I *can* remember how to be fun again. Teach me how to be fun again.

'So you girls need to fill me in on stuff because my sisters are very diplomatic. Tell me about Jag. Good uncle?'

'Better than that melon, Simon,' Eve says quite directly. 'He wears Jordans so he's super cool. Have you met Max yet? He's all right too and you'll like him because he's covered in tattoos. Maya and Cleo have said he's nice.'

I love the camaraderie between all these girls. I can't but wonder where they learnt that from.

'And how's school for you two? Any boyfriends?' I ask, digging for goss like a good aunt.

'Tess likes a boy called Callum, he always waves at her on his paper round,' Eve tells me, retching slightly at this revelation. Tess has no hesitation in hitting her around the head.

'He's at my school. He's friendly.'

'But is he cute?' I say matter-of-factly. 'Do you want to snog the braces off him?'

Tess's face rises to a blush. 'Well... look, don't tell Dad because I think this will freak him out. When people talk about his girls going out with boys he always talks about buying a gun.'

'That's what dads do. But you won't have to worry about your dad if I'm around because if this Callum treats you badly, I will jump on a train and kick his face in, yes?'

They both smile. This feels more like the aunt they know and it's good to see that parts of me never left the building. From the rear, Joe suddenly appears and scuttles past us at demonic speed and Eve chases him down to help Will, who is still weighed down by his rucksack. She catches him and throws him up in the air.

'What are you two gossiping about?' Meg suddenly says, appearing at my shoulder.

'Your daughter's first tattoo. Has she not shown you?'

Meg's face blanches even if she knows that to be a complete lie.

'It's on my back,' Tess teases and skips away to find Maya and hold her hand.

'Meggsy, they're kinda awesome, eh?' I say, my gaze drawn to the way Eve walks, just like her mum.

'They are. Good gene pool.'

'The best.'

'If she gets a tattoo though, I will kill you. Actually maim you with a brick.'

'I love you too, sis.'

'Here... We got you a gift,' Meg tells me, handing me something wrapped in tissue paper. I rip it open to find a shiny gold badge with the words 'Birthday Bitch' on it.

'I love it.'

She waits for me to remember something, her expression hopeful. 'Thought you might...'

* * *

Mum did make a shitload of sandwiches, eaten mainly by Joe, who it seems likes jam so I look forward to train farts later when there may be more a fruity tang wafting around the carriage. I've had a jam sandwich too, a pre-mixed cocktail in a tin and about twenty mini sausage rolls, and I couldn't be happier. Afternoons like this warm the soul – just picnicking on the grass, meandering along the paths and trees, soaking in the sun of a late summer's day. Less cool for Beth perhaps, trying to shield her sweaty boobs as she breastfeeds, and Grace, whose little Cleo gets a little dramatic in the heat. But for me, to have this noise and volume of people around me is the absolute best. I adore them all, even some of these random men I don't quite know.

And Mum even brought a birthday cake that got slightly squished in transit and the whole group sang to me while I stood barefoot on the grass, in a playsuit and straw hat. I blew out all those candles and I wished. I wished so fucking hard to remember them all before running my fingers along the frosting and getting told off by Mum. To cap off the day, we've now stopped at what looks like a mini funfair and, because I'm the best aunty there is, I've bought all the little people ice cream, using Dad's wallet of course, and going for extra dayglo sauce on mine like the seventeen-year-old person I am on the inside. It's a sedate funfair because it's Kew and posh so there are old-fashioned carousels with weathered-looking ponies, vintage toy cars and an inflatable slide that looks like a castle. I'd like to say they bring back fond memories of my youth but my mum banned us from these places when we were younger because fairs were where young girls went to smoke crack cocaine and get impregnated by wrong 'uns. She may have a point, I think I snogged a lot of boys next to the bumper cars and maybe let a few touch my boobs, but there's much less chance of that here given the music is mainly coming out of an accordion, and there's a man in a straw boater and white trousers so see-through you can see the colour and fit of his undercrackers.

'Right, I've bought a load of tokens so you girls go mad. Look after the little ones,' Meg's husband Danny announces, handing over a load of gold coins to the older girls. There's a mixture of screaming, joy and wonder as they disperse and the rest of us perch on benches to take some respite from the heat and wander away on walks for coffees and to calm down restless babies.

'Should one of us supervise?' Mum says worriedly, eyes darting everywhere.

'We can see them, Mum,' Emma says. 'The older girls are pretty sensible.'

Meg nods in agreement but she still sits there, perched, ready to run at the slightest sign of trouble.

'Well, seeing as we have a moment,' I announce, trying to

distract her. 'I just wanted to say thank you to everyone while we're here, gathered in my honour.'

Jag laughs and that smile makes me see what Emma fell for.

'You've all uprooted your lives for a bit, for me. And it's not gone unnoticed. I'm sorry I was such a spoon and fell off that bike and worried you all but I'm so grateful for the way you've all shown up. You've been at the hospital, by my bedside, you've accompanied me to appointments and even to our old school. So, thank you.'

Everyone is silent for a bit and I can't quite tell if it's the emotion of the moment or the heat but Emma and Meg shift looks at each other before laughing, quite offensively.

'What?' I ask. 'Don't laugh at me.' Grace and Beth both do their best to stifle their giggles too.

'It's just, we're not used to earnest, pensive Lucy. It's new,' Meg says.

'And I don't think I like it,' Beth adds.

Even my parents sit there, smirking.

'Oh, then piss off the lot of you. I was trying to be nice.'

'You are nice. You just show it in different ways,' Grace mentions. 'I mean, I like sensitive, well-meaning Lucy.'

'I don't,' Emma contributes. 'It's freaking me out. Please make a joke about sex now.'

'Or not,' my mother interjects.

'But you would have done the same for us. You have done the same for us on many occasions so shush,' Beth says, more sincerely this time.

'It's been interesting, in any case...' Meg says. 'We all know Emma still talks in her sleep and someone in this family doesn't think they need to flush after every wee.'

'It's an environmental thing,' Beth says. 'I am saving the planet.'

'But it smells and it's gross.'

'But hasn't it been fun too?' I add. 'When was the last time we all painted each other's nails and shared clothes and had one of Mum's greasy lasagnes?'

'My lasagnes are greasy?' Mum asks, offended.

'The meat is swimming in something. You like that sauce in a jar too, it's not good...' Meg says jokingly.

None of the sisters will admit to this much but there's a moment as we sit here and take stock of the fact we won't be together like this for a while, not until Christmas at least. When do the opportunities otherwise present themselves? Births, funerals and weddings, no? Maybe I was the one thing that brought us together for this short while. I'm taking credit for it.

'Mummy, Mummy... you've got to... quickly...'

The moment is suddenly interrupted by a young Violet, who runs over breathless. Our looks scatter to all corners of the park.

'Vee, is someone hurt?' Emma says, rising from her bench.

But then we hear it, it's Eve fighting with someone. Another adult? 'I don't care if you're a grown-up. I don't know you. Why do I have to respect you when you're being so rude?'

Meg rolls her eyes to hear her daughter's tones and rises from her bench but, as we look over, we see Joe sobbing at the top of a giant inflatable slide, his other cousins doing their best to pacify him. Beth dashes over.

'I don't care if there's a queue. He's a baby and he's scared,' shouts Tess, getting stuck in.

Meg smiles as the woman her daughters seem to be harassing rolls her eyes, looking around to find out who these little firecrackers belong to. Joe is sitting in an older cousin's lap, his arms gripped tightly around her as he bounces down, a big mass of limbs and giggles right into Beth's arms and she wipes his panic-stricken face down.

'Are these your daughters?' asks the angered lady in the queue, arching towards Beth, gunning for this fight. She really wants to do this? Meg and I know exactly what we need to do and we head over leaving Emma and my mother sitting there, wondering what sort of event will have us barred from Kew for life.

'They're *my* daughters,' Meg announces, walking over.

'Then you need to teach them some manners.'

Tess's face goes a bright puce colour. 'Mum, she was being awful. Joe went up there and freaked out and she told her kids at the top to just push him down. Who does that? He's literally a baby.'

Her kids run in circles beside her. They're not in the near vicinity of quality as my nieces and nephews. 'Everyone was waiting to use the slide. Maybe if he was supervised properly by adults then we wouldn't have this problem.'

Meg and I look at each other and laugh.

'I don't understand what's so funny. Your girls need to learn some respect. They're very rude.'

Meg is on a light simmer. She never blows over completely. It's a frothy mix of complete disdain and the storm is brewing. It's going to be quick, sharp but very very painful.

'Girls, where are your manners? I taught you better.'

Eve looks like she might break things. 'I'm not saying sorry.'

'No, thank me for giving you the tools to deal with witchy bitchies like this. You are so welcome and I am so very proud.'

Her girls beam. The woman immediately looks horrified. I may laugh a bit louder.

'This is a children's play area. I'm going to report you.'

'To who?' Eve asks. 'The Kew Gardens police?'

The young girl makes a very good point but, gosh, look at you. I adore you. The queue assembled for said slide doesn't even move, I think they feel this is far better entertainment.

'Well, the slide is free now. Why don't you trot on up there? I'll take a great pleasure in pushing you down,' I contribute.

'Are you threatening me?' she shrieks.

I place my upturned palms into the air and shrug. 'I believe you just told your children to do that to my three-year-old nephew. And I wouldn't push, love. I'd kick you so hard you'd launch like a space shuttle.'

Meg closes her eyes. Whilst she stepped over the line and gave her a firm what-for, I've barged my way through. The line is very far behind me, faint and in the distance.

'That is a threat. Did people hear that?' She takes out her phone, pointing it in my direction. A hand appears to block the lens. Meg. That's some reflexes, like a bloody cat. She points the camera at Tess instead.

'Get that phone away from my daughter,' Meg warns her.

'I'll do what I like...'

And that is when it kicks off, true Callaghan style. These incidents happen once in a blue moon. I hear it went down like this when Emma had finally had enough of her cheating husband, Simon, and we all confronted him one Christmas. Mum broke his nose. And a memory suddenly bubbles up of all my girls standing around me, the lights are purple for some reason, I'm in a bandeau top, there's a song I know in my head like lift music. I know this song. But Meg's voice is louder, tearing me away from my memory. Beth is trying to level it all out and failing. A boy has just said something to Eve. And there's a left hook. Good arm, girl. Did Maya just bite someone? It's a big mess of voices and insults. Where do I fit into all of this? I turn and Emma and Mum are sitting there shaking their heads at all of us. The line behind us disperses. The man with the straw hat and the boater has his phone out filming it all. Professional. We're going to be banned from this place. And I don't know how and why I do this but it feels right, to soak up the last of the sun, and I grab Joe and Maya.

'Come with me,' I whisper. We run over to the slide and we climb the dodgy ladder to the top. Joe's eyes search for me. This wasn't a good idea the first time round and it's high, Aunty Lucy. But look at the view, little Joe. Look how we can see all the trees and all the buildings and all the sky. Don't look down. I wrap my arms tightly around his tense little body. Why is that man waving his cane at me?

'LET'S GO DOWN TOGETHER!' Maya shrieks.

And that we do. I may scream. People look up from below to see what that sound may be. Mum looks very alarmed from down there. I won't drop the baby. Have more faith. The rush of air between my ears, the thrill, the speed, you forget the joy of a slide, the static on Maya's hair. This is bloody brilliant. But as I get to the bottom, there's a strange sound. Almost like an explosion. People inhale deeply with shock. That man with the cane stands there over us as I sink slowly into the ground.

'How old are you?' he says in a voice not befitting his posh outfit.

Seventeen in my head, actually thirty today since you're asking. Did you not get me a gift?

'Not for ages twelve or over, you've burst my sodding slide.' I know because I'm no longer on a cushiony soft surface but have hard ground under my back. He then looks down at my chest. Perv. Oh. It's more than that, I've landed quite awkwardly and had a bit of a nip slip situation. Maya cups her hands around her mouth and giggles.

'BOOB!' Joe shouts loudly, smiling.

I didn't drop the baby though, that's because I'm a bloody excellent aunt.

15

'So you're banned from Kew?' Darren asks me, laughing into his cocktail.

'Well, not the town of Kew but I suspect we won't be going back to the Queen's Royal Gardens any time soon.'

'Only you could get yourself into that sort of trouble, eh?'

'Not me, the whole fam.'

Fam. That's a new word I've learnt from the past decade that seems to be a part of modern vernacular. My fam. My bloody awesome fam. After I burst a slide, showed a bunch of families my nipple and everyone laughed, Meg was threatened by a balding man in a Barbour coat (whatever), we all shouted our best insults and the babies learnt many new words. It was the best birthday present I've ever received bar the time Beth gifted me her old Reebok pumps. But then the crowd dispersed, we all found a pub garden and had a merry dinner almost as some sort of victory feast for taking on the playground bullies of Kew.

When the last pint was ordered, we then did what we've apparently been doing for years, we went back into our corners of the world, to live the different strands of our lives in different

houses, with all our new extra family members. It was the
saddest of times but we masked the sadness with alcohol and
the knowledge that we'd just lived through another family anecdote to wheel out in years to come. I won't lose them all. Beth is
still on maternity leave so is going to stick around and Meg says
she'll pop down on the train every so often but the girl band are
embarking on solo projects for now. They will rise through the
charts once more, no doubt, and come together for the odd
reunion tour.

'You do like flashing. It's your thing. I've seen your boobs
more times than is really necessary and we've only been intimate once,' Darren informs me.

'What did we do?' I ask curiously.

'We had drunken half sex where you don't even know if it
counts towards your numbers because you're so pissed and you
don't even know if it went in properly.'

I knock my head back in laughter at him recalling it so
frankly. I like Darren. Not in *that* way but he's been round to
Mum's occasionally to have a cup of tea and he seems invested
in me and my life and wanting to get it back on track. But also
not in that way as, since my accident, he and Cass seemed to
have formed a relationship. From the sounds of it, the trauma of
potentially losing me forced them together one evening and
they've been inseparable since. Presently, they're at the night-
away stage of their relationship where they shared a bathroom
and didn't freak out at hearing the other poo.

'So you and me never did more than that?' I ask.

'Oh, I was so in love with you at one point but you are an
uncontainable force, Lucy Callaghan. It would take a larger-
than-life man to be able to fit into that orb.'

'Like Madonna?' I ask.

'Yes, I'd have been a rubbish Guy Ritchie.'

Cass comes back to the table with a tray of shots and drinks
and puts an arm around me.

'So... I guess we should say happy belated birthday?' Cass says, holding a shot glass aloft.

I pick up a glass and toast them both. 'To thirty...' I down the sambuca shot and let it scorch the inside of my throat. This should be bigger, shouldn't it? It was supposed to be drinking, dancing and general carnage in a field until the sun came up on my thirtieth year. But it was all scrapped because of that blinking bus. Instead we replaced celebrations with family picnics and I've opted for quiet drinks with a select few. However, Darren and Cass serve a different purpose here too.

'So, is she coming?' Cass asks, looking at her watch.

'I told her eight.'

'She was never very reliable,' Darren adds with a hint of disdain in his voice.

'One would think you didn't like her?' I ask. Cass laughs.

Tonight, I'm meeting Imogen, who I apparently had been half seeing before the bus. Well, that was my impression from the many times we'd shared pictures of our genitalia with each other but, according to Darren, it was more of a friends-with-benefits arrangement. I've been doing this a lot recently, having casual drinks and coffees with people from my contacts list who I believe I've slept with. Leo was the Batman fella I shagged in Emma's utility room at Beth's birthday party. Apparently, I threw a cake at Emma that evening. Leo was lovely and, apparently, we had three months of wild healing sex before I broke it off in the nicest possible way by setting him up profiles on many dating sites through which he found his current girlfriend, Natalie, who works in marketing and whose only flaw seems to be that she doesn't like baked beans.

There have been other meet-ups. There was a man who cried because my situation made him think about the fragility of life and everything he hasn't achieved in his own, and a banker who apparently was heavily into his kink and left me with a business card saying he'd love to come round and clean my house while I shout abuse at him. I live with my mother, I thought. Mum might like that though, especially if it gave her a break from the dusting.

'She's just a flake, an unsociable one at that. Bloody hard work. And she just shags you and leaves...' Darren says.

'I did the same with a lot of people...?' I say.

'I don't think so. You were never cold with people.'

'She's just not that fun, Luce,' Cass says, hooking her arm into his. 'Oh crap, she's here. Don't turn around...'

I turn around. Obviously. Imogen has arrived in a suit, to a bar. It's very fresh from work and her work is in the City, automatically feeling more important than mine.

'Lucy?' she says, examining my head. 'Wow, that's a look. How are you?' Immediately, the tone of her voice grates. She comes over for a double air kiss. I was attracted to this?

'Imogen?'

'Yeah?'

Yeah, she's not Tony. I liked Tony immensely. She's aloof, if attractive. Her hair is black, slicked-back, she's got a stud to each ear. She's so preened to the point of nearly being boring.

'There's a spare drink going here if you want, Imogen,' Cass says, waving at her.

'We've met, right? Sorry, I'm terrible with names.'

'Darren and Cass.'

'Yeah. So I didn't really get your message? You were in an accident?'

'A bike accident.'

'And now you don't remember a thing? I'm not sure that's how amnesia works, is it?'

'Are you a doctor?' Darren asks her.

'No, actually. But I've seen documentaries.'

This isn't awkward. At all. There's a very conservative look to her and she reaches to take the White Russian offered, sips it and then flinches.

'I've been meeting a lot of people recently, trying to fill in the gaps,' I say.

Darren smirks and I kick him under the table.

'So, did you want to get out of here?' she says, looking at Darren and Cass dismissively.

'Oh no. God, I meant I have no idea who I became over the last ten years. It's all a mystery so I've been trying to work out who I am. Who I went out with.'

'We didn't really go out,' she mumbles. 'We just slept together for a while. It was open.'

'Didn't we go away together?'

'Well, yeah... look, I can't drink this. I'm going to get some wine,' she says bluntly, not offering to buy anything for anyone else and taking her bag with her like we might steal it.

As she walks away I lean into Darren and Cass. 'What the hell? She is awful? I slept with her? She's so shiny and cold.'

'It's why we called her the Fridge.'

Having not drunk huge amounts in the past months, the shot I had earlier forces quite a loud laugh out of me and Imogen turns from the bar to look at me. She's in a suit. I'm in a cropped top and jeans. This is a very weird mismatch but at the same time I'm semi-intrigued how we fell into bed together.

'You used to say she was very skilled. I always thought you were just addicted to the orgasms. The mismatch in personalities was interesting to you, a challenge. Apparently, she was very good at making you...'

'Come?' I say.

'And more,' Cass says, whispering but not.

Darren puts a finger to his lips and looks up to the ceiling. All I know is at seventeen, I didn't even know an orgasm was a thing, at least not something you experience with another person. It was something I did by myself, for myself, not even knowing what that sensation was really. I scrunch my face up in reply.

'Surely I could have done that myself without having to interact with her, or even found someone a bit warmer.'

'We often questioned your decisions when it came to your sexual partners. You had sex with a fifty-year-old hot yoga instructor once. He'd come for drinks in leggings.'

'I did?'

'His name was Roger. Bendy as fuck, saggy balls,' Darren tells me.

'We'd get school reports on them all, Luce. They gave us life.'

Imogen suddenly appears back at the table. 'The wine selection here is horrific. Not sure how long this has been lingering in their fridge.' She puts her bag down on the table, blocking Cass out of view. 'What were we talking about?'

'Yoga,' I reply. 'Do you do yoga?'

'I'm not into that hippy shit,' she says blankly.

'Oh. So remind me why we slept together?' I say bluntly. I have no idea who I am but I have a feeling I'm not the sort of person who's going to fake a whole evening of conversation for the sake of it. She seems perturbed to have to speak so openly about it in front of my friends.

'It was fun?' she says, not looking too entirely sure.

'Your face is really reading fun right now.'

'I don't do sarcasm.'

'I do.'

Darren and Cass sit that much closer to each other to take this all in, hoping I might do us all a favour and just get rid.

'I don't get why I'm here then? You said it was your birthday? Is this it? Is this the party?'

'Yeah?'

She looks around. Was she expecting balloons? Vol-au-vents? She seems upset that she even had to buy her own drink. She studies my face, disappointment framed in her impeccably groomed eyebrows.

'You've changed,' she mutters.

'Getting hit by a bus will do that. I was under the impression we maybe cared about each other so you might give a damn that I nearly died or that it is my birthday...'

'Happy birthday?'

'No card?'

'People don't do cards any more.'

'These two got me a card.'

Darren identifies himself as the card-giver by putting his hand in the air. It had a monkey on the front wearing lipstick and a beret.

'Look, what we had was just casual,' she adds. 'I don't even know your last name. We'd have sex and that was it, you were never so uptight about it before?'

Darren and Cass look at each other with bated breath, waiting for my response.

'In fact, you were more fun. If you've had some accident and some sort of lightbulb moment about what we were then I can't sign up to that. I'm sorry.'

I'm unnaturally quiet for a moment as I study her face. She's pretty, there is no doubt about that, but I can't quite tell where the sexual attraction is here. Why you? Why women? This still confuses me. I was always under the impression that people knew about their sexuality from a young age. But at seventeen, those feelings were still deeply embedded somewhere. I don't want you. I don't want to kiss you, see your boobs or have your fingers anywhere near my bits. So what I do is just nudge my drink forward and have it spill in her general direction, over what looks like quite an expensive handbag.

'Fuck. Lucy. Grow up,' she says, picking up the bag and trying to wipe it down with her hand. 'This is bloody Prada.'

I sit there and cock my head to the side, staring into space.

'Well? You're not going to at least apologise?' she demands.

'No, I'm having a lightbulb moment that maybe you're a bit

of a bitch and I'm disappointed in my older self that I would
have ever gone near someone like you.'

And with a smile, she picks up her sodden Prada and leans
into me. 'Bye, Lucy.'

'Piss off, Imogen.'

And she departs, not even acknowledging my friends but at
least leaving us with a full glass of red to share. My eyes follow
her as she vacates the bar, not even bothering to turn and give
me a second glance.

'That was what I was into?' I ask Darren and Cass, still a bit
silent from the confrontation.

'Drama fuelled your soul. I think you thought it made the
sex better. Who knows?' Cass replies and she comes over to kiss
me on the cheek, noting my unusually pensive look. 'Hey, you
know where we should go tonight? Velvet Boulevard.' Darren
gives Cass a strange look at the suggestion. 'C'mon... Not for
any other reason but just for the fun? To see who's working?'

'Is that a new Tube station I don't know about?' I ask
innocently.

Darren still doesn't look convinced. 'It's a sex club that you
and Cass used to work at,' he explains, my eyes widening. 'Not
like that, you used to do bar work there, it paid very well. Even
if you did have to serve drinks in your underwear.'

'Nice underwear though,' Cass tells me. 'They'd give us
vouchers to go buy our knickers from Agent Provocateur – we
were in mostly for those sorts of perks. We could go. To bring
back your memory and all that...'

'What's the other option?' I ask.

'We get ratted here and then we have to carry Darren
home.'

'Then let's go, bitches.'

* * *

'LUCY! YOU BLOODY DIAMOND! COME HERE, GIRL!' I don't know who this man is but he's twice the size of me with a very square head and the tailoring of his suit is immaculate. 'I heard what happened, look at your hair? You look like me!'

'I do... And you are?' I feel knowing his name is important given he literally has me in a bear hug with my toes scraping off the floor.

'Are you serious?' he tells me, looking slightly insulted.

'Kyle, she lost her memory in the accident, remember?' Cass tells him.

'I thought you were pulling my leg. Really?' he says in deep East London tones, putting me down. 'Then what if I told you I was your husband and you were totally in love with me.'

'I'd ask you how I take my tea...'

'Milk, no sugar, 'cause you're sweet enough...' I wink at him and he roars with laughter, lifting up a red velvet rope and letting us all inside the club. 'Any trouble, girls... you come get me. Let yourselves through to the back.'

Cass gives him a kiss on the cheek and we enter the club, heading for a side door next to a cloakroom operated by someone in bunny ears and a corset. I used to work here? I guess it would beat an evening shift at Sainsbury's. Darren and Cass have explained the many side hustles we were all involved in to keep us alive and in London rents. We all did the princess party scene as that was decent money, cash in hand, and there was everything else from back-up dancing and pantomimes, to bar work and private ballet lessons, to bored expat housewives in West London's Holland Park. This bar work paid very well but Cass and I drew the line at being in the rooms at the back. Stuff happened in there that people spoke about in whispers. All we know is that the rooms have to be deep-cleaned every night. The club must get through a lot of Dettol.

Darren and Cass lead me through to a large dark dressing

room that has a window that I will assume is one-way as one girl sits there with her boobs out, corset undone and eating a packet of smoky bacon crisps. Do we talk about what's beyond the window? There's the bar I obviously used to work behind and Cass wasn't joking, the current girls there are in PVC thigh-high boots and masquerade masks. But around the place, people are just scattered enjoying sexual endeavours of varying descriptions. There's two people shagging on a sofa, looking very enthusiastic about it all. Is the balding fella in the cage all right? Can we check on him? Is he locked in there? What is also bizarre is that we can't hear any of it, only see, so it's like when we'd watch porn at a sleepover with the volume right down so someone's parents in the next room couldn't tell what we were doing. Seeing this through my inexperienced eyes makes me stop in my tracks though, as does Darren, who I suspect is not very into this scene.

'You girls used to tell me about this and I never quite believed you. It really is a thing, eh?' he says, putting his head to one side to study the angles by which one man is suspended off a wall. An older busty woman in a velour tracksuit and flip-flops sits there staring out of the window and turns to look at us. As soon as she sees my face, she jumps up in shock.

'As I live and breathe, it's Miss Juicy Lucy,' she says in a squawking London accent. She comes over and wraps her arms around me, holding me tightly in an embrace. Luckily a gold chain with her name gives me a clue as to who she is.

'Tia?'

'See, she's only remembered the important people in life,' she says to Cass. 'How are you, girl?'

'Confused?'

She roars with laughter and urges me to come and sit down next to her.

'I can't tell you what a treat it is to see you. When I heard what happened, no word of a lie, I sobbed.'

'So, I worked here?' I ask her.

'You did. One of my best girls behind the bar. You and Cass did the occasional shift for me.'

The way my eyes keep catching what's behind the mirror amuses her. I suppose I was never so prudish when I was mixing people's cocktails. Darren and Cass escape to get some drinks and possibly wash his eyes out with vinegar.

'I never partook in the...'

She shakes her head. 'That's what Olive does.' She gestures to the girl with the corset undone, still demolishing her crisps and sitting there with her boobs out, staring into space. She puts a hand up to acknowledge me.

'So, all these people...' I ask, craning my head around to see four people all at different angles to each other like some sort of puzzle of flesh.

'It's all kink, babes. High-end Mayfair kink. I'm the manager here. I check everyone is behaving themselves and keeping to the rules. I look after my girls. I looked after you.'

'Thank you,' I reply, bemused.

'Oh, you were always a dream to work with. Bloody hilarious. We used to sit here well into the night and chat shit, watching the punters.'

'Is the guy in the cage all right?' I ask.

'Gareth? Oh, that's his thing. He'll sit there all night. We just have to bring him drinks and, later, someone like Olive will go shout at him and he'll lick her shoes. It's his thing.'

I grimace but look over. It's not right to kink-shame but I do worry about the tummy bugs he could contract. Still, I'm glad he's happy.

'The foursome come here about once a month, like date night. They order the chicken wings in advance, arrive separately, get it on and go back to their townhouses in Hampstead like it never happened. Him on the rack is Larry. He's into his pain especially when it comes to his nipples...' She then lifts a walkie-talkie to her mouth. 'Can we watch out for Mr Smith in the leather mask for inappropriate touching, please...'

I turn my head to her. Inappropriate? Here? It's all a bit inappropriate, isn't it?

'We're big on consent and boundaries. Safe words for days,' Tia informs me. 'They're new though...' she continues, gesturing over to a couple in the corner. 'Bless them... we get a lot like that...'

The couple in question sit in the corner of a sofa, looking as confused as me, wide-eyed and lost.

'They're married and want to spice things up but it's possibly a step too far. Nice as a fantasy but a bit more in your face in real life,' Tia explains. They both literally don't know where to look, she's working out if she should be crossing her legs. He looks like he's trying desperately hard to suck his tummy in. 'And someone get some complimentary drinks over to the new couple, please...' she continues, mumbling into her walkie-talkie.

'And so you just orchestrate things from the back here?' I ask.

'I manage it all, babes. I give people what they want within reason and then I send them home. No judgement, all smiles... Olive, can you go to the blue room. Mr Hussain has asked for you.'

Olive salutes, pouring crisp crumbs into her mouth before she does and pulling a wedgie out of her arse. As she laces up her corset, she grabs a flogging tool from her make-up desk. OK, then. She leaves the area, as another girl walks in. She has nipple tassels, which jiggle as she walks, and a very high-cut see-through bodysuit on. As she sees me though, she stops and looks to almost tear up, running over to embrace me.

'No bloody way! Luce!' I think I know who this is from social media and I think she may have messaged me.

'Hayley?' I guess.

'Yes, you silly bitch.' Her embrace is warm and familiar and I realise she may be more of a Darren/Cass mate as opposed to Imogen. 'I was there that day when you got squished by the bus. I'm made up you're here. You're not working, right?' she asks, shocked.

'No, just a brief birthday visit.'

Darren and Cass re-enter the room with a tray of drinks, and she waves at them.

'I forgot your birthday? I'm an awful friend. We'll remedy that later. Of all the places to bring her though, Cass.' Cass shrugs as Hayley walks over to her make-up station and pulls off her nipple tassels without even flinching. She then throws on a hoodie and comes to sit down next to us, grabbing a bottle of beer.

'Tia, they said to bring you tea?' Darren says quizzically, handing out the other drinks.

'Yep. I don't drink on this job. Tea all the way. I hope them bastards got it the right colour.'

'They also...' Darren pulls out some biscuits from his coat pocket. '...said you'd go ape without these.'

She puts a palm to the air in praise. 'I likes your new fella, Cass. I like a man who knows to spoil his girl.'

She winks at him and it's clear Darren doesn't know whether to be scared or flattered. She grabs the packet of Jaffa Cakes and puts her feet up, completely undeterred by the people in the background performing some pretty energetic gymnastic moves to get the angles desired.

'We thought it'd be a good way for Lucy to see what this place used to be to her...' Cass says, offering me a cocktail. 'Despite how it looks, you used to love working here. Behind the scenes, it's pretty close-knit, almost like family. We had such a laugh.'

Tia offers Cass a hug, who, in turn, raises her mug of tea to me.

'And you work in the back rooms?' I ask, turning to Hayley.

'But in a non-contact form. Olive and I have personas, it's all very dominatrix-led. I like it, it's very cathartic.'

Hayley then does what the majority have done of late which is to study my face. *You don't remember me, do you?* she's thinking. And there's a look of disappointment. *We were mates. We used to sit here, chat and share bottles of Jäger into the night,*

'So this amnesia thing. How long do they think it'll last, lovely?' Hayley asks, swigging on her beer.

'Who knows? I've tried everything. I'm tracking down most of the people I've ever slept with. We paid for me to go to a hypnotherapist. I even got all my sisters to live with me in my family home but nada...'

Hayley reaches over and grabs my hand. 'Oh love... we miss you. You know that...'

Darren puts his arm around me. 'She's still here. She poured a drink on Imogen before. It was quite a thing. Proper shades of old Lucy...'

'The Fridge?' Hayley says. 'Thank god, she really was hard work, that girl...'

I pause for a moment to take that in. The idea that these people know my life better than I know myself is disconcerting but they make me feel safe, that I'm part of this bubble and I feel loved, cared for. Family. Even within the confines of this very unique place. The sound of a man part screaming, part calling out in pleasure, rings through the corridor behind this room and I'll assume Mr Hussain is in good if very firm hands.

Hayley catches me looking at the mirror again, watching a couple peruse through a bowl of sex toys and lube like they're rifling through a tub of Halloween sweets. 'How many people had you slept with at seventeen then?' she asks.

'Three and a half, really...'

Darren sniggers, knowing somewhere down the line he became a half figure too.

'This must be an education then?'

'Like a bloody intensive course. I'm told this was my scene though, I didn't shy away from this part of sex.'

'It's probably why you and I were friends, allies maybe?'

In that case, I feel I need to sit here with a notepad and pen and re-learn all of this, quickly. To make up for lost memories. Not just ten years gone but over a decade of sexual experience and endeavour just vanished. I probably lay in so many wet patches and learnt so much in that time about my body, my likes, my orgasms and now I have to learn that again. I'll have to reset my counter, no? Like, where has that woman got her...? Oh. That's new.

The door of the backstage area we seem to be in suddenly swings open and Kyle from the front door comes in.

'Did someone say birthday?' he says, with a cake in hand.

'Yes, Kyle!' Tia says. 'We do this properly if we're celebrating our Lucy. Cass, babes... there's candles in Olive's make-up station.'

I don't want to think why Olive has candles but everyone hustles to attention, clearing spaces on tables as Cass side-hugs me.

'You bake quick, Kyle...' I laugh.

'Nah, it was Darren here. Mentioned it at the bar and we always have cake in stock.'

'For customer birthdays?' I ask.

They all look at me smugly. Oh, people do stuff with the cakes. That would be sticky, with massive potential for getting fondant in your crack.

'This hasn't been touched, right?' I ask.

'Straight out the box, you dirty mare,' he cackles. 'How old are you?'

'Thirty.'

'Dirty thirty,' Hayley says, grinning.

Or maybe some version of it. Everyone starts singing, which

is surprisingly tuneful and there's a touch of harmonising at the end as a treat. I see it all, the smiles and the love in their voices, the reflection of my candles in the mirror of the room perfectly illuminating that foursome, still going strong, changing positions so they won't get cramp. And a shade of my own reflection in that mirror. Lucy Callaghan, she belonged here once.

'Come on, blow out them candles, girl,' Tia squeals.

'Make a wish,' Darren whispers.

I wish for it all back. That's what I wish for. All of it. And I close my eyes and blow.

But as the candles go out in a shadow of smoke, we all get distracted by the thud of a pair of pale middle-aged butt cheeks getting pushed and squished against the window. Christ, they're hairy. They're squeaking as they move up and down. Squeak, squeak like a mouse. We all burst into hysterics. I certainly did not wish for them.

16

Over from the steps that I'm sitting on, there's a couple lying on the grass, legs entwined, and I really want to throw my coffee over them. Don't worry, it's not hot coffee, it's iced, and I'm slightly fuming they messed up my order because I asked for vanilla not hazelnut, but iced coffee will do the trick here. It would stain and it might wake up these two numpties from whatever love-misted-googly-eye shite they're invested in.

I think it's the way she's talking to him, the way she's testing him. *Do you think I should cut my hair?* she says, hands cupped around her face. *No, you look better with long hair*, he says sweetly. *Are you saying I'd look bad with short hair? No, you'd look beautiful with whatever hair. I can't believe you said that. I was just being honest. Over-honest. Come here. Give me a hug.* She leans away from him. He tries to smooth it over by initiating a kiss. She smiles.

For god's sake, if you want to cut your hair, cut your hair. Do it for you and no one else and yes, he's right it wouldn't suit your round face, you'd look like Angela Merkel, but hair grows so, essentially, it wouldn't be a biggie. And mate, why did you let her do that? Why did you let her make you feel bad for being honest? Don't let her manipulate you like that. There is no such thing as over-honest. It's not even a word. You both deserve my iced coffee in your laps. They both notice me gazing over in their general direction and glare at me. I pretend to drink my coffee and throw a bit of my croissant at a pigeon. The pigeon gives me a look. Come on, mate, back me up. He doesn't care.

It's been two whole months since I woke up and I want to say things are better but it'd be a lie. My hair is growing so I now look like a hard-ass Charlize Theron in an action movie, and physically my strength is returning with some reluctant thanks to the torture merchant who is Igor. Hey, Igor. I know a club in Mayfair where you could be paid big bucks for the sort of masochism you dole out. However, my memory is still in nowhere land. Mum continues to panic every time I leave the house in case I wander into a field and forget why I'm there but I venture out nonetheless. I mean, I binge-watch (new lingo) the hell out of this new Netflix thing and I spend a lot of time in pyjamas, don't get me wrong, but I also meander through life. I get on buses and trains and explore my manor because a lot can change in London in ten years and if this is my life now then I need to imprint it into my new Lucy brain.

As it turns out, the brain needs work, the levels need refilling because, when we talk about old Lucy, it turns out she was also a clever clever bitch. I mean, this isn't a huge surprise as I grafted at school, I was destined for university, but it turns out I liked university and the experience a lot more than the average person and once my three-year degree was finished, I just kept going back for more. The sisters would argue it was so I could be a perpetual student and drink and sleep my way into oblivion for a lifetime but Dad explained it differently. I understood the sheer unpredictability of showbusiness so everything I did was to put me at some advantage, to fill the CV. So now I have all these bits of paper to my name but, unfortunately, none of the remembered wisdom to back them up so it makes sense to come to old university campuses to see if the knowledge can be infused through my bones. Maybe just being within their walls can make me feel all them super smarts again. It can be a chance to observe all these students and imagine myself as one of them.

London was always my city of choice for university. The city is my lifeblood and if I wanted drama, theatre and the arts then that flows through the veins of this place. I went on an open day to Birkbeck with Grace and the grand, historic buildings were slap bang in the middle of swanky Fitzrovia but a stone's throw from Soho. It felt like a London I wanted to get to know immediately. What would I have been like as a student? I hope I was cool and nothing like this sad case couple in front of me. Maybe I was part of a gang, like the ones sitting over the way. I reckon they are all besties (also new lingo, look how quickly I learn). Or maybe I was the berk lying in the middle of this grassed area, already smoking and reading Proust on his own. Would I have been attracted to the arrogance? I think I'd have liked to have brought him down a peg or two and made fun of his cravat. I sit here with my crap iced coffee, large sunglasses and trainers thinking how I've missed all of this and now I'm here like some drunk after the event, trying to recall a time when I lay on this grassy quadrant. Hungover, no doubt.

* * *

'Excuse me, is this the year one philosophy module?' I ask. A girl turns around to look at me. She seems to have been beamed in from the nineties in wide-leg denim and a tie-dye cropped T-shirt.

'Yeah,' she replies, giving me the once-over from tattoos down to trainers. I should have left my iced coffee for her. I know what she's thinking: *How nice! A mature student! They've let you in to combat some sort of thirty-something crisis. I'm younger than you. I'm better than you.* But yes, with more debt ahead of you and I have the better tits. I don't say that out loud. Groups of students stand around the lecture theatre waiting to go in and pangs of both pity and sadness dart through me. This feels like it should be me, starting this journey into university and the rest of my life. I bet I was a precocious sod, wasn't I? I would have strolled in here like I owned the place and put my feet up at the back.

I follow them all into the room and watch as they take their seats, turning off phones and scrambling around with laptops and bits of paper, that whiff of anticipation in the air. *I will take notes and then I'll take on the world with my new biros.* The girl I approached before catches my eye to see me not taking anything out of my bag. Yes, us mature bitches just take all that knowledge in without needing to write it down.

'Morning all. My name is Dr Jill Rigby... welcome to Identity, Mind and Free Will, and a new semester.'

Jill is dressed in wide-leg checked trousers and a black polo neck jumper, with glasses on the top of her head that she reaches up for occasionally to check that they're still there. She looks up and scans the room as the screen changes above her. When she sees me, she stops and smiles, shaking her head.

'So, first rules of my lectures, you listen, you write as much as you want, but no technology, no computers, no recording, no mobile phones. If you can't listen and absorb what I am trying to say then you shouldn't be here.'

I don't even have a pen out.

'What if you've done this course before and you're here for a second round?' I ask. Everyone looks at each other. *Someone asked a question. She didn't put her hand up first.* Don't ask permission to ask questions. That should be a life rule for you all.

'Then welcome back,' she says, looking at me. 'Just no heckling if you know the answers.'

She studies my eyes. There's a warmth and familiarity there but her face does not ring any bells bar the fact she looks a little like Rachel Weisz. Are you Rachel Weisz? The thing is, you're not. You're Jill and all I know is that I think you helped me realise that I am bisexual.

* * *

'Lucy bloody Callaghan,' Jill says after the last student has left the room. She comes over and embraces me tightly, a hand tenderly going to the top of my head.

'Everyone is obsessed by the loss of my hair,' I say.

'I was going to say it suited you. Not many people can carry that off.'

'Why, thank you. The low-maintenance thing is a winner.'

The hum of people behind the lecture theatre door makes her tidy all her sheets and books away from her desk, stuffing them into her bag. It was a successful lecture from what I could tell – the way the students were engrossed and no one seemed to fall asleep. I stayed to listen to how she spoke, how she moved across the room, the tiny ways she'd add inflections at the end of sentences to try and get a low murmur laugh out of the room, the way in which she obviously knew and cared about what she was saying. We were a couple, apparently, for a year when I was at university, and all of it was new, so very new to me at least, so she felt like an important person to meet in the flesh.

'We can chat outside, it's sunny. How does that sound?' she asks. I nod and follow her as we make our way outside the lecture theatre and through the winding corridors of the building, outside into the courtyard I was in before. As we queue for drinks from the outdoor coffee vendor who tainted my last order with hazelnut, she's quiet with me, I think a little awkward, but not in an Imogen the Fridge way. More that she's sad, that she doesn't know what to say.

'So you're a doctor now?' I ask her, trying to break the silence.

She nods.

'You weren't a doctor when we met?'

She shakes her head, smiling. 'When we met you were second year and I was doing my master's.' She bites her lip to relive the memory. 'You were kinda dating Tony.'

'You knew Tony?'

She laughs and gets her phone out of her bag to show me a photo. 'Tony was my best man at my wedding, you were there too? We got married round the corner from here and then had a reception on a boat. You and Tony did a Kate and Leo at the bow and had to be restrained for your own safety.'

I inspect a few photos on her phone where I have my mouth open in absolutely every one. We'll blame the excitement, the alcohol, but also the fact I am a fan of open water. I'm not wearing a bra either, which seemed to be a rule I lived by.

'I was at your wedding, even though we...?'

'Lucy, I love you dearly but we were never meant to be a couple. You never wanted that but it didn't mean we didn't stay friends. I think Tony helped in that respect. He became a common link between the two of us.'

'Your wife... she looks nice?'

'Amelia... she lectures in law. And...' She scrolls through her phone. 'These are our boys, Rafe and Xander.'

The family picture in front of me is drenched in happiness and I smile. I don't even know anyone on that phone but you can tell these people are exactly where they need to be.

'That's a beautiful family...'

'I'm so lucky,' she says, staring back at her phone.

'So, just to be frank and open... You were my first lesbian experience? Am I right?'

Jill blushes, looking around her before she answers.

'Sorry, I didn't mean to just come out with it like that...' I say, trying to backtrack.

'Well, you wouldn't be Lucy without the frank and open. Yes... I was your first. And in the interests of frank and open, I was the first person who ever gave you an orgasm through your G-spot...'

'Really?' I say. I don't look round, I don't care who hears that.

'That's what you said at the time. Unless you were lying, you cow bag, but you were always one to speak the truth...'

'I...I...' Jill seems surprised by my hesitancy. 'I'm confused with how and when this developed. You know my situation. Currently, I don't remember these feelings of being bisexual. I'm trying to get to grips of how and when...'

She roots in her handbag and offers me a sweet. 'Lucy, there is no handbook on this stuff, of how someone discovers their sexuality and who they are. It's a pretty private and ongoing process. When I met you, there was just a spark and you wanted to act on it in other ways than just being friends. I've been out since my late teens so I guess I held your hand and walked you through it...'

'And did it end badly?' I ask, worried I may have hurt someone who obviously cares for me in some way.

'No, not really. We were at different stages of where we were. I wanted a partner, a family, commitment and you wanted...'

'Something else?'

'You'd just discovered your G-spot so you were quite up for finding other people who'd explore that in greater depth too...'

She doesn't look hurt or disappointed that we never were but I feel an embrace from her, a feeling that we hold each other in some esteem, in some emotion.

'Can I say something?' She gestures.

I nod.

'You look so lost, Lucy. I don't know why but it's making me a little sad for some reason.'

'How so?' I enquire.

'The Lucy I knew was so sure of herself and where she was going in life. No one was going to tell you different. Your confidence was like this elixir, it was certainly what attracted me to you.'

I pause as she manages to analyse that so accurately within half an hour of just being in my presence.

'I'm still me. I'm just... you covered a lot of it in your lecture. I feel I've lost a sense of who I ever was: my identity, my mind... I can't seem to find it. I can't seem to work out how I got to being that person.'

She takes a large sip of her coffee and puts a hand into mine.

'It was all through the process of living the last ten years. You don't just grow as a person overnight. Maybe you need to give it time. You spent the last ten years learning, becoming. It's why you did so many degrees. You always just wanted to be better. A better actress, a better dancer, you were so driven.'

'Maybe that's what's missing... my drive. I remember having it at seventeen. I just can't seem to locate it at the moment...'

'Well, can I do anything? Is there anything you need?'

'I need my damn memory back, that's what I want. I want to be me: that Lucy who is supremely confident, who walks up to a man or woman, flirts mercilessly with them and has random liberating sexual encounters.'

'Have you not slept with anyone since...?'

'The accident... no. I saw Tony's penis in a pub though, don't judge.'

She laughs. 'I knew that already. The Lucy I knew wouldn't care for people's judgement though, she would never have said that at the end of a sentence.'

'I guess I'm just scared,' I say, my voice trailing off to admit that emotion out loud.

Jill looks over at me in disbelief at this person before her and I feel sheepish. Lucy Callaghan was never scared, of no person, thing or thought. People describe her to me and I picture her out and about dressed like some sort of female gladiator taking on the world. She was a force of nature. I don't feel like that very much at the moment. I feel like a low-level earthquake that flips over a few garden chairs, capable of a few tremors but little else.

'Tony's back in town next month. You should give him a call.'

'So we can have sex?' I say, horrified.

'So you can have sex with someone who'll look after you. Have you felt the need/desire since the accident?'

'I think I have. Tony helped. I've buttered my own bagel if you know what I mean?'

She chortles. That feels like a Lucy thing to say.

'You were always very sexually liberated. You were one of those people not tainted by fear or shame. You did and tried it all.'

'She sounds awesome.'

'She is awesome.'

And therein lies the problem. For the past few months I've kept looking to this other Lucy as another person, comparing myself to her constantly, thinking I need to live up to her, to become her. Maybe she's always been there.

'But maybe going out, having some fun, it won't help you remember but at least it'll help you to live in the present rather than reminiscing about a past you can't remember and you can't relive...'

When she says those words, my face blanches a bit with an emotion I can't quite describe. I think everything I've done up to this point has been an attempt to turn on the lights again, to find that girl I used to be. But maybe this is it. Maybe I need to accept I'll never find that house again, I need to build a new one, brick by bloody brick.

'So you're saying I need to get shagging?' I ask.

'You need to stop walking around this university thinking it'll bring it all back. Let me help?'

'With the shagging?'

'No, silly. But I'd love to help enrol you in a course here maybe. If you need to start from scratch.'

Start from scratch. Would that start here, again? Do I need to find another lesbian to help me rediscover my bisexual side? How does one find that? Tinder? Her eyes shift to the side to the young man I spotted before, reading Proust.

'He would have been your type, back at uni?' she tells me.

'Really, he looks a bit earnest.'

'You would have shagged that right out of him.'

I laugh and her face relaxes to see someone she remembers. The man in question may be older than his teens, some master's literature buff. The leather satchel is the redeeming feature, the badly fitting denim is dubious. If we were to hook up then I'd be mercilessly cruel about the cravat.

'How would I have approached him?'

'No nonsense. *This is me, if you don't like this shit then you're missing out*,' she says. I think she may be mimicking my accent. It's not terrible and, for a moment, I understand why I would have been attracted to her. She's pretty but it's cerebral, it's kind. I reach over and kiss her on the cheek.

'Thank you.'

'I'm not sleeping with you, Lucy.'

'No, for coffee, for explaining that time in my life to me.'

'We had a lot of fun. There's a saying that describes you to a tee. You lived your best life.'

'My sister said the same thing to me.'

'The sisters. God, you loved those girls, all those nieces. I'd never known anyone who loved their family so much, it made me slightly jealous.'

'I have nephews now too,' I reply, getting out photos from our jaunt to Kew Gardens.

'It was your best feature, how hard and ardently you loved those you cared for. I never felt anything less from you, even as a friend.'

She stops for a moment and finishes the last dregs of her coffee, then turns to her left.

'Hi, my name is Jill and this is my friend, Lucy, and I was just wondering if you were single?'

What the actual hell? I smile and wave as he gives me the once-over.

'I'm Pedro and yes, I am single.'

'Like Pedro the Pony,' I say.

'Who?' he asks.

'*Peppa Pig*. I have nieces. Peppa has a mate called Pedro.'

From Jill and Pedro's quizzical looks, it would seem this is not the angle I should have chosen to prove to this semi-good-looking man that I am cool and sophisticated.

'Only through art can we emerge from ourselves and know what another person sees,' I suddenly reel off.

Jill looks at me like my mind is having a small malfunction.

'Proust,' I say, pointing to his book. He looks impressed but it's most likely I can quote that as I once saw it in a hypnotherapist's office.

'I watch Peppa and I also read philosophy, it's a very dangerous combination,' I say with my most winning smile. He smiles back. 'Now tell me, Pedro. What brings you to Birkbeck? And let's talk about that cravat...'

17

I stare at the ceiling of a room in a student flat near Bloomsbury. Pedro is not big on interior décor. It turns out he's from Seville so makes do with a dresser that's falling apart, sheets that smell vaguely of oregano, brand-new shiny textbooks and an old birthday card that he's Blu-Tacked to the door of his wardrobe. I'll also be frank, he's big on pubic hair too. Christ, I was waiting for chicks to fly out but A* for effort and enthusiasm and asking me what I liked rather than just ploughing ahead. Would recommend, would come again, hopefully, will come before I leave. Pedro confirms his student status to me as he's now having a light nap while I count the cobwebs hanging in the corners of his room. I roll over and study the spines of his textbooks and examine the used condom strewn on the carpet. Why do they do that? Like, wrap it in something at least, right?

After introductions, Pedro became quite chatty telling us about his course, his part-time job working as a barista and blabbed some bullshit about Proust that I think he thought was smart. Jill observed the interaction and, as soon as he initiated some flirty contact by touching my knee, she got up and excused herself to go to a tutor group session. Before she left, she held me close and told me to be present. I shouldn't be retracing steps, I should be going down a newly forged path. Ones that involve random Spaniards.

Pedro snuffles lightly in his sleep and rolls over. There was a spark there for a brief moment when we got in through the front door and he whispered something Spanish in my ear, his breath warm on my neck. Did I enjoy that? It was less awkward than I thought I would be. I remembered how to put a condom on, which given everything I've forgotten feels like a skill worth noting. My recollections of my teen sex involved trying to work out what fitted where, like those baby wooden toys where you're getting the shapes to match up. This felt like more a dance with moves and rhythm that maybe my muscles still remembered in parts. I felt pleasure deep within me, which was a relief but also a release. It felt good. It felt like I still worked. Would do again. Maybe not with Pedro and the big bush because I feel I need to floss now and your dental hygiene shouldn't be the first thing you think about after having sex.

As I lie here, I think about how many times I may have done this, on a variety of beds with different people, and I won't lie, it actually arouses me. A lightbulb flickers away inside of me. Not to remember but to think what is now possible. Thanks, Jill.

I've not changed. I'm still a nosey bitch so instead of lying here I get up, put some knickers on and head to the kitchen. Pedro is not big on snacks and this is a reason why we would never have a future together. I pour myself a glass of water and sip it as I walk into the living room. Pedro does do plants though and throws, so many throws, like a true student. And books, many books, their spines bent back and withered. I sit down, boobs out, on a very uncomfortable sofa to take it all in. It's like a version of my house share without the charm, the nudists or the ladders. My eyes are suddenly drawn to a book on the shelf that seems to be a photo album so I sit on the edge of the sofa and run a finger down the spine to remove it from its place on the shelf. Pedro on his travels. He doesn't wear bad denim all the time, he wears short shorts and goes up mountains and likes a picturesque backdrop to show how he conquered those mountains. How does one do that with your pubic hair situation? He must chafe like hell. He also likes his photos of nature. Seriously, who takes this many pictures of trees unless they have some sort of bark fetish? Does he look back on these and go, *Oh, I remember that oak from that hill I climbed in Bologna. What a trunk.*

However, after a while, the pictures start to change and a young lady with brown curly hair and hazel eyes suddenly appears in the photos. They like a sunset and a selfie at dinner, these two. She is very present in all these photos to the point where I go to the bathroom and open a cupboard. That's women's moisturiser, that's women's shampoo for frizzy hair, that's a lady shaver. I go back to the bedroom and open a drawer. Pedro, there are women's undergarments in this drawer. You absolute helmet. I stand over the bed, wearing only my knickers, the photo album in hand and drop it with some force over his crotch. I don't worry too much because his pubes will absorb most of the force.

'Oooof...' he says in grunted Spanish tones. He observes me standing there, seemingly not too bothered about having my tits out in his room. 'Are you going?'

'I am.'

'I had fun, can I have your number?' he asks.

'Yeah, it's 0781... you-have-a-girl-friend...'

He looks down at the photo album and twigs why I may be a tad confrontational.

'Oh, we broke up.'

'Which is why her pants are still in the drawer. Unless they're yours but hell, I don't judge.'

He pats the space in the bed next to him, beckoning me to sit down. I don't move.

'They're not mine. They're...'

'Your girlfriend's.'

'Seriously... we've just broken up. She hasn't had time to move her things out. Please, stay...'

He continues to pat the bed like one would for a dog, encouraging them to jump up.

'You fell asleep and... you have a girlfriend...' I say, collecting my belongings from around the flat.

'I don't...'

But before he has the time to answer, a door opens and a voice rings through the flat.

'Pedro! Pedro? Are you here? My lecture got cancelled.'

You do. It's the look in his eyes that catches me first, they almost drain of colour, the whites of his eye glow, every sinew in him stiffens. He suddenly scrambles around in his bed, rearranging the sheets and throwing my bra at me. I catch it like a pro but the panic doesn't seem to flow through me as much. *Pedro, she's home! How are you going to get yourself out of this little pickle?*

'Please, put some clothes on...' he begs.

You see this scene in the movies quite a lot, don't you? The wife comes back early and the husband who has his secret lover in the bedroom has to make a mad scramble to put his dick away and hide said lover in a wardrobe or under the bed or push her out through some open window so she can scale down a drainpipe. They are scenes masked in shame and secrecy. But maybe this girl deserves better. I roll my T-shirt on very slowly and Pedro stands up to try and throw a sheet over my body like a toga. *How many other people have you shagged behind your girlfriend's back, Pedro?* He stuffs my coat in my bag and takes the used condom and places it in one of his coat pockets. *Mate. That's really grim. Use. A. Tissue.*

'I'm making tea! Do you want tea?' rings a voice from the kitchen. *I'll have tea if you're making.* I hear her talking to someone on the phone. We don't have a lot of time, Pedro... do we? He goes to the window of his room, which opens out into the street.

'Please... Please... I beg of you. Please, Lucy.'

'Did you not want my number then?'

'I will pay you to move quicker.'

'I believe that's called prostitution. I'm offended.'

'She will kill me, please... don't do this...'

'Do what?' I stare at him for a moment. You cad. How many times have you done this? In the actual bed you share with your girl? The girl you've shared all those moments and pictures with. How long will you keep doing this to her? All the way through university together? Through a marriage? After you have kids? This girl deserves better. I'm not leaving out of a fucking window. I put on my clothes, stuffing my bra in my bag, and barge past him, sauntering through the flat until I find the girlfriend in the kitchen, dunking teabags in and out of mugs, AirPods in, chatting to someone animatedly in Spanish. Pedro chases me down clumsily like he's escaping a hurricane. Mate, you have no idea.

'Hi! I'm Lucy...'

'*Disculpe, hay una chica aquí...*' she mumbles, looking at me curiously. Pedro appears at the door and smooths down his hair, hoping it might mask his damning guilt.

'Gabriella.' She even reaches out and shakes my hand.

'God, you're so beautiful. Pedro, you didn't tell me how beautiful she is...'

'Thank you...' she says. 'Who are you?'

'I met Pedro at the university.'

Pedro is a funny colour now. The sort of colour of raw chicken that's gone past its best before date. He's also sweating a great deal, droplets of sweat just forming in globules on his brow.

'Well, would you like tea?'

God, you're sweet too. I shake my head. The thing is I didn't want to cause a scene or leave a note anonymously. I needed to meet her first so I could look her in the eye and make sure she isn't too fragile or that the news would leave her in danger.

'This is my number, Gabriella,' I say, slipping my number to her on an old receipt I've found in my bag. 'I'd guess both of you are very new to London so do give me call if you need me.'

'Why would I need you?'

'Because I just slept with your boyfriend...' I say with steely eyes. 'He didn't tell me about you because I'd never have slept with him if I'd known you existed. I am so very sorry you are hearing this from me and not him. It gives me no joy to bring you pain but the way he tried to just push me out of a window makes me think, Gabriella, that you deserve better.'

I will not feel shame in this but I can at least make this better for her. Pedro looks like he might throw up. She stares at him and then back at me.

'For how long?'

'It lasted about twenty minutes.'

'No, I mean... I had my suspicions he was seeing another woman.'

'Oh, no... we just met.'

Pedro. You bloody whore of a man. Gabriella shakes her head and I hear a very angry Spanish voice projecting through her AirPods, which she places on her kitchen counter. There is then a barrage of Spanish words that my GCSE can't quite translate but I think I hear the words for pharmacy, sausage and the colour green.

'This was not your job to tell her...' he tells me angrily.

'No, it was yours, you lying piece of *mierda*!' she screams, storming out of the kitchen and into their bedroom. I stand there in the hallway peering through, still on nosey bitch mode, watching as she opens bags and stuffs them full of her belongings. Pedro cries on his knees, she tosses some Proust at him, right into his eye. Good for you, girl. She then starts chucking stuff out the window Pedro asked me to jump out of so I absent myself and go out into the street. I hope she throws him out by the scruff of his neck. I cross the road and watch as passers-by get sucked into the drama. That's a laptop, girl! I hope his thesis is on there and it's not backed up. Pants, socks and shoes follow and the shrieking sound of Spanish anger resounds down the street like the scene from a better film where a douche gets his comeuppance. My phone suddenly rings inside my bag. It's Beth.

'Hey, babe.'

'Hey. Where are you? Who's shouting?'

'A Spanish girl called Gabriella has found her fire.'

'Did you help her find that?'

'Naturally. She's just thrown a kettle out of the window.'

'Is it a good kettle?'

I watch as crockery starts breaking on the pavement like something out of a Greek wedding. I wish I understood Spanish a bit better.

'I slept with a Spaniard, B.'

'OK, someone's going out into the world again and having fun. That's good?'

'No. His girlfriend came home while I had my tits out in their bedroom.'

'Oh. Shit. Why are you still there?'

'Because. Drama. I kinda started it, I want to make sure she gets out all right. I'll leave if the police show up. He had a lot of pubes.'

'The Spaniard? More than me?'

'Enough to have donated pubes to at least two other men.'

'Why would you donate pubes?'

'For merkins, maybe.'

Beth is silent. Possibly wondering if I've hit my head again.

'Anyway, when you're done, go to Mum's. It's the reason I'm calling. I'm coming round.'

'OK, for dinner? You bringing the boys?'

'Nah... I just found something out and you need to know... Meg will be there too.'

The tone of Beth's voice changes and, for a moment, I stop looking across the road, at the builders heckling the scene from the scaffolding next door, at the old woman with a shopping trolley who seems to be stealing some of Pedro's stuff, at the people filming the drama on their phones.

'Everything OK, B?' I ask.

'Yeah. I don't want to say it on the phone.'

'Is it the boys? Will? Are you OK?'

'No. It's just... Oscar. You had that name Oscar on your phone. Oscar from the 9th of February. We've worked out who it is...'

18

Having sat in my fair share of doctor's surgeries of late, I really am not thrilled about sitting in another. This one is unnaturally sterile, from the plastic plants to the shiny leaflets, and staff in matching tops. All whiter than white. It feels like the sort of place where one would come to either get some fillers or an intimate wax. Instead, I'm here with two sisters who look abnormally anxious on my behalf.

'Stop shaking your leg,' Meg says, sitting next to me, clutching a hand around my knee.

'All right, Mum,' I grunt back.

I do like that look she gives me when I compare her to our mother. It's a look that gets me through the day. Beth cranes her head every time a door opens and closes. She was the one who put two and two together and got Oscar but she looks like she just wants answers, to find that missing jigsaw piece. Frankly, I'm disappointed that somewhere this posh doesn't have a hot beverages machine.

'Are you sure this is the place?' I ask, looking around. Since we've been here the lady in reception keeps smiling at me and then looking sad that I don't remember her. Because this place doesn't feel like a place I'd frequent. Although mildly ridiculous, the sex club I understand, the university also feels logical, but this is completely not where I thought I'd end up.

'The number of this place is on your phone. He's the only Oscar we can link you with,' Beth says.

'I really hope you're not having an affair with this man,' Meg says.

'Lucy wouldn't do that... not with everything Emma went through...' Beth says, defending me. She's my favourite sister now.

'Would I though?' I ask. 'Maybe he's got a giant schlong. You'd expect a doctor to know his way around.' Meg closes her eyes, hoping the receptionist didn't hear that. 'You two are too much. It could be a very simple explanation that we're in a book club together, or share an allotment... or run a multi-million-pound drugs ring.'

'What if he's your actual father and it turns out Mum had an affair with him thirty years ago?' Beth says.

Meg isn't playing into this and I'm disappointed that she lacks the imagination.

'No, the most likely reason is that you were probably having sex with an old man.'

'You sound jealous. B, do you have any sweets? You always have sweets,' I ask, sighing out loudly.

'That's because I'm the best sister.' She rifles around in her handbag and pulls out a family bag of Haribo. This is why we keep Beth. Meg's hand reaches over my body to steal some and I elbow her out of the way. She always seems to think she's entitled to the gummy cola bottles. A woman from across the way looks over at us curiously trying to figure out the dynamic of this sister sandwich, wishing we'd conduct ourselves with more decorum but working out why we don't quite match. I wish I knew. Like I wish I knew why I have a connection to a doctor at a high-end fertility clinic in London.

* * *

It started after I slept with the Spaniard and then unearthed his cheating to scenes of drama where the actual police did indeed show up, though not before Gabriella called herself an Uber and got the hell out of there. Beth rang and I walked through the streets of London and listened to how the sisters had done their best investigative journalism to find out that one of the numbers on my phone belonged to this fertility clinic, Vitro (which, knowing me, they thought was a nightclub). Further digging led them to discover one of the doctors here was called Dr Oscar Jacobs. Oscar. So he wasn't an old lover, an adversary, the name of a child whose party I once commandeered. No, it was the name of a fifty-something-old doctor who liked a lemon-yellow tie and whose beard looked like he'd borrowed it off a man of the mountains. The mystery had been unearthed and, frankly, it was slightly disappointing, to me at least.

To the other sisters though, it sparked some surprise. Lucy was interested in her fertility? Lucy avowed to us with much indignation that motherhood was not her thing. She liked her vagina, she wanted to preserve it for the future and not have it ruined by the spoils of childbirth. Why would she be here? Had she suddenly grown up and realised she wanted a future with more stability? With children? The only other reason Emma could think I might be connected to this place was because of STDs, while Grace reckoned it was because maybe a doctor had realised my vagina had broken some world record and he was analysing it now for research. This was unusually hilarious for Grace but they're both still cows. That said, we got in contact with the clinic and made an appointment. Let's get some confirmation about why Dr Oscar is pinned to my notes.

A door suddenly opens to the left and a couple leave, one crying, I think with joy, but the three of us sisters go quiet for a moment, trying hard not to stare as they make their way to the reception desk. They are followed out by someone I will assume to be Dr Jacobs as he looks exactly like his profile picture on his website. He looks around the room and grins widely to see me, putting his arms out in preparation for a hug. We hug? OK then. I stand up.

'LUCY!'

'DR JACOBS!' I reply as he wraps his arms around me. I guess he may have seen my vagina so I will afford him this level of intimacy but Beth and Meg look completely bemused by his warm reception of me. He stops hugging me to stand back and study me, looking at my head. I wish people would stop doing that. He's working out what to say next as his gaze bounces towards me and my sisters.

'You've brought company this time? Is everything all right?' he asks.

'Oh, these are my sisters, Beth and Meg. Do we know each other?'

He looks at Meg, wondering if this is some elaborate prank.

'I'd hope so with the number of times you've been in here? Seriously? Is everything OK?' There is concern there, which makes me less dubious about him.

'I was in an accident about two months ago and I'm having problems recollecting events.'

His expression drops for a moment and he ushers us into his office, away from the gaze of others.

'You were? Lucy!' he says with some shock, closing the door. 'It explains the new look. What happened?'

'I tried to take on a bus. And lost,' I say, as we all enter the room and take our places on a long white leather sofa.

His shoulders slump for a moment and he looks me up and down in what I hope is not a sexual way. Dear god, I hope the familiarity here is not from the fact we slept together. You're lovely but you're old.

'So retrograde amnesia?' he asks.

'Possibly dissociative...' Meg intervenes. 'The psychologists can't decide at the moment.'

'So you have no idea who I am or what this place is?' he asks.

'I know you're a doctor and this is a fertility clinic but basically...' I get out my phone and scroll down to the note where his name is pinned with the date. 'This was on my phone so obviously quite important. Maybe it was an appointment? Have I done a party for your kids maybe? But you said I'm here a lot. Did I work here? Was it because of something else?'

'Was she ill?' Beth asks.

He pulls a chair over to the sofa, looks over the top of his glasses to read the note on my phone but then smiles broadly.

'You have no record of your time here?' he asks.

'The one thing we learnt with Lucy is that she does not have much of a paper filing system,' Meg contributes. 'Her inbox was like a car crash too.' She's not half wrong. When we tried to look through my emails, there were 6,475 unread, the majority of which seemed to be confirmation of password changes and Boohoo discount codes.

'Then this might be a bit of a revelation...' He wanders over to some bookshelves in the corner of his office and retrieves a file that looks like a catalogue of sorts. He runs his fingers down the dividers and page numbers and then brings it over to us. All three of us sit here waiting, wondering, part of me hoping that this is a very complicated coffee menu. He sits down and turns the folder around. It's a picture of my face. *Lucy, 29, BA in Drama Studies and English Literature, MA in Philosophy in Literature, DipEd in Dance Psychotherapy, blonde hair, blue eyes, 5'11.*

'What sort of clinic is this?' Meg questions, slightly worried as this seems to be a catalogue of women, and all our minds jump to the wrong conclusions. Do they farm women? Christ, was I an escort? Is this a ruse for something?

'Lucy was an egg donor.'

Meg and Beth go deathly quiet at the reveal. I won't lie, it takes me a moment to process that as my mind just goes to the kind of eggs one can eat with bacon and I picture myself here donating them to the good doctor for his breakfast. I hope I carried them in a wicker basket. Eggs?

'She was one of our more popular donors too. I mean, you're very attractive and well-educated and your profile always appeals to our many couples looking for donor eggs so they can start families of their own.'

Meg can't seem to speak. Lucy did good things too? The same Lucy who does drinking and jokes and cartwheels at inopportune moments without knickers on?

'How many times has she done this?' Beth asks.

He scans over some records. 'Twice.'

'But she's Lucy, she occasionally smokes and drinks like a fish. How would she have been suitable?' Meg mumbles.

'But...' Beth says, working it out. 'She was fit and active too. Remember she used to go on those months of health kicks and diets. She'd tell us she was detoxing her body.'

'She was an ideal candidate,' Dr Jacobs explains. 'I apologise, this is a lot to perhaps get to grips with...'

We all sit back in the sofa to absorb the information. 'Did I ever say why...?' I ask the doctor.

'Well, without sounding crass, it paid well so I think that was attractive to you but you also once told me you never wanted children of your own so you didn't want all these good genes to go to waste. You were always very amusing, Lucy, but I did get the sense that behind the financial rewards you wanted to do a good thing.'

Beth starts to tear up now at the thought of it all, this secret altruist who used to harvest her organs to pay her rent but also leave some sort of legacy in the world. It brings a smile to my face to know that next to that all-singing, all-dancing and all-swearing Lucy, there was at least a part of me that was trying to do something decent. Meg's brow tells me different though.

'I just can't get my head round this... the ethics...'

'Lucy was very relaxed about it all. She was offered counselling as a donor and she understood her rights and those of the parents. She was always very popular in the clinic, very chatty. I think we knew everything about you, more than a normal doctor should. You had a cat with an amusing name...'

'Pussy?'

'That was it. You used to show us pictures and ones of all your family. You persuaded my receptionist, Janine, to leave her husband.'

That's why she was smiling at me. It's quite an image to think of me with my legs akimbo chatting to Janine about her shit husband and how she could do so much better in life. But then again, it's not a surprise.

'I could never quite tell if you came in here all chatty to mask your worry about the procedures or if it was just what you were like,' Dr Jacobs continues.

'No, it's all her,' Meg adds.

He smiles, telling me he'd already thought as much. 'Look, I can send you away with all the literature and forms you signed, just to verify it. Maybe if the circumstances have changed, we can also review those documents,' the doctor says calmly.

'No, it's OK. It's just another thing new to process,' I reply. 'So you just scooped the eggs out? Like frogspawn?'

Dr Jacobs laughs. 'To a point.'

'And now there's a whole jar of them stored in a fridge somewhere?'

'Yes, Lucy. In ice cube trays.'

'Really?'

'No.'

This does make Beth and Meg laugh for which I'm glad as it breaks this strange tension in the room.

'So, we know why you're pinned on my notes then. This date, 9th February. Was it an appointment I had then?' I ask.

He pauses for a moment, wondering whether to divulge. Given that he's obviously had me in stirrups and foraged my eggs out of me, I don't think there are any more secrets we can keep from each other. He goes over to a desk drawer and rifles through it, before he pulls out a card and brings it over.

Oscar Avery, 7lbs 12oz, born 9th February 2022

A picture of a baby wrapped up like the most edible wrap sandwich you could imagine lies next to the words, his eyes closed, hand tucked under his cheek. He looks familiar.

'A lot of egg donation is anonymous. You find out about the donor and then that's it, but the Avery family wanted to know you more and asked for contact. Mum asked us to send on certain details with her thanks.'

'And they named their baby after the doctor who helped them get pregnant,' Beth concludes, tears rolling down her face. 'Lucy, that's your baby.'

'But it isn't...' I mumble. 'I helped to do this?'

Dr Jacobs nods and I laugh, in shock, in wonder. That's a baby, a real-life baby. He's so cute it hurts my bloody eyes.

'Oh, Lucy...' Meg says, holding tightly onto my arm.

Are they proud of me, finally? Look at me doing big girl things when you guys weren't looking.

'Though come on, right, is he not the most handsome little bubba you've ever seen?' Beth smiles through her tears while Meg studies my face as I take it all in. Does she see the glow? Because this really does make my heart hurt with joy. I helped a family make a baby. While I was trying to take on the world, I did something good in these last ten years, I tried to do something good, for balance.

'How many other of Lucy's eggs have been turned into babies?' Meg asks, making it sound as if they've been grown from the ground like the cutest of potatoes. She has a point though. Is the doctor going to bring out a catalogue of babies that I've enabled? Are they on every continent?

'Three, Oscar being one of them.'

My eyes widen for a moment. 'So I'm basically building an army.'

'Of sorts. You used to joke and call them your minions.'

'That's quite a scary thought, Lucy. Three little babies out there running around just like you. God help the world,' Meg mutters.

I pause for a moment. The enormity of the situation, the consequences, feels huge but it's countered by the fact that out there, a couple – a few couples – got to start a family, have a baby. I don't care if they inherit none of me but just to have let them borrow my biology feels good.

'Are you OK, hun?' asks Beth as I sit there staring at the baby picture in my hands.

'Do you think I can meet him?' I ask Dr Jacobs. Meg and Beth look at each other anxiously. 'I know the boundaries, I'm just curious.'

'I can certainly ask. I'm glad you're OK, Lucy,' he says, putting his hand in mine.

'Oscar. That's a good name.'

And for a moment, my mind wanders to this baby of mine, who isn't really mine at all. And I'm holding him and kissing him on the forehead before I hand him over. *Hey, kid. Go take on the world and have a shitload of fun. Ask all the questions, drink all the drink, laugh and love so very hard but only the right people because there are a lot of douches out there. You don't belong to me in any shape or form but, by god, you are real and you are destined for greatness.* Oscar. That's a really really good name.

'Lucy... Lucy?'

And as my mind wanders, something weird starts happening. It's strange because I can feel Dr Jacobs' hand in mine but I can't. Why can't I bend my fingers? Grab his hand, come on, Luce. His hand is right there. I look down at my hand but it doesn't seem to be mine. I open my mouth to speak and can't make the sound come out, my jaw feels loose, numb. Come on, Luce. Speak. But the feeling extends to my right eye, to my neck. Fuck. Breathe, Lucy. Tell them you can't feel anything.

I can hear Meg screaming as my body collapses into itself. *Get out into reception and tell them we need an ambulance here, immediately.* Beth scrambles out of the room, her handbag dropping to the floor and its contents tumbling out. Sweets everywhere. Don't waste the sweets. *Lucy? What's wrong? I think she's having a stroke of some description. Lucy! Don't you dare, come on. I'm here. It's me, Meg. I'm here.* I feel her hands gripped around me, her breath to my cheek. *Doctor, please. I don't know what to do. We need to lie her down.* There's a sharp pain to my head, an excruciating pain, and my body suddenly loses control of itself. *I think she's having a seizure. Control her neck. LUCY! CAN YOU HEAR ME?* I want to say yes, so very loudly. I want to scream it. I'm here. I've always been here.

19

My head feels like someone is sitting on it. The last time I felt like this was in Ibiza. I had one of those nights where I ended up in a bar in a wrestling ring, wearing a bikini. There was a sea of foam involved, The Weeknd in the background, a Viking hat and an inflatable palm tree that I'd stolen from the garden of someone's villa. I wrestled a very skinny lad from Sunderland who tried to sit on my actual head so I flipped him over, trapped his bony arse in a body scissors move and it took four grown men to pull me off him. I won a voucher for a free seafood dinner that evening, and a medal that I lost in the sea.

Hold up.

Ibiza.

2015.

I was supposed to be on a yoga retreat. That didn't last long. I stole the goat. I went into town and just checked myself into a hotel, partied and drank and joined a hen party. Laura from Wigan was marrying Jamie. Don't tell Jamie but Laura had a bloody amazing send-off. We really did pay tribute to her single life for one last time. One morning at that hotel, I went to the breakfast buffet and threw up in a serving dish full of French toast. *I remember.* Lucy remembers little details like these for posterity but also for the anecdotes. *She remembers.* I really do bloody remember. I'd jump up and do a jig if my head didn't hurt this much.

'Mum,' I whisper.

It's the unmistakeable silhouette of Mum's bob haircut that I see first and she drops whatever she's reading onto the bed in shock.

'Lucy?' she whispers.

'Yeah. That's me.'

She grabs my hand tightly and kisses me on the forehead. 'I need to get someone, wait...'

'No, don't. Just stay here for a moment.'

It's normally quite difficult to get my mum to do what I say but she stays, the grip on my hand tight. I feel it all but, compared to last time, my brain feels like it's been picked up and shaken around like a snow globe, the flakes settling.

'What happened?' I ask.

'There was a blood clot, they went in and removed it but it explained a lot, it was hidden, pressing against lobes or something. Emma can explain it better than me but it was why your memory had gone. It was just bloody lucky you were in a doctor's office when it happened.'

The memory floods back to me, the blurred vision of my Meg and Dr Jacobs over me, and it's welcome, not to relive it but to actually have a memory, to have it and be able to put the pieces all together again, not have them scattered about and not fitting together. A tear rolls down the curve of my cheek and my mum scoops it up with her finger.

'Do you know who I am?'

'You're Meg.'

She stops for a moment then smiles. 'How old are you?'

'Thirty, fucking thirty. How did that happen?'

She sighs with relief, her breath trembling.

'Have I been asleep for long?' I ask.

'It's now 2031.'

'Really?'

'Not really.'

'That's not funny.'

'You said I was Meg.'

'Because that was funny.'

She does a very Mum thing of patting down the bed, studying all the monitors around my bed like she knows what all the readings mean.

'Would you have sat there then for ten years, waiting for me to wake up?' I ask, attempting to calm her down.

'I'd have stopped for occasional toilet breaks. I don't think you'd have appreciated me peeing in a bucket in the corner of the room. But yes. I'd have been here every day.'

We pause for a moment to take that in.

'You've been asleep for about twelve hours. They explained what they did to your head and your dad threw up so they've taken him home. The sisters are doing shifts.'

I reach up to feel bandages, wires still flow out of every arm. They put that one up my pisser again, didn't they?

'Did the sisters all come back to London?' I ask, slightly annoyed that I'd have disrupted their routines again.

'Of course, they're all crashing in various houses. I met Max, Grace's new boyfriend.'

'Thoughts?'

'He's pleasant. Possibly trying too hard to impress me because he's scared of me. Also, so much hair.'

I smile. 'Talking of hair... Did they shave my head again?'

'Yes.'

'Hair grows.'

'That it does.'

Mum can't seem to find the words but stands there just as I've asked her to do. It's a version of Mum I've not seen before and it's slightly unnerving. I can't tell if her stoicism is strength or fear.

'Talk, Mum. You're scaring me.'

'*I'm* scaring *you*...'

'Do I look awful?'

'Yes. Not as bad as when that bus hit you, mind...' Her hand reaches to my mine. I remember this hand. 'You have more lives than a cat, Lucy Callaghan...'

'Where is my cat by the way?'

'In my house. Her new favourite thing is to sleep on the toilet and then attack anyone who goes near it. I had to pee in a shower tray the other day.'

I try and laugh but even that hurts.

'What's my cat's name? I don't remember.'

She looks mildly perturbed. 'Your cat is called Pussy.'

'Oh yeah, I knew that. I just wanted to hear you say that word out loud.'

She laughs and shakes her head at me. I take a few deep breaths as the pain in my head starts to throb. I want to say it's bad but I can liken it to a couple of insane hangovers I've once had.

'Can I get someone now?'

I shake my head. 'I quite like having you to myself. That rarely happens.'

She perches herself on the edge of the bed. 'Are you in pain?'

'Pain is relative. It was far more painful living without my memory for a bit. You replacing all my knickers. Or sharing a bathroom with four sisters again.'

'I forgot how much shower gel you get through. Can I at least tell your sisters you're up?'

'Wait, just a few more moments.'

She studies the edges of my face, hands gripped around the steel railings of my bed. When I was in my first coma, Mum would spend weekends here camping out in the Premier Inn next door. Dad said she'd hardly slept, she'd just wander here in the night and read to me. My Lucy loved reading, she told the nurses, so she'd sift through the classics and read them to me, stopping occasionally for vending machine tea. We all have different versions of Mum in our head, she's our fiercest critic and our loudest cheerleader, but I suppose we all love so hard because of her.

'I guess you know why I was in a doctor's office then,' I ask her.

'Your sisters did say. They tried to cover it up but I got the truth out of them. If you needed the money, you could have come to me or your father, Emma?'

'It was more than that, Mum. I just wanted to put something out into the world that had meaning. It can't always be about me even though I'd like it to be.'

She smiles. I was expecting more of a bollocking there but she seems to be holding back. It'll possibly come later as not even she is so callous to give it to me both barrels when I'm in a paper dress.

'Tell me what you remember,' she says.

'God, everything. It's like a librarian has been in and helped me restock my brain but fuzzy memories of who I've seen and who showed up in the last few months.'

'You saw Tony,' Mum reminds me.

'You have a thing for Tony.'

'Because I think he's one of the few men I've met who is your equal, Lucy, who understands your value. No one else really comes close.' She puts a hand to my face, tears forming in her eyes.

'You can cry if you want, Mum. I will allow for a public show of emotion here. I nearly died. Twice.'

'But you didn't,' she replies a little smugly. 'And I never really had any doubt.'

'Because of your secret medical degree?'

'Because you're made of sterner stuff, Lucy.'

'That's all you.'

'Well, that's stating the bleeding obvious,' she says, laughing.

'Mum?'

'Yes, Lucy...'

'What do you think about my last ten years? What I've done with my life?'

Hello, existential Lucy who has never really shown her face before this. I don't think I ever sat still long enough to consider these questions. I just did what was in my gut and what felt right and time ticked along without me ever gazing at my watch in doubt or regret. Mum looks out the window for a minute, at a sliver of sky visible through closed blinds.

'Lucy. I remember when I held you in my hands for the first time. You were so close in age to Grace and I just remembered, this mass of curls, and thinking, a fifth daughter. How the hell are we going to do this?'

'I was a mistake, wasn't I?'

'A happy accident.'

'A mistake. But well done for letting Dad hop on when Grace was only three months old.'

She ignores that last comment, which is standard Mum.

'But there's always a moment when you're holding a baby and you're studying its little face and these miniature little hands and you just wonder about the path, where they're going to go, what they're going to do.'

'Did you think I'd end up on this path?'

'No. But then did I think Emma would be divorced? That Grace would be a widow? I never thought that either. I didn't think I'd end up with all these grandchildren.'

'You're avoiding the question.'

'Your path is unfamiliar to me, Lucy, so I can't comment. I

never thought I'd end up with five daughters either. There is no wrong or right path. It is a bemusement to me though that your path seems to be laden in troublemaking and pictures of penises.'

'They are funny though, aren't they? The penises.'

'You youth just have too much time on your hands. Back in my day, if you wanted to send a girl a picture of your penis then you had to set the timer on your camera, take the film down to Snappy Snaps and then probably be banned from that branch.'

I laugh. 'Spoken like someone with experience. Did Dad make albums for you?'

She shakes her head at me.

'Seeing as I've been at death's door though and we're alone, then why are you sometimes the critic, the judge? I never quite know what you think of me. I don't think any of the sisters truly know...'

She smiles. 'Lucy... All you girls are my proudest moment. But you're my force of nature, my whirlwind baby. You're not on a path, you're raging through fields and you let people know you're in the room. I've given up trying to understand it but I like your energy. I've always liked that. Any criticism of that always comes from a place of love.'

'Of honesty?'

'Maybe of trying to protect you all from the bad. Your dad describes it like this. He always says I spend far too much time getting in the way of you and your sisters. The truth is, I hate seeing any of you hurt or upset. It lights a fire in me. When it comes down to it, I'd jump in front of moving traffic for my girls.'

'A fitting analogy.'

'Apologies. But he's right. I wished it were me who got run over and not you. I'd do that a million times over.'

I pause for a moment to hear the emotion in her voice.

'If a bus hit you a million times over then you'd certainly be dead, Mum.'

She doesn't see the humour in my retort.

'So please don't do that. I quite like you, Mum.'

'Quite?'

'Yes.'

She narrows her eyes at me as I cough and she encourages me to sit up in bed.

'Are you OK?'

'I'm bloody starving.'

'What do you want to eat?'

'Toast. And tea.'

'I'll see what I can do. What sort of tea?'

'Builder's brew. Sugar please.'

'Strong as tits?' she asks.

I nod, smiling.

'Good. I'm going to get the doctor now.'

'If it's the same doctors from last time, can you get the one who's reasonably good-looking? Not the one with the comb-over,' I say.

'She feels better, doesn't she?'

'She's getting there. Tea would help. The service is so slow in this place.'

'Oh, piss off, Lucy.'

20

'OH MY GOD, LUCE,' Cass says as she throws her body over mine. Darren stands there with his face in his hands. You're crying, aren't you, mate?

It's been an afternoon of it, people filtering in and out of this room with grapes, flowers and bento, sheer relief on their faces to know I'm both alive and also back in the room. Everyone from parents to sisters, to teeny tiny nephews and nieces who enjoyed playing with the controls on my bed and nearly folding my body in half. But the love is real, all these people, and the best thing is knowing who they are, how they fit, how they belong in my life.

'I think it was the shock of knowing you two got together... What the actual hell, guys?' I mumble.

Darren looks almost effervescent with joy to have his old Lucy back. 'It works. And essentially, it was all because of you.'

'Then I'd better be a best man or something, name a child after me.'

'Deal. So what do you remember now after the accident?' Cass asks.

'Oh, all of it, it's a very strange feeling. Thank you though for sticking with me when my mind was being an absent bitch.'

'Well, you owe me thirty quid so I have vested interests,' Darren says.

I laugh and hold both of their hands as they stand either side of my bed.

'I can't believe you took me to Velvet Boulevard on my birthday though? You literally took me to my workplace.'

'We didn't know what to do. It was that or Heaven and we didn't think you were ready for a gay nightclub. We've told all the gang down there you're OK.'

I smile. That's the biggest relief of all maybe. To not have to start again but slide into old routines, to go to auditions, do the odd work shift and shag the odd random. It wasn't a perfect or orthodox life but it was mine and it made me happy, so much of it made me happy, and if I could speak to my seventeen-year-old self who thought this didn't carry value or that it was time wasted then I'd tell her to rethink all of that doubt. Life isn't a straight clear path, it should never be, and I've enjoyed my last twelve years being a complete rollercoaster.

'So what now, Wonder Woman?' Darren asks.

'More physio, rehab and then back into the world. I'll have to buy a new Elsa dress, grow the hair out, I'll make it work.'

'You always do,' Darren says. 'And when you've made it work, we've all got a date in a field, yeah? We're going to call it Lucy's Comeback Fest. I'll even make the T-shirts without complaint.'

I hug him warmly. I might even get them from Marks & Spencer.

There's suddenly a knock on the door and I turn my head to see an unexpected visitor. *You? Really?* How far and wide has news travelled of me being back in hospital? My eyes go to Darren, who studies the visitor at my door.

'Cass, maybe you and I should grab a coffee or something?'

Piss off, that was not what that eye signal meant, which makes me wonder what sort of friend he really is. Grace would have read that in a heartbeat.

'Guys, this is Josh Reid. I knew him from school.' I attempt to sound as deadbeat as I can to show that his presence here is not welcome but instead they all shake hands. 'These are my mates, Darren and Cass.' Josh's eyes scan down to Cass's boobs and, immediately, I'm hoping Darren might smack him.

'I can go if it's not a good time?' Josh says.

Please go, jump in the river.

'Oh no!' Darren exclaims. 'We'll let you guys catch up,' he says, winking at me. Really? No. Don't leave me with this wankpuffin. They exit the room, leaving Josh standing there with another supermarket bunch of flowers, pretty much wearing the same outfit as last time. I really hope he's changed and showered in that time.

'Hi.' That's his opener.

'Hi, come in?' I ask. Rather than stand there with your crappy flowers. He comes over to the bed and sits on a chair next to me.

'You're the last person I expected to see here,' I tell him, quite bluntly.

'Oh, well... it was on social media. Farah from school, your mate – she put it there and then a mate told me and, yeah, I thought I'd come and see how you were...'

'Apart from the hole in my head, it's all good.'

He laughs at that despite it not being particularly funny.

'Are none of your family here?' he asks, obviously not keen to bump into the likes of Emma or my mother again.

'They don't keep vigil constantly. I allow them to eat occasionally. I think Beth is downstairs.'

'Oh, that's good.'

I wish they were here so they could help me beat you up. The last memory I had of Josh was in my bedroom at my family home and I felt completely powerless, still overcome by all that emotion I felt for him as a seventeen-year-old. Even when I found out the truth of what happened to us as kids, it was heart-breaking, a complete revelation. Now, I have all that informa-tion, all that power. I know what happened in that nightclub and how, essentially, he was a bit of a lad getting his leg over with other girls, damn the consequences to other people and their teenage hearts. As a thirty-year-old, I barely give him a second thought.

'Glad you got through the second op all right,' he says, putting the flowers down on my bedside table.

'Yeah, lucky that...'

'You'll need to grow your hair out again.'

'Yep.'

'Not that your hair looks bad...'

We sit there in silence for a moment, like he's a young man come to visit a great-aunt he doesn't quite know.

'Sorry, Josh, why are you here?' I ask, trying not to draw this out.

'I just wanted to see you.'

'So this is for your benefit, to make you feel better about your life?'

You can tell that turning this on him is confusing and, I'll be frank, I like that.

'I came because I wanted to... I don't know how to say this...'

He looks all around the room, the eye contact is poor, the delivery worse. Spit it out, boy.

'When you showed up again in my life, it just got me thinking about stuff, about the direction my life has gone in and my relationship, my marriage. There was a time I really loved you. I was an idiot for what I did at the time and how I treated you. And...'

Holy crapballs.

'I think part of me wonders if you are the love of my life. I think I'm still in love with you.'

The actual holiest of crapballs.

'Josh?'

'Yeah?'

'No?'

His face falls somewhere between crestfallen and insulted. I've just done something super romantic, right? That's what all girls want. To hear that they're loved, validated and someone wants them? No?

'What are you doing?' I ask him.

'I'm telling you how I feel. I'm just being honest.'

'You don't love me...'

'Well, isn't that up to me and how I feel?'

'So you want to have sex with me?'

'Well, I...'

'You said you wanted to be honest.'

'I guess... You're really fit.'

'That's not love, Josh.'

'Nah, I mean... I think it all means something. Why did you think *I* was still your boyfriend when you woke up? You forgot everything else? Why did you think about me? Maybe it's a sign.'

'It's a sign I had a complete brain scramble. You are married with kids, don't do this.'

'But—'

'But what, you want to shag? Or have an affair? Or leave your wife and start a life with me, see your boys every other weekend? Yeah, I'm not the girl you're looking for if that's what you want.'

'You don't think we were in love back then? The more I think about it, it was the most in love I've ever been...'

Really? More than with your wife, the mother of your children, your own sons? What an awful thing to say. If I could,

I'd drop kick him out of this window. He stands up, almost asking me to throw him a bone. And that's when a memory comes flooding back to me. We're standing outside some toilets...

'Don't go to university, Lucy. Please...' he begs.

'But it's London. It's literally just down the road. It's not like I'm going to Glasgow. You can visit whenever you want?' I answer.

'Don't you love me?'

'I do. Of course, you know that.'

'Then stay. You can do all sorts of distance courses these days. I've looked some up for you.'

'Where has this all come from? Why don't you want me to go?' I try and hold his hand but he won't let me near it.

'Because you'll meet people, guys, other blokes, I've heard what goes on at university.'

I smile. I know what goes on at university because of my sisters and it sounds brilliant.

'You must not love me as much then,' he states callously.

'Josh. Are you asking me not to go to university or are you telling me?'

'I'm not doing anything. I love you.'

'This isn't love.'

'Well, piss off then.'

'I want to do something with my life, Josh.'

'That doesn't include me. You think you're better than me? Smarter than me?'

'I've never said that.'

'Seriously, go to university, live your life. Fucking selfish is what it is. Fuck off.'

'No, YOU FUCK OFF.'

Josh keeps looking at me as I play that moment in my head. Tears rolled down my eyes that evening to be called selfish from someone I loved, on the day I got my A-Level results, my birthday, on a day that was supposed to be about celebration, he shat all over it. That's not love.

'It was first love maybe. It was very pure and untainted by real life but you know what, Josh?'

I let him come in a little closer to hear.

'I'm really bloody glad we didn't end up together.'

He immediately looks insulted. Good.

'Your love was dependent on me staying, me being close, it was built on conditions and stopping me from living my life, from growing. What an awful way to love someone.'

'I was young.'

'It was vindictive, even then. And after we rowed, you went and hooked up with Chloe Hilton in the loos at Oceana. Farah saw it. You didn't even lock the door, that's so rough.'

He doesn't even try and apologise for that.

'Well, yeah but we all do stupid stuff when we're young. It wouldn't be like that now...'

'It *won't* be like that now? Are you on drugs?'

'I can't stop thinking about you.'

'Then read a sodding book... you're doing it again! So you feel something and I have to react. This is how I'm reacting...' I squeal, my face contorted in disgust, like I've just trodden in something I shouldn't have.

'Then this is how you're gonna be – alone and single at thirty?' he retorts, thinking for one second that I may be scared of that prospect.

'I'm not alone though, am I? I'm surrounded by love and friendship and people who really care, who've been there this last decade and held me close and have never let go, despite me. You think I want to be defined by you swanning in here telling me you'll have me and make me less alone? Fuck off. I'd rather sit on a cactus than have your knob near me again.'

'Whatever. Look, I'm just telling you how I feel.'

'Next time, write it down. On a Post-it note and shove it up your arse.'

He grabs his flowers and storms out. I hope he saves those flowers for the grave he'll have to dig when I tell his wife what he's been up to. I punch at a spare bit of mattress beside me. That hurt. At the doorway, two heads suddenly appear, Beth and Meg, wondering if it's safe to enter.

'Did you see who that was? Did you hear what he said? Go and chase him down, Meggers, and trap his dick in the lift door. Go!'

Meg stands her ground. They slowly enter the room, both with wide grins on their faces.

'That's not funny. What an utter wet wipe, thinking he can come in here and sweep me off my feet, like I'm some girl that needs saving, that needs to be told clichéd tripe like that.'

'Luce, calm down. Your blood pressure, babe,' Beth says, coming to sit down next to me. She takes my hand in hers and tries to stroke out the clawed nature of my fingers.

'Correct me if I'm wrong but didn't I get punched by Chloe Hilton that night?' Meg asks.

'You did. You took one for the team,' I tell her. 'And Beth also jumped on in there and slapped her so hard her chicken fillets fell out of her bra.'

Meg stares into the distance to relive that memory, the sisters in full flight, it was a beautiful thing, like geese flying in formation towards the sun.

'I was so drunk, I have zero recollection of that night. Did Josh really come in here confessing his undying love to you?' Beth asks curiously.

'Yes. I am fuming.'

Meg sniggers a little to hear it.

A lesser girl, poorly and broken, would have relented but not me. *Wow, you love me? Even when I'm broken, bald and at my lowest ebb? You'll still have me?* Seriously, eff off as far away from me as humanly possible. Because I'm not nearly done. I am not broken. I'm going to get Igor back in here and I'm going to work my arse off and find someone who'll sort out my hair and there's going to be a comeback, bitches.

'You may have just broken his heart though?' Beth mentions.

'And? Just a shame it couldn't have been his face. That, what he was going on about, is not love. What's in this room... this is love. This is what's kept me alive and looked out for me all those years. He's not part of this story, he's not even a side note. He's a typo, a mistake.'

Meg and Beth look at each other and smile. I like a rant, it's cathartic and I think it's the reason I have such good skin as I get all my bad energy out into the world rather than let it fester in my body, but there was something in there for these sisters that is all true.

'Who am I in your story then?' Meg asks.

'You're a novel, babes. You'd all get your own novels. Main characters for sure, starring roles. I'd change your mumsy jeans and have you in better outfits though.'

'Bitch.'

'And that is love...'

21

'And that is good, Lucy. I am impressed.'

My hands release the clamps and I put them down on the table Igor scribbles some notes on a clipboard.

'Are you writing that I'm your best patient?' I mutter, craning my head over to see his notes.

'No,' he tells me bluntly. 'My best patient is a sixty-three-year-old woman called Norah who's just had a new hip and makes me muffins...'

'I have muffins.'

'Not like Norah. Unless you were being sexual, which, in that case, you can put your muffins away. In fact, if you wanted to know what I was writing, I actually wrote that you're less of a whiny cow at thirty.'

'Thank you,' I say, feigning gratitude. 'We'll blame my late teenage hormones for that version of Lucy.'

A smile, I think I got a smile. I'm breaking you, Igor, and it's fun.

'Your sister tells me you were a dancer, you were into your fitness before all of this happened.'

'Yeah, the job kinda dictated it.'

'Well, once you're discharged here then I want you to take things very slowly. Low impact to start, any pains and niggles, then you ring me.' He hands me a business card.

'Are you giving me your number, Igor?' I say, my hand to my chest, acting flattered.

'Yes, I am. Because it's my medical duty and my wife and your sister are very good friends.'

'You're married?' I ask him, slightly stunned. That's a woman of some strength and stomach who would be into that hair.

'I am married. I even have kids. You missed out there.'

'Plenty of fish, Igor. I am sure I can find another merchant of torture elsewhere.'

'I doubt it. In any case, your sister has pre-booked appointments with you for the next three months so I am not rid of you yet.'

Igor, there were times when I actually hated you and wished many unkind things but you, sir, had much conversational wit at least.

'Don't get hit by any more buses, Miss Lucy. I will be in touch.'

He puts his notes back in his bag, shakes my hand and carries a kit bag out of the room while I sit on the edge of the bed and rotate my ankles.

'Good toes,' I say, straightening them like pokers, bad toes, flexing them at right angles. Low impact, my arse. I have a ballet session booked in a few days and I'm dying to get back to it but, hell, what Igor doesn't know won't hurt him.

It's been two weeks since I woke up and it's been days of lying in this room, staring at the walls, hearing the faint bleeps and alarms from medical machinery nearby, scoffing down sandwiches and sushi that my family have sneaked in for me, and entertaining a selection of people who've come to be by my bedside. Tony rocked up with Jill, the sisters, a few nieces, Kyle from Velvet Boulevard brought cake (purchased from outside the club) and Dad has moments when he sits here and reads in perfect silence, falling asleep with a book at his chest, and I watch, wait and make loud noises to wake and scare him.

Recovery will be a journey but today I'm being sent home, to Mum and Dad's, to start before I go back to the shared house. Mum is ecstatic this begins the countdown to Pussy leaving her house but I will be glad to be out of here at least, making steps in the right direction.

'Is that what you're wearing?' Emma asks as she stands at the doorway.

I'm in a cropped top, zipped hoodie and leggings, I didn't realise that I needed to wear an official leaving outfit but it's comfortable, it's me.

'Go on, tell me I'll catch a death, Mother,' I say to her haughtily.

She rolls her eyes then comes to sit on the bed next to me.

'How are you feeling?' she asks, stroking my head.

'Ready.'

'That is like the best word to describe you, ever.' She releases a small breath of air that feels loaded with emotion and I grab onto her arm.

'I'm good, Ems. Please don't worry.'

'Do you know how it feels being your sister? There's always worry, this air of unpredictability. You're like a spring, where will she bounce to next? What will she say? What will Lucy do?'

'Isn't that the beauty of me?' I ask.

'Perhaps. It keeps us on our toes at least.'

'You need it.'

She picks a bit of fluff off my top. 'Bounce high, little one, yeah?'

'Always.'

She gives my scar the once-over and then moves to the

cannula in my hand, the bloody bane of my life for the past fortnight. Don't tell people but I've pissed all over it at times when I've had to wheel my drip to the toilet. That can't be good.

'Isn't that a nurse's job?' I ask her as she unwraps some cotton swabs.

'I asked for the honour,' she says. 'Though they were lining up to do it. You've made friends, eh?'

'It's a gift.'

'Miriam who does catering is obsessed with you. Apparently, you've told her you can get her tickets to *The Lion King*? I've been asking you that question for years.'

'Yeah? I know one of the swings.'

'You slept with one of the swings?'

'So rude to just jump to that assumption.' The answer is yes, though. But of course I wandered out of my room here and got to know the people. I mean, what else was I going to do here for two weeks? Just lie here and think about the meaning of life?

'I'm also going out for drinks next week with Zahra and the nurses. Oh, and did you meet that man who got skewered on that construction site?'

'Skewered? You didn't sleep with him, did you?'

'No. He's, like, sixty. His new name is Kebab but his wife's been in and they're lovely. They've booked me in for their granddaughter's third birthday.'

Emma looks me at strangely. I've been recovering but seemingly also on the hustle. She places a swab over my arm and removes the needle, sticking a plaster over the place where it once was. I look down at it and then wind my arm around. Freedom, at last.

'Come on, you. They're waiting downstairs. Do you want a wheelchair?' Emma asks.

'No? You could give me a piggyback?'

'No. Take it slowly.'

As I step out of the room, Zahra and a few nurses are

standing around to offer hugs and their goodbyes and we wander through those brightly lit corridors, Emma with my bag in hand, looking official in her smart doctor garb and name badge, whereas I look like someone she's taken in for the night. What have I learnt about this place? It is sobering to see people at their lowest, their physical beings failing on them, but geez, this place is held up by spirit, people fighting to get better and the kind souls who help them to do that. I grab Emma's arm with silent pride to know she is part of that.

'What will you do in your lunch breaks now? Where will you go?' I ask her.

'Oh, I might actually be able to eat in peace and not have someone steal all my lunch.'

'Boring. I might have to come back and just harass you weekly.'

'Only weekly. Any more and I'll push you in front of another bus myself.'

We both laugh, entering a lift that also holds a withered older gentleman in a wheelchair hooked up to an oxygen tank. He wears his standard paper dress, covered with a dressing gown. There's a look to his face that says he doesn't really care for the aesthetic, confirmed by the way his legs are apart and he's flashing his todger at us. I smile with wide-open delirious eyes at Emma, who pretends she's studying the poster on the lift wall very very intently.

'Where are your shoes, mate?' I ask.

He turns to look at me, not impressed. 'It's not like I'm going running, innit?'

'Very true. So what's going on with you?' I ask, pointing my finger around.

'Shitting emphysema.'

'I got hit by a bus.'

'Well, that was stupid.'

Emma laughs. It was, wasn't it? At least he's honest enough

to tell me to my face.

'You fixed up now?' he asks.

'Who knows?' I reply, spying a packet of cigarettes in his dressing gown pocket. 'What about you?'

'No. Lungs are buggered.'

'Could be worse, at least you've still got a willy,' I say, glancing down.

He looks down and howls with laughter, coughing and wrapping himself up. The lift doors open and we let him wheel himself out, waving as he does. This floor is busier, shops and outpatient clinics fill the spaces, but Emma navigates us through the doors outside. I've been out since I woke up but that hit of autumn sunshine is always welcome, the warmth on my face, the sound of my city in the background, sirens and traffic, the low buzz of London in my ears. We walk a short way to the hospital gardens, the Thames and the unmistakeable outline of the Houses of Parliament in the background.

'They're over here,' Emma says, pointing to a bench. 'I'm going to put your bag in my car and head back, all right?'

I nod and walk over. Meg stands up and embraces me hard.

'Is that what you're wearing?' she whispers. I ignore her. 'Luce, this is Holly and James Avery. Holly, James, this is Lucy. And this is...'

'Oscar?' I say. 'I mean, it'd be weird if you brought another baby with you.'

I went for humour, I don't think I should have opened with humour. They look like any other couple you'd see. She's small, slender with mousey hair, and he's all crewneck jumper and well-fitting jeans. Do we shake hands? Or not. The emotion of the situation is too much for Holly and she comes over and grabs me, her frame wrapped around mine tightly. I hug back.

'I can't believe it,' she says. 'It's actually you.'

'For one night only...' I reply.

Meg gives me a look like I need to dial back my weird brand

of Lucy. We all sit down. I won't lie, I wish they'd stop staring but I guess they're trying to work out how much of me is their son. I peer over into their buggy and he's wide awake, bluey-grey eyes like mine, seeming deep in thought but likely just wondering when he'll next see milk. I smile. He's a bloody good-looking baby but I expected as much given he's half me.

'I'm sorry I sprung this on you. Before everything happened, I was quite content to just let you get on with your lives, I didn't want to intrude in any way. I guess...'

'Oh, we get it...' James replies. 'We were shocked when the clinic got in touch and told us what happened and we just wanted to know you were OK.'

'I'm getting there.'

Holly lifts Oscar up from his buggy and he sits there contentedly in her lap, playing with her necklace. I bend down to say hello and he laughs. That sound is perfection.

'So just to be sure, it's my egg and James' juice?' I ask. Meg scrunches her face up to hear how I've phrased that.

'Yeah,' Holly explains. 'And then it was implanted in me via IVF. You were our third go, other attempts with my eggs and other donors hadn't worked.'

Well, I can only think my eggs would have held on for dear life, they would have had stubborn grip. James holds Holly's hand at that point and I notice their rings, there's the silent understanding that they've walked over flames to get this far, and look at them now, it's a brilliant portrait of family, of a couple deeply simpatico, who've lived and bonded through something together. This is love.

'And the pregnancy, the birth... everything was OK? You're OK?'

She nods, glad that I've asked. 'He's a bit of a night owl but he gets on with everyone, he finds everything funny at the moment.'

'That'll be Lucy all over then,' Meg contributes, beaming so hard.

'And what do you guys do?' I ask.

'James is in PR and I'm a teacher. We live in Streatham. You're a dancer? Actress?'

'Of sorts.'

I don't know how to describe what I see in front of me but all of it has such purpose, such meaning, and that feeling just flows through my veins, the best tonic I could ask for.

'Can we just ask why? Why did you donate your eggs?' Holly asks.

If they want the truth then it started with an advert in a lift at university. Seven hundred and fifty pounds for my eggs? The first thoughts were that it was a bloody good deal and I figured that I probably had hundreds of the things given I was in my prime. But as I got more deeply into the process, the reason changed.

'I never want kids. I knew that very early on in my twenties as my sisters started having babies. For one, they made childbirth sound horrific.' Meg sits there and doesn't disagree. 'But motherhood just never sang to me in the way it did my other sisters. I never knew why but I'm very happy with my life and my work. And it never felt like I was missing out either. I was handed all these nieces and nephews and I just felt I had so many little people to love, what they give me is enough. I adore being their aunty. So it made sense that if I wasn't going to use this resource to its full potential, I should see if it might be useful to someone else.'

They both nod and hold hands again. It's very lovey-dovey and I'd jest if I knew them better.

'They give you counselling when it happens so you can run through that thought process with them. It all makes sense to me at least. And seeing you now makes me realise it's probably one of the best things I ever did in the past decade and I've done a lot, I tell you, Oscar...'

Oscar giggles cheekily and I laugh with him.

'I know I told the agency that we'd have some contact but, just to clarify, now we've met in the flesh...?' Holly asks tentatively.

'Oh, seriously... as you were. Whenever in the future a moment presents itself then let him know who I am, he's welcome to meet me if he ever wants, but you three just get on and do your thing. Maybe send me a Christmas card once in a while but, in all honesty, I'll take this moment and hold it close and you just... live, look after him, he's brilliant.'

I'm making Meg cry and that to me is everything but look at him. He's perfect, they're perfect. There are other babies out there too and I am sure they are all bloody miracles as well. I hope they have love, I hope they love so hard, they feel it in their tips of their fingers, I also hope they give this world hell when they're older. My genes almost dictate it.

'Would you like to hold him?' Holly asks me.

I nod. Hell, come here, kid. Come sit with Lucy. He sits on my lap, facing me, and wraps a hand around my finger.

'Hey.'

He sits there quietly and takes it all in, looking me in the eye.

'I'm Lucy. Nice to meet you.'

His hair is curly, just like mine when I was that age. I pull at one of his blond curls and make a 'boing' noise to make him giggle.

'Bounce high, little one. Bounce high.'

* * *

After some brief conversation and baby cuddles, Holly, James and Oscar don't stay long and we wave them off as they stroll into the sunset, into the crowds of Westminster Bridge. As they leave, the emotion is far too much for Meg, who bursts into tears and I have to sit there holding her, which to be fair is a bloody liberty as I was the one who nearly died and also the one who was supposed to be sharing a moment with my biological child.

'All good?' asks Grace, from behind us. 'Meg, we told you to be here because you're the strongest, why are you sobbing?'

Beth gets tissues out of her rucksack and hands them to Meg, who blows her nose noisily.

'Because it was amazing. Look what she did, she made that family so happy and that baby is just adorable.'

Emma hands us both cups of coffee. 'We kept our distance so they wouldn't think we're descending on them en masse to stare at the baby. They'd think we were trying to steal him,' she explains.

'It's all good. I got to meet him, time to move on,' I say.

'Are you OK though?' Grace says, all the sisters glaring down at me, thinking the moment may have triggered some emotion or even regret in me. How do I just move on from something as life-changing as that?

'I'm perfect, that baby is with the right people. He'll be grand.'

Emma gazes over at me in a weird way that almost speaks of some pride though she'll probably never say that out loud. Beth looks like she knew there was good in me, somewhere about my person. Grace's face speaks worry, concern. When you found out about Oscar, you stroked out, don't do that here, again.

'We have a question though...' Beth asks. 'Why did you never tell us? You tell us everything.'

'Not everything...' I say indignantly.

'Luce, I feel that I know everyone you've had sex with quite intimately and I've not even met a tenth of them in real life,' Grace tells me. 'You used to describe their penises to us.'

'You want to know all the things I've done for money...' I tell them.

'No!' Emma shrieks. 'What have you done for money? Please not that...'

'Ems, seriously? I do have some class about me...'

The sisters all look a little dubious at that statement.

'I knew some of you would have your reservations about the ethics. Maybe I didn't want to be talked out of it. It felt important, like a good thing to do.'

Beth puts her head on my shoulder.

'But what if it'd gone wrong?' Emma asks me. 'You were put under sedation.'

'And I put your name as an emergency contact so I'd have been fine.'

'So why was he pinned? As a note?' Beth asks me.

'To remind me occasionally of something good in my life. I have plenty good but when I'm at a horrible audition, I'm waiting in the rain for a bus or I'm having to scrub a theatre toilet because a punter's had too much Merlot then the note gives me a little boost.'

I get up and urge the sisters to walk with me. It's too nice an evening not to at least have a promenade along this place. Emma and Meg lead the way, linking arms, while us younger three follow closely behind like ducklings.

'So you really never want kids?' Meg asks me. 'You don't think you'll change your mind?'

'Gracie adopted so I have options. I'll just steal one of yours if I really have to... I've known for a while that I don't want the norm. I may meet the love of my life one day, it could be a man or a woman or anyone, but I know I just want to keep living and moving and not being stuck in some everyday like you boring spanners...'

They all roll their eyes at the same time. If the eye-rolling was a synchronised event in the Olympics that moment could have scored high, medal-winning points. *Oh, Lucy. She's back in the room, isn't she?* And against all their better judgement, they love the bones of me. I know they all do, it's why they're all here. *You left your kids with husbands and our parents to see me discharged from hospital and watch me meet my biological baby. I'd die for the lot of you. My best bitches.*

'So what's the plan now?' Beth asks as we stroll along past City Hall, through the crowds gawping up at the London Eye. It's a big Ferris wheel, people, move along.

'Food? There's a Wahaca up there?' Grace suggests.

'We could go on a big rager? I am out of hospital and recovered. I could call Darren and Cass and make this a big night?'

'No,' Meg says politely.

'You're not allowed alcohol for two more weeks,' Emma warns me. I stick my tongue out at her.

'I was kinda joking,' I tell her.

'We never know, Lucy.'

'I was actually talking about what now for Lucy, after today, next week? Is there a plan?' Beth adds.

'I've been asked to do a party next week. Cass and Hayley have bought me a new Elsa wig. Just hope I can remember the sodding words to all the songs. Apart from that, nothing. I plan to eat all of Mum and Dad's food and for Pussy and I to annoy Mum as much as we can.'

'Please can you give your cat another name?' Grace asks. 'One of my girls drew your cat the other day in her schoolbook and labelled it Aunty Lucy's Pussy.'

'And that is the joy of my Pussy. I'm so glad you got to meet her. Isn't she the best?'

'I've never met a more disagreeable creature in my life,' Emma says, she who was once married to Satan himself.

'That's all me. I trained her to be like that.'

Meg is laughing. That's also the most perfect sound.

'But to answer your original question... I don't know, Bethy. See where the tide takes me next.'

We keep walking, taking in the sights of kids running up

and down the pavements of Jubilee Gardens and the street performers and mime artists that line the way. I dive into Grace's handbag and throw them all her loose change. Just before we get to the British Film Institute and the space underneath inhabited by booksellers, I pause and look up. Waterloo Bridge. *Hey there. I feel like you and me know each other now. I crashed into you, my blood is part of your fabric now.* It feels like bumping into an old flame that burnt me quite badly and ran me over on the way out. I break away from the sisters and look out over the railings into the river. Beth and Grace stop in their tracks and join me, Grace's arm going around my shoulder. Meg and Emma come into the huddle. I don't think it's emotion that's caught me or even some philosophical moment where I'm thinking about the meaning of life. But I just feel lucky. I am so lucky to be standing here.

'They sent me a bill for that bike, you know... because I didn't return it. Three hundred fucking pounds.'

'What?' Emma asks angrily.

'Dad paid it. I remember coming off that bike and flying and you know the first thing I thought? I mean, I swore like hell but I also thought about all of you. You four.'

Meg's nostrils are trembling again, setting herself up for the cry.

'I thought that this was all happening because Grace didn't teach me how to ride a bike properly...'

Grace pouts with tears in her eyes.

'But I thought how shit that I'll never get to see you sisters again.'

We all stand there, overlooking the river, to take in that revelation. It's always been us five and for all I forgot in the last decade that is what remained. Ten years of life, like being inside a pressure cooker with everything having been thrown at us for good measure. It's transformed us as women, as mothers, as daughters, wives, widows and sisters, and still we stand, we remain, we're here, different evolving versions of ourselves and still moving, still growing, still together. I'm really glad we're still together.

'Nah, just joking. Didn't give you girls a second thought. All I thought was I should have bloody walked.'

Beth punches my arm while Meg shakes her head at me, laughing.

'Here...' I say, reaching into my pocket and getting my phone out. 'Find a space, we'll send this to Mum.' I angle my arm out in front of me and all the sisters get into view of my phone screen, trying to work out their angles and the amount of teeth they should be showing. I gurn quite attractively. Pure cheese.

'Give us a look please before you post that on social media...' Meg asks.

We all pause to see it. Sisters, five. All alive. Just. Meg's eyes scan to the line of smaller thumbnail pictures under the one we just took.

'Lucy, why are there pictures of your vagina on your camera roll?' she asks.

Beth and Grace stand there smirking.

'Oh my god, Lucy. That's a hospital bed...' Emma says, grabbing my phone. 'Your thigh is hanging off the railing. Did you have sex in the hospital?' Her tone is making me think that this is not the done thing.

'Maybe?'

'That'll be a yes then...' Grace interjects.

'Lucy, seriously?' Emma replies. 'Who was he? Who does that? You were ill.'

'Have we just met? He was from X-ray, his name was Rhys. He liked showing me his bones.'

Emma stares hard at Meg, who is trying hard not to laugh.

'So, sisters...' I say, pacing slightly ahead of them. 'Who wants to hear about his penis?'

EPILOGUE
2028

The Callaghan sisters: Where are they now?

Meg Morton continues to live up North in the Lakes with her silent lumberjack husband, Danny Morton, and their youngest daughters, Eve and Polly. Their eldest daughter, Tess, is on an art foundation course at Central Saint Martins in London. She has a boyfriend called Ace and a tattoo. Meg still blames her aunt Lucy for all of it but deep down loves that her daughter has ended up in the city she grew up in, and is thankful she inherited her father's artistic talents as she herself has problems drawing stick men. Danny and Meg are still very much in love. They've never been dogging. Honest.

Emma Callaghan-Kohli is still married to the very lovely Jag. She's one of the most noted paediatric cardiac surgeons in the country, and recently went viral after one of her surgeries to separate conjoined twins went live on YouTube. She shares custody of her girls and Iris, her eldest, has recently decided she'd also like to study medicine at university. Her ex-husband, Simon, lives alone and his hairline is starting to recede quite badly, so much so that he decided to go for hair plug surgery, which now makes him look like carpet has died on his head. Her sisters still call him Satan.

Beth Callaghan turned forty this year and is still very tired. To celebrate this landmark birthday, she went to Glastonbury with all the family and sprang the huge surprise on them that she and Will, her long-time love, had also arranged to get married there (by a hippy called Zenith; no one knows if the ceremony is legally binding). Her sons, Joe and Jude, gave her away. Later that evening, she and the sisters managed to get a selfie with Beyoncé, who was in attendance. This was a peak sister moment and all of them have that selfie framed in prominent places. Jay-Z and the sisters' dad got on very well.

Grace still lives in Bristol with her girls and still doesn't understand the economic value of lingerie. She's still with her boyfriend, Max, who cut the ponytail off for charity one year but grew it back as he looked naked without it. Her daughters still have matching haircuts but are different in every way. Maya is a keen footballer but she's learnt not to bite kids who kick her. Every year, they all go on what they now call 'The Big Tom Adventure' where they find somewhere on a map and explore the hell out of it. Next year, they are meeting their Aunty Lucy in Japan so they can eat sushi and mochi for days.

Lucy. She's had quite the six years. After her brush with death and that bus, she performed at a posh London party where a film producer was in attendance and liked how she had both guest banter and excellent improvisational skills when she forgot the words to songs. They kept in touch and he invited her down to an audition for a real-life version of *Frozen* that he was trying to cast. Someone called Ashley was at the audition. Ashley was really quite awful.

Lucy got the part. In fact, she nailed the thing, in a really good wig, and won the Golden Globe for Best Actress in a

Comedy or Musical that year. She mainly made the headlines though as she swore twelve times on stage when she went to receive her award and then at the after-party was caught dancing quite inappropriately with Robert De Niro. She was nominated for an Oscar and took her mum to the ceremony. She lost to Meryl Streep (boo!) but when asked on the red carpet what she would do if she won, she swore again but said, quite mysteriously, that she had an Oscar so it didn't really matter. Fact checkers were never able to understand what she meant and started romantically linking her to Brazilian foot-baller Oscar, for no discernible rhyme or reason.

Disney are trying hard to purify Lucy for their means as the kids love her to bits but it's a battle they can't seem to win. Naturally, the tabloid press have a field day with her too. She enjoys her new lifestyle and is attached to lots of different models, actors and rap stars but never seems to stop moving. People label her, the social media comments say all sorts and beg for her to stay with the one person and find some fairy-tale ending but she doesn't care. She's Lucy. She doesn't buy into fairy tales. The media also love Lucy because she has no filter, she calls out injustice in Hollywood and has no reason to protect or respect people who treat her and others unfairly. At a table reading for her last film, she was caught on camera pinning an actor's hand to a desk with her elbow after he tried to grope her. Said actor had to have two fingers in a cast for a month.

She currently is living in New York where she's starring on Broadway playing Ophelia in *Hamlet* to critical acclaim. In her dressing room, she pins a card to her mirror from an Ophelia she once knew. New York isn't home. Once her stint is over, Lucy is looking forward to returning to London, back to the home she grew up in, sitting around the Sunday roast table with her family and her tales of legend; her best one will involve a very famous actor from the Marvel franchise, a fire extinguisher, running away naked from the NYPD and her bra getting caught in a post box. She brings her cat everywhere with her. Disney paid her money to rename the cat. To the world, her name is Pearl but, behind closed doors, she is still called Pussy. She's still the most miserable damn cat you'll ever meet.

A LETTER FROM KRISTEN

Dear lovely reader,

Hello again! Or maybe you're new? Either way, thank you so much for reading – you really are a superstar and I feel so incredibly lucky that you chose to read my book. If you want to keep up to date with details of my writing, just sign up at the following link. Your email address will never be shared and you can unsubscribe at any time.

www.bookouture.com/kristen-bailey

I really hope you laughed with Lucy. She's featured in many of my other books and we've been laughing with her for so long so it was a relief to finally let go of the reins and release her into the world so we could tell her brilliant story. An important note from me about this book: I didn't visit a sex club to research this book. I watched *Sex/Life* quite a fair bit on Netflix (Episode 3) and a few raunchy films and documentaries too when the kids were in bed. Seriously, I research my books thoroughly but even I have my limits. (I also would have had to have shaved my legs... Who has time for that?)

If this is your first fling with the Callaghan sisters then you'll also be glad to know that they all have their own books. *Has Anyone Seen My Sex Life?* (Meg), *Can I Give My Husband Back?* (Emma), *Did My Love Life Shrink in the Wash?* (Beth) and *How Much Wine Will Fix My Broken Heart?* (Grace) are all available as e-book or paperback. Nothing would give me greater pleasure than if you were to go and catch up with the other sisters.

LUCY! Aren't you a gem of a character? You're funny, free and wild and I think you may be an inspiration to us all to live life to the fullest without worry, care or shame. That said, you also love people so hard and throw yourself into everything with all your being. I hope you'll always be like this. Don't change.

Am I Lucy? Well, I'm a little bit of all the sisters but since we first met Lucy in Emma's book, my husband has noticed a change in me. I was once the diplomat, the people pleaser, but since creating Lucy and bringing her to the page, it's been transformative. I mean, I've got some way to go but I'm much better than I once was at calling people out and telling them to piss off. And sometimes, we all need to do that. God, if Lucy has taught you anything, it's that life is really too short to put up with people's nonsense. So that mum on the school run who talks behind people's backs? Tell her to her face to behave better. That guy at work who makes the borderline misogynist comments? Shut that shit down. Be more Lucy in every way. She embraces life so madly and fully so, please, do the same. I hope I don't come across like some crazed motivational speaker now but, seriously, promise me her story has inspired you. Go out there and try everything, be strong as tits, do what you love, do who you love and don't look around for validation or an excuse. Do it for you.

That said (and this is hard to say out loud), this book marks the end of the Callaghan sisters' adventures for now. Don't be sad because I'm sobbing as I write this so I'll do all the crying for us. Hopefully, in the last five books, we've been able to show you a snapshot of ten years of their lives and all the comedy, drama and adventure that's come with being a modern woman. What can we learn from these sisters? That there's no real way to exist as a woman these days, it's a constantly evolving beast.

You can be happily married, but you can also be divorced, widowed, live in supposed sin or just stay single. Have kids, don't have kids, adopt kids, have a career or stay at home, have both? Be gay, be bisexual, be straight. Defy convention about what a woman can be or what box she is supposed to be in. All the sisters' stories ring true with me in some ways and point to times in my life where I've learnt, grown and become. It hasn't been linear, it's come with a multitude of complications, emotions and setbacks, but the important thing is to always emerge on the other side, a little more ready to take on what life throws at you.

What I've loved about the Callaghans too is how their stories just resound with love. I never tell people I write romantic comedies because, to me, romance is kinda corny. It's more than meet-cutes and bunches of flowers. What I do write are books about love and the many infinite forms in which that can exist: a love for family, mundane love between couples who've been together for years, lost love, new love, maternal love, platonic love, a love for friends, unconventional love, a love for life. I hope you've enjoyed reading their stories because the love has been there in spades within this marvellous family and I hope this may be why people gravitated towards them so much. Crikey, I will miss writing about them so very much but I will hold them close for a really long time. Love, always.

OK, enough with me being all soppy! I will sign off here. Before I go, I'd be thrilled to hear from any of my readers, whether it be with reviews, questions or just to say hello. If you like retweets of videos of people falling off things then follow me on Twitter. Have a gander at Instagram, my Facebook author page and website too for updates, ramblings and to learn more about me. Like, share and follow away – it'd be much appreciated.

And if you enjoyed *Am I Allergic to Men?* then I would be overjoyed if you could leave me a review on either Amazon or

Goodreads to let people know. It's a brilliant way to reach out to new readers. And don't just stop there, tell everyone you know, send to all on your WhatsApp groups (just be careful if you are attaching images...).

With much love and gratitude,

Kristen xx

www.kristenbaileywrites.com

facebook.com/kristenbaileywrites

twitter.com/mrsbaileywrites

instagram.com/kristenbaileywrites

ACKNOWLEDGEMENTS

CHRISTINA DEMOSTHENOUS! I will shout that name forever because you're a brilliant editor and it really is a joy to work with you. I've been trying to work out why that is and, essentially, it's because you're so damn kind. All of your emails, edits and notes always have a lot of love that shines through them, you care about the work but also the author. Even when you're telling me to stop swearing, you're so bloody nice about it, and there was a lot of swearing in this one (over one hundred forms of the f*** word in the first draft – sorry!). Thank you for being the ultimate champion, the most wonderful human and for sharing my love of good trainers and wrap dresses.

At Bookouture, a shout out to everyone behind the scenes who make the magic happen, especially Sarah Hardy, Lauren Finger, Rhian McKay, Becca Allen, Alba Proko and the incomparable Sarah Durham, who, if you're listening to this on audio, you would have heard embody the spirit and joy of Lucy. Thank you for bringing my words to life with such care and enthusiasm.

Now on to the Oscar-style list of people who've randomly helped with this novel along the way. You don't know these people but you should because they are bloody brilliant. Emma Harris is my all-time favourite school-gate mum. She's a provider of wine, incomparable chat and counsel and one of the most formidably talented and wonderful people I know. Thank you for showing me that as a mother, the key is balance but also pursuing the things in life that make your soul sing. Thank you for all your stellar knowledge and voice notes about theatre and dance. WINE! SOON!

When I wrote the hypnotherapist scene, I was in random conversation with Will Simpson, who basically created Cosmo for me. He immediately leapt onto that page but, I'll be honest, the character came alive when I added your voice. That's because you are calming, kind and the best sort of people. One day, I hope to be able to gift you a dreamcatcher pendant, you won't have to wear it. Now shake my hand.

Before I was a writer, I studied psychology at university and it was good to be able to dig into the annals of my acquired knowledge to talk about Lucy's condition. Learning about people and their behaviour is a massive part of being able to write characters and move them around a page so a thank you to the infinite number of teachers, lecturers, study mates and tutors who instilled my love of the subject.

Since joining Bookouture, I can't dispute that there have been a number of book bloggers and reviewers who've championed the Callaghan sisters at every turn and have done a stellar job in promoting my books, coming on book tours and being such wonderful channels of support and friendship. Javier @ Diagnosis Bookaholic (bestie and Spanish translator oracle), Lucy Moore @ The Book Club Bitches, Emma @ Star Crossed Reviews, Gemma @ Between the Pages Book Club, Fireflies & Free Kicks, Janice @ Jan's Book Buzz, Sharon @ Stardust Book Reviews, Els @ B for Bookreview, Vik @ Little Miss Book Lover 87, Honolulu Belle @ Books & Bindings, Jen @ Nothing Like A Good Book, Jo @ Tea & Cake for the Soul, and the wonderfully kind and lovely Gavin Dimmock. Love and thanks for being there from the beginning but, that said, there have been dozens of others who have read and reviewed my books, and offered myself and so many other authors brilliant levels of support. I am in awe of all of you and the work you do for the book community.

And here is a list of random people who I adore so very much. You either read my books, share all my book spam, give me writing suggestions, inspire characters, are wonderfully supportive, or are always on the end of a phone or messaging app. You make this writing lark a lot less lonesome: Sara Hafeez, Graham Price, Mike aka Gurney Harlech, Barbara and John Bailey, Elizabeth Neep, Luke Travis, Eva Verde, Jo Lovett-Turner, Drew Davies, Leigh Gill, Pip Sumner, Sophie Ranald and Shirley Golden.

You don't write about sisters unless you've had sisters and so I thank Leanne, my one and only bestest sister. When I wrote this book, I had some building work done and I moved my whole family in with hers. Literally eleven people under one roof, testing her Wi-Fi to the max and literally life imitating art, or maybe it's the other way round? Those three months inspired a lot of this story. We got through a lot of cereal, laundry and toilet paper but we also brought back all our old dance routines and performed them nightly to our very confused children. We weren't even drunk. Shout out to the best night where we (sort of) won all that money on *Pointless* by knowing all the very obscure films of Emily Blunt. Thank you for being the better sister. You know it's true.

I should also thank my brother too or he'll get the hump but the truth is you've always been our third musketeer and I am sorry we dressed you in that yellow Snoopy swimming costume when you were younger and took photos. Thank you, Jon-Jon, my unofficial twin and the most wonderful little brother that everyone loves (except me, I think you're occasionally a smart-arse and I will always live to beat you at Scrabble). And to the other man in my life, my wonderful father, Barry, who always asks me how my writing is going and who gifted all my books to his cleaner without knowing what they were about.

As said, I'm not Lucy. Oh, I'm a complex combination of all the sisters but my Lucy moments I learnt from my mum, who's always been pretty bad-ass. I have a resounding memory once in a multi-storey car park when a man took her car park space and she followed him to the lift, had a go and then turned to his wife and questioned her judgement to be married to such a twat. I think I was ten when that happened. My mum calls people out. If she hears her grandchildren have been spoken to badly at school, she calls me up and questions why I haven't been waiting outside the school to take matters into my own hands (obviously, I've never done this…). But with fire comes love and someone who cares deeply for her clan. Thank you for helping me find my fire when mine is lacking. To note, she still does buy me underwear every Christmas even though at the time of writing I am forty-one years of age.

Nick Bailey. If I wasn't a Lucy then my husband certainly was and it's wonder he made it out of school to become a reasonably well-adjusted adult. His stories could fill novels and, as I was a goody-two-shoes at school, I thank him for giving me a list of all the times he misbehaved at school. He did make a French teacher cry. He can't remember why. Besides being my favourite wrong 'un, thank you for all that you do for me. Those words will never quite be enough. Thank you for screaming at me to back up my work, for loving me in such quiet yet reassuring ways, for your patience when I spend half an hour choosing what to watch on the Netflix.

Bambinos. I have four of them and the joy, the laughs and the pride they give me is unparalleled. It can't be easy having a mum who writes and is scatty AF but you never hold it against me. In fact, you sometimes show up with tea and biscuits, which shows me I've done something right. However, being your mother isn't always easy and this is where I'm going to get a bit emotional. My editor always applauds the authenticity in my hospital scenes. I'd like to say it's because of my tip-top research but it's mainly because I've spent a bit of time in hospitals with my little people. My youngest son was once rushed into hospital with a severe blood infection and septic hip, and my youngest daughter has a chronic heart condition. Being strong for my kids in those moments were the most challenging times in my life but I'm under no illusion that the reason they're both still here is because of the NHS. I rarely get political but the last couple of years and my own experiences have shown me how very lucky we are to have this establishment in our country and to have such wonderful people work within it, helping others with such care, empathy and dedication. Look after it, protect it, hold it in the esteem it deserves. A special thank you to Dr Elliott, a paediatric orthopaedic surgeon in Southampton General Hospital. We were on her service for five years and I thank her every day for saving my boy.

As this was Lucy's book, my next paragraph was going to be aimed at the people in my life who perhaps have tried to stop me from getting this far – a disparagement list if you will. However, both my editor and copy-editor suggested it may not be the best idea, which is both a shame for me and you, as it was quite a funny end to this novel, and filled you in on a few of my crapbag exes and lordy, I have some STORIES. Anyway, without naming names because you know, lawsuits, I channel my best Lucy at this very moment and stick up my middle fingers at all those people. I don't hold grudges (much) but if you're ever wondering if I'm writing about you then the answer is probably yes. But it's usually because I have to create a completely unlikeable character and need the inspiration. None of what you tried to do worked. I'm exactly where I need to be.

And there we are, the Callaghans have come to the end of their story. Thank you, Meg, Emma, Beth, Grace and Lucy. You're all parts of me, my favourite imaginary friends and, for the last three years, you and your families have been like some sort of invisible lifeline, you've kept this writer company and it's been a joy to bring your stories to the page. The rest of your lives are unwritten for now but, in my head, you'll always be dancing to TLC, throwing cakes at each other and telling Lucy to get off the table before she breaks it. You will always be my best bitches.